Also by Marilyn Wallace

So Shall You Reap

A Single Stone

the Seduction

A PERFECT CRIME BOOK

Doubleday

New York
London   Toronto   Sydney
Auckland

the

Seduction

Marilyn Wallace

A Perfect Crime Book
published by doubleday
a division of Bantam Doubleday Dell
Publishing Group, Inc.
1540 Broadway, New York, New York 10036

Doubleday is a trademark of Doubleday, a division of
Bantam Doubleday Dell Publishing Group, Inc.

ISBN 0-385-46907-1

For Molly Friedrich,
with affection and gratitude.

Acknowledgments

I'm grateful to Kate Miciak, as always, for her editorial astuteness and enthusiasm, and for understanding my intent and helping me achieve it.

Thanks to Katie Supinski, who explained rag rugs to me, and to Mac Scott, who made me a straight-shooter. Any errors, of course, are mine. Again, as ever, thanks to Bruce Wallace and Judy Greber, whose careful manuscript readings and friendship I couldn't do without.

the Seduction

9:00 a.m.

We face each other, two sisters, one dark and edgy, the other a pale, serious redhead, both slender and watchful. We know that even if we seem to be talking to each other or entertaining only tranquil thoughts, we are really waiting. Waiting for him to make his move; waiting, too, to make ours. As the morning passes, the house will grow hotter, the air denser with the threat of rain. Our breathing will become more and more labored. The past and the future will recede, and only the moment for which we all have been preparing will matter.

Hazy morning light streams into the living room. It passes first through the leaves of two sugar maples, then seeps from the sheer curtains framing the window to splash like finely-crafted lace across the oak table separating Rosie and me. In the center of the table, a bowl of rhododendron flowers sits on a doily of shadows. Each blossom is the same bright pink as the mark on Rosie's mouth where she's been biting her lower lip.

A sudden image, of a trail of amber honey and a sightless, staggering insect drunkenly following the glistening drops unaware of the web that's about to snare it, makes my skin prickle. Not being able to act is driving me crazy. That, and the weight of the gun in my pocket.

I understand him now. I think about the way we gathered information, drop by drop, how we discovered that some of it was in front of us but meant nothing until we'd found the proper container to hold it all. I sense him; it is an unexpected consequence of the past week's events. I didn't anticipate this absorption, this taking him inside me. I hate having him in my head like this.

"If you'd lived through that, Rosie . . . can you even *imagine?* You wake up and your memories are with you all the time. You play at being just like other people, doing your job, having normal conversations and all the while this *thing* is living in you, a monster that was created when—"

"He did a good job of pretending. For a long time. I don't want to talk about him." Rosie leans over the wicker basket; her strawberry hair falls forward, hiding her eyes. She plucks a white broadcloth shirt from the pile and holds it with a determined, steady hand in front of her. "You see? The whole thing about making a braided rug is that each piece of fabric stirs something in you. This one—you used to wear this when you were, what, sixteen? You wore it the last time you went dancing at the Edgewood. I mean, back then, not last week. You were big on making statements in those days, Lee. Wore this if you wanted to prove you didn't follow the rules, right?"

I hide my wariness behind a grin and a shrug. "Things change. Anyway, I've always been more than a pair of jeans or a suit or a handbag with someone else's initials on it."

"Well, what *did* it mean when you tied a piece of black lace to the top buttonhole? One more thing to get the guys to notice you? Not that you ever had to try very hard. I bet you got the lace idea from one of those magazines you were always reading when you were supposed to be doing math homework."

She's full of surprises, my older sister, little bits of perceptions squirreled away, round and hard like nuts.

"What's this, the wisdom of hindsight?" I ask. "And before you answer, Rosie, fair warning. The next item in that pile is your pleated skirt. You practically lived in it, that and the red crewneck sweater and your gold hoop earrings, your entire senior year. You even wore those huge earrings to bed. I mean, weren't they uncomfortable? What did you think—you wanted to be wearing the proper accessories in case

Prince Charming galloped up this godforsaken road in the middle of the night to rescue you?"

Rosie's sea green eyes sparkle, and I can't tell if she's angry at me or laughing. "At least *I* never pretended to be cool. I was always so behind the times, I practically invented retro. But back then—God, it was embarrassing to think anyone might find out I longed for Elvis and for circle skirts. My biggest dream was to be in a spotlight dance on *American Bandstand*. I had this fantasy, I never told anyone before and it's still privileged information, sister privilege, that some hunk with smoldering eyes and a motorcycle jacket would come to my window and proclaim his undying love by serenading me with 'Earth Angel.' See what happens—this is why you make rag rugs. Can you imagine doing this thirty, forty years from now, two old-lady sisters dipping into the past?"

In the silence, the clock on the mantel marks each second. *Tock tock tock*, without emphasis or variation. The light angles across the fabric-filled basket, snagging on the split-twig handle, moving to a flimsy yellow remnant that has been folded carefully and laid on the pile. Neither of us comments that the clock echoes our heartbeats.

My fingers skim the yellow fabric, and I'm surprised by a hot rush of resentment. "Is that really what I think it is? Aunt Christa's bathrobe, the one she used to call her negligee?"

"Why do you say it that way, like an accusation? You were the one she chose. Aunt Christa didn't tell *me* her secrets." Rosie's forehead wrinkles.

"Sorry. I got caught by that old feeling. Whenever she giggled, I felt as though she wanted to switch places with me so that she could be the little girl and then I'd have to be the grown-up. It never occurred to me that you might want to be in my place, listening to her go on and on about men and clothes and her body. I hated what she expected of me." I stand, pace the length of the room. A muffled silence descends when I step back onto the rug. I touch the brass candlesticks, move a cut-glass vase half an inch farther from the edge of the mantel, feel the cold, reassuring handle of the gun in my jacket pocket.

"Okay, so the idea is to cut strips two inches wide and sew them together, lots of them, until the piece is very long, maybe thirteen, fourteen feet. Then you fold each edge of the whole strip lengthwise and sew a seam. I use an overcast stitch. It holds better." Rosie's best instructive voice can't conceal a quaver.

the Seduction

I make no mention of it as I place the shirt on the gleaming surface of the hardwood floor, just beyond the boundaries of her most accomplished rug, a five-foot-long oval that swirls with life and color. Deftly, Rosie cuts a straight strip and demonstrates how to fold it and where to sew the seam.

"When you've sewn the long seam, see, you end up with a flat tube. You plait four tubes together and then you curl the plait into an oval. You use this heavy thread to stitch the oval together. It's really—"

"Wait!"

A noise crackles the air outside the house. I stand on my toes and strain to see the source of the sound, like footsteps on fallen leaves, except that it's summer and damp and there won't be dry leaves for months. A sudden gust of wind whips the thinnest maple branches and sends Andrew's empty lunch box clattering down the porch steps. A smudge of a cloud pushes across the sky from the west; the room seems cooler. But he isn't out there, not where I can see him anyway, and I turn back to my sister.

Rosie continues to smooth the white broadcloth, her hands working along the side seams, her face without expression. "Storm's coming, that's all."

"Okay, I get your point. He won't show himself until noon. I hate waiting."

Rosie picks up the scissors and studies me. She's trying to be steady enough and certain enough for both of us, so that some impetuous action of mine doesn't make us any more vulnerable than we already are. It's clear to me that she doesn't want her options limited by my rashness.

"It's pretty important to make the strips as straight and as even as you can, but the nice thing is that you don't have to measure. It's like impressionism. Like finally getting permission to color without having to stay in the lines."

The sudden explosion of my laughter makes Rosie jerk her head up.

"Sorry," I say when I catch my breath. "Here we are, waiting in your living room for this monster to show up, passing the time by talking about rag rugs. Or maybe I should say, you're teaching me about them, the way you've been trying to teach me about things all my life, and then you say something about impressionism and staying in the lines. It's just . . ." I don't say, *I can't tell what's real and what I should be afraid of anymore.* I say, "It sounded funny."

Outside, the first patter of rain on the porch roof turns quickly into a fierce downpour. Rosie dabs with a tissue at the trickle of sweat between her breasts. "I haven't felt a whole lot like laughing for a while. I'm glad something's funny."

"And *I'm* glad it's going to be today," I say harshly. "I'm ready for him, Rosie. It's going to be over soon."

Rosie cuts another line parallel to the seam of the white shirt. "You're that certain?"

I look out the window; rain slashes at the tender green shoots in the garden. My mouth is parched as chalk dust. "I'm sure. Because of everything we've discovered. Because we finally figured out what he's thinking. Which means he's no longer the one defining the rules."

"We don't have to play his game, you know."

My sister is good at talking herself into a steadiness she doesn't feel. "And is that why you've got those scissors clutched so tightly in your hands, Rosie? Because you're not playing his game?"

Rosie sighs and lays the scissors in the basket.

"I've been imagining him, Rosie. The pictures keep getting sharper and clearer, like photographs emerging from a developing bath. I see him sitting at this bare table, clutching a spool of black satin ribbon, forming those bows, all those perfect, shiny bows. Funny, I never see his face. Only those hands and that slippery, smooth ribbon. It's like he's two people at once, part of him wounded and guilty, the other gloating over his evil tricks and . . ." I don't want to say any more, but I stand directly in front of my sister so that she can't pretend I'm not serious about what I know.

"I don't care about him," she says in a voice I hardly recognize, with a conviction that startles me because I have assumed we've grown beyond surprises in the past week. "I don't give a damn about the terrible events in his past and I don't want to spend another second trying to understand him. I just want to make him stop. I want him to leave you alone. I want him to leave *us* alone."

I catch my breath in anticipation of her next words. She means, *To leave Andrew alone,* most of all, but she doesn't say it aloud. I won't either, not now, not when I need Rosie to be concentrating on this moment and the next one, and not on her son. Andrew is far away and safe, which both of us would admit if we were truly calm, really rational. Hands folded in her lap like a Renaissance madonna, my sister's eyes betray her.

"You're not thinking of changing the plan, are you, Rosie? He'll just go back into the shadows. He'll disappear until he thinks he can come out again. And God knows what damage he'll do then. No, the timing has to be his. We have to wait."

I resent his assumption that my life's purpose is to read his sick, cryptic messages and respond to them. A feeling of violation racks me with anger, and to keep from shouting I plop into the chair and push my head against the high back of the chintz-covered cushion.

"All right," Rosie says, agreeable, her old self again, "I won't do anything for now. I'm not going to promise forever, Lee, but for a while, I'll wait. Help me sort out these pieces, will you? I need to do something so that I'm not just thinking."

Revulsion tightens my gut. I will take the old white shirt and Rosie's skirt and lay them smooth and make them neat. I will pretend, along with my sister, that we are preparing to make a rag rug, and the time will pass.

He will be here soon, in this room, and we will be ready for him. Rosie, and me, and the gun.

1

The subway station always felt the same when I stepped off the F train, dank and gloomy, as though time and seasons didn't exist so far below the ground. I fell in with the crowd snaking between the tile walls toward the trickle of light beyond the exit sign, my purse tucked against my side and my eyes on a nonexistent object in front of me. Funny, how that New Yorker's unfocused gaze felt inborn, like my other city tricks: carrying my keys between my fingers so that I'd have a ready weapon; veering away from doorways to avoid nighttime lurkers; checking the little mirrors high in the corners of elevators before I stepped inside.

I emerged onto Sixth Avenue and stopped short, shading my eyes against the glare. Oh Lord, the city was trying to hold me, keep me in its clutches like a tantalizing, possessive lover. All that glinting sun washing the sooty pallor of the buildings with a honeyed patina. . . . Mike would have whipped off his lens cover and shot half a roll of film. Even through the exhaust fumes, he would be dancing with eagerness to capture the promise of summer in black and white.

the Seduction

But I would walk away from New York's allure for a while. This day was a going-away present from the city, a teasing sendoff to protect me from the enchantment of the tropics, to ensure my faithful return. The travel agent had tried to discourage me. The heat. The absence of nightlife. The skeleton staffs at the hotels. Blah blah. But an off-season resort, a beach too hot for crowds was *exactly* what I wanted. Cozumel in June would be deserted, a perfect opportunity to let the tension melt from my body. And I'd get the pictures I needed to finish the project I'd begun with Mike. I would keep my promise.

All my life I've been drawn to attractive, arrogant men. Mike Crutchfield had been the most recent, the most attractive. Mike had quickly charmed me into believing his particular brand of arrogance was merely a wall he'd built to protect his soft spots. And it had worked . . . until four months ago. No wall, but a double-edged sword, that defensiveness. *Guess it cuts both ways,* Mike had whispered from his hospital bed, his voice so soft I'd wondered if I heard him.

I pictured the Memphis cop. Fat, greasy-haired, balling a ketchup-stained napkin in his fist as he told me Mike had done nothing to provoke the stabbing. Just a Yankee, taking pictures in the wrong bar, Mike told the cop in the ambulance on the way to Emergency. Always knew it would be what did him in, he rasped as his blood stained the bandages, should have asked permission, should have seen them watching. . . .

I passed the Wollman rink, trying not to remember the evening last December when we argued about whether it would be magical or just plain corny to go ice skating under the stars, hold hands, fall down and laugh together. Turned out we were both wrong—it had been fun, and I'd filed it in the collection of memories that reminded me that Mike really had been part of my life for a short, sweet time. I missed him terribly, still.

I found myself walking faster toward my office, trying to outpace the sound of his voice in my head. "I'm going to find out what I do when I'm not surrounded by safety," he'd said as he swung his leg over his motorcycle, kissed me, and roared away. "I don't want my images to be predictable," he'd written in a postcard from the Smoky Mountains.

I pushed through the revolving doors and walked to the elevator bank. Funny, how I'd reacted to the cop's phone call as though I'd always known it was coming. Mike said he loved his motorcycle, his camera, and me. Ironic which one had killed him.

. . .

When the telephone rang—it had been bleating at me all morning but I'd taken each interruption as proof that the clock *was* moving forward —I flipped a permission form into my "out" box and reached for the receiver.

Maria Vasquez rushed into the conversation at her usual, breath-defying speed. "You ready for your vacation? Staying in your apartment is going to be *heaven*. I wasn't *meant* to share a three bedroom apartment with five roommates. Listen, Lee, you sounded funny last night."

"Not funny. Sad. Confused. You're the one who tells me it's part of the grieving process, so I was trying to get angry." Angry at what? At Mike for getting himself killed? At a society that made everyone fear strangers and clamor for the gladiators to spill more blood?

After a silence Maria said, "I'm sorry, honey. You get your film and stuff?"

"Got the film. And the lenses. He had more faith in me than I had in myself. I never quite believed him when he said he wanted my pictures in the book. I still think of it as *his* book, even though he'd sold it as *ours*."

As though my eye, my perception of light and shadow, my knowledge of figure-ground balance matched Mike Crutchfield's. Mike had conceived of *Lush Life* as a mix of natural images and intentional tableaux, opulence and abundance that stopped just short of fetid and overripe. *Get us a few more shots of the richness of nature,* he'd told me as he hooked a bungee cord around his duffel bag and secured it to the rack. *Green. . . . We need some riotous green,* he'd whispered from his morphine stupor in the hospital hours before he died. My lover, my friend. My teacher.

"How'd the wrap of the winter issue go?" Despite the lilt in Maria's voice, I suspected her delicate features were crinkling with impatience, urging me to let it go.

"This is *City Magazine,* remember? We got it off on time but just barely. New feature writer insisted I make his name bigger on the masthead. 'I'm the photo editor,' I told him but he still didn't get that I have nothing to do with print specs."

"You tell him a bigger *name* won't compensate for other deficiencies of size?" Maria chortled, a rich and throaty sound.

"Go ahead, laugh. You wouldn't think it was funny if—"

the Seduction

Before I could finish my sentence, my office door flew open and Stewart McClaren burst inside. He sauntered across the room, a lean, cool study in denim and leather, and planted himself in front of my drawing table.

"Lee Montara," he said as he lowered his thick lashes, "this is your lucky day. Go ahead, open it." His eyes hung closed a beat too long, as though the sight of me stirred a languid, overwhelming pleasure in him. He draped his tobacco-colored leather jacket over one shoulder. With his other hand, he held out a large portfolio secured at the top with two black bows that looked like laces from a pair of wingtip shoes.

I slipped a loose push pin into a carved teak box, then motioned him to the chair beside my desk. "Pinky's birdseed's in the blue ceramic jar," I said into the receiver. Surely even Stewart would get the message: Not everyone believed, as he did, that the sun rose and set—and magazines failed or succeeded—on the strength of Stewart McClaren's charisma.

Maria offered a cheerful *hasta luego* and I hung up. I presented Stewart with a cautious smile and a raised eyebrow. "What's this?"

"You're doing Milan, right?" Through a cloud of cedary cologne, he waved a graceful hand at the portfolio. Prince Stewart commanding the handmaiden.

Well, the handmaiden was about to become the Ice Queen. Stewart McClaren needed to understand that every photo editor in New York City was *not* panting for him. We weren't *all* intimidated by his antics, didn't care whether he pulled another stunt like the one, four years ago, that the magazine community had attributed to him. After a photo editor rejected his pictures, a carton arrived in her office. Scores of magazines had been cut up, squares missing from selected articles. When she'd checked the credits, she discovered the missing pieces had all been Stewart's photographs.

The next day, in the mail, she received a copy of the magazine she worked for. This time, the neat, square hole on the credit page marked the place where a picture of the editor, seated at her desk, had appeared.

"Page proofs are all in." I didn't wait for him to look up from the portfolio; he might consider a pause an invitation to press his point. "The winter book is closed, Stewart. We print on Monday."

He proceeded as though he hadn't heard me, tugging at the black laces, turning back the leather cover, spreading two contact sheets and twelve glossies on the desk.

The Duomo loomed from nowhere into a vacant sky. Trolley lines slashed across a bank window. Stewart's photographs were compositionally interesting, certainly, but they were all wrong for the magazine, too quirky, too lacking in the kind of narrative Mike had taught me to look for, unacceptable . . . even if Stewart *had* brought them in a month ago.

"Sorry, Stewart, but these don't work for me. Our readers want adventure, not confusion."

"Montara, you're doing yourself a disservice." He shrugged extravagantly, using his shoulders the way another man might use his hands or his voice, as a means of calling attention to himself. "Let's talk about what great pictures these are over dinner. How about, say, nine? I've got reservations at a dynamite fish restaurant."

Now, my smile held real pleasure. "Stewart, I'm out of here in ten minutes and on an airplane in three hours. Listen, our demographics are consistent. *City* readers have advanced degrees and make pots of money and they hate not understanding the pictures."

"And they don't want to be patronized. My photographs aren't easy, Montara. They *are* fresh. You've seen my *Vanity Fair* spread. You can't afford not to have me in your glitzy book." The corners of his thin lips turned down in a pout.

No temperament today, I thought impatiently. Not ever, not with me. "Didn't anyone ever tell you that restraint and a little class are business advantages? Don't threaten me, Stewart. Make me love it. That's all you have to do. You want to sell your portfolio? Make me long for it because I can't do without it."

He reached out and traced the knob of my wrist with his index finger, pulling away a second before I jerked my hand back. His voice was low, thick. "Don't forget to pack something white and flowing, Lee. We'll have a terrific time, you'll see. You like pompano? The restaurant does a great pompano. I'm staying at La Playa Blanca too. Best hotel on Cozumel."

Cozumel? What did he mean? *La Playa Blanca?* I felt my face flush with anger, but I pushed the portfolio toward him and forced myself to speak calmly. "Take these with you. It'll be easier than having Cindy mail them."

His hand shot forward. The photos churned, scattering along the carpet. "Don't play games with me, Lee. You must know you're driving me crazy. I think about you all the time, awake and asleep. Your violet eyes, your restless, beautiful hands, your long dark hair . . ." His sigh rattled the air.

What was he talking about? Driving him crazy? I'd seen Stewart McClaren maybe three times in the past six months, once at a museum and twice at parties. Hustling, on the make for assignments and exposure, the way free-lancers always are. Standing too close and whispering, the way Stewart always did. He never exchanged ten words with *any*one without steering the conversation back to *his* pictures, *his* last shoot.

"This is some tactic to land a spread in the magazine, right? Our pretty blond receptionist friend tell you where I was going?" I pushed out of my chair, too angry to sit. Twenty stories below, a river of lunch-hour strollers flowed south along Fifth Avenue toward Rockefeller Center in a constant, silent ooze. I tried to fix my mind on white sand and golden sun and the delight of snorkeling in azure water, on palm fronds and hibiscus to shoot for Mike's book. But Stewart McClaren cast a thin, dark shadow over the blue-meets-blue horizon line. I shoved the empty portfolio across the desk at him. "You'd better take your things and go."

"Hey, lady, you know, when someone tells you they're crazy about you, you should give them the courtesy of a response. But, okay, we'll talk about it tonight, on the beach."

He grabbed my shoulders and pressed his body to mine, his chest flattening my breasts, his breath damp against my cheek. "You didn't mean pictures, did you, Lee? You long for it already, don't you?"

I slammed my heel down on his instep. The action bypassed all thought, shocking me at first and then pleasing me.

He yelped and leapt back, glaring, then grabbed his leather jacket and strode into the hall.

"Cozumel. Shit," I hissed through clenched teeth. I snapped off the drawing light, tossed my keys into my purse, and slammed the office door shut. The warren of work spaces in the graphics room was quiet, the hall empty. Except for Cindy, her blond head bent over a copy of *GQ*, the reception area was as silent as a deserted battlefield.

"You shouldn't have told Stewart McClaren I was going to Cozumel," I muttered over my shoulder as I passed the desk.

Cindy's expertly arched eyebrows rose. "Lee, wait. I didn't— Maybe he checked with our travel agent."

I was sure the travel agent valued the *City* account too much to give out a personal itinerary.

"Actually, Cindy, it doesn't matter. I've got a solution. You have a bathing suit, don't you?" I plucked an envelope from my purse and tossed the airline ticket on Cindy's open magazine. "If you take a cab," I heard myself say, "you can just about get packed and make the flight."

The elevator doors closed behind me, damping the sounds of Cindy's astonishment.

Vacation: Well, I'd certainly vacated my life. Maria in my apartment. Cindy in my airplane seat. Where did that leave me? Without a destination, without a plan, that's where.

I pushed the sleeves of my jacket to my elbows, glanced at a window display of gaudy flower ties draped over men's sandals. As the sun warmed my bare arms, my stride lengthened, but neither my route nor my destination mattered, not really. I could walk to the East River or to the Hudson. I could stand all day on the observation deck of the Empire State Building if I wanted to. What difference did it make?

And then I laughed aloud, surprised by the gift of sudden understanding. This was precisely what Mike had sought when he maneuvered and juggled and constantly rearranged his life—the intoxication of possibilities.

It was delicious and it was true. No one, not the new feature writer or Cindy or any of the free-lance photographers who framed my life like a flat, neutral border, had any idea where I'd be ten minutes from now, ten hours from now. Ten days from now I'd surely be on the twentieth floor of a Manhattan office building working on the New Orleans issue for spring. At the moment I was a leaf on a pond, susceptible to the currents and whims of every breeze.

I nodded at a comic book vendor with reddish dreadlocks and a grin that carved his cheeks into soft, cinnamon-colored mounds and revealed a gap where a front tooth should have been. His black eyes reminded me of hot, dry countries where people collected water in clay jars.

"Hey, miss, what you need, it's all right here."

And why not? A little courage, courtesy of Wonder Woman and her golden lariat and silver bracelets. Some adventure with Tin Tin, a crystal ball, and a colorful gypsy troupe. I grabbed up both comics, lay a few bills in his cigar box, and strode off.

I had ten days to fill, and a promise to Mike I would absolutely keep. Those last three or four pictures were critical, and I was going to get them. Some other aborted vacation, I'd stay in New York. I'd get half-price tickets to shows and spend hours in the cool of the Frick garden. But now Mike was everywhere in this city, and the memories would blur my vision.

Taconic Hills. Rosie had been saying forever that she wanted me to spend some time with her. Maybe this was the right moment and Taconic Hills, sleepy and undemanding and certainly lush, the right place.

"I miss you, Lee. We're sisters but I feel like you've been keeping yourself away from me forever," Rosie had said last week when I'd called her to tell her about Cozumel.

Not forever, I had wanted to shout. Sometimes you push me away when you judge me.

But that feeling never lasted long; it always gave way again to the affection, to the permanent bond between us. It would be good to see Rosie, to hear her calm laughter and listen to her dreamy, distilled observations. Rosie liked to give advice; a different perspective wouldn't hurt.

If I could find a rental car—it was Thursday so maybe it would work out—I'd be on the Henry Hudson Parkway before the worst of rush hour traffic. I could be in Taconic Hills by dinnertime.

I continued downtown, filled with pictures of picking strawberries and making jam, of hunting with Rosie through dusty old church rummage shops for five-dollar treasures. Andrew and I would go for walks to the creek and discover salamanders and turtles and build dams out of rocks and twigs. I'd bring lots of film and work on composition and available light, and I'd finish *Lush Life.* We'd all sit on the porch in rocking chairs, reading, silent, glad for each other's company, and Stewart McClaren would vanish and Rosie would finally forgive me for leaving home.

A little time nestled in the domestic bosom of Rosie's peaceful country life would surely restore my balance.

2

Rolling meadows and trees in full leaf whipped by in an emerald blur as the cool air lifted my hair from my face. Mike would have loved this ride. Not as free or exposed as motorcycle travel, and not as dangerous, unless a state police cruiser was clocking me. I forced myself to slow down, checked the side mirrors as I swung onto Route 199 from the Taconic State Parkway. Nothing. Not a car, not a truck on the road behind me. The dark blue sedan that had been following me for twenty minutes, that speck that made me wonder for a brief moment where Stewart McClaren might be, had disappeared.

I hummed along with a Bonnie Raitt tape, finally shouting a chorus out the window, startling the cows in one field. The mingled scents of cut hay and wildflowers charged the air with end-of-semester memories, the first hint of summer solitude.

Ten whole days without clocks or schedules—a small sigh of contentment stirred in me at the thought.

The edge of the eastern sky shaded off into dark blue. I chugged up the long unpaved driveway, checking off familiar markers. The rut on the left that had bumped Rosie from her bicycle twenty years ago, tossing her onto the ground on her delicate, breakable wrist. The granite boulder pushing out of thick undergrowth like a stubborn, half-buried chin. The big, battered mailbox. I rolled to a stop beside the three pine trees, soldiers guarding the cornfield to the right. A scraggly line of rhododendron bushes flanked the other border, as always. The two-story colonial house seemed to have sagged a little, but the eyebrow windows above the front porch looked down jauntily, winking a greeting.

Andrew bounded down the steps, his yellow hair tousled, his six-year-old body clad in a polo shirt and jeans, and my heart lurched at the sight of him. How long had it been? Months? Half a year? He was impossibly taller, arms and legs leaner, his round indistinct child's face beginning to have a shape to it.

"Auntie Lee!" His arms clasped my neck and his legs twined around my waist before he slithered to the ground.

"Hi ho, kiddo." I bit my lip to keep from exclaiming over how big he'd gotten, and he rewarded me by grabbing my hand and tugging me forward to the porch.

"Come see the race car I'm making. Dad's gonna help with the steering when he gets back from the senior trip. Lucky stiffs, they get to miss a whole week of school. He's leaving . . . maybe tomorrow. This is the front bumper."

He chattered away, pointing proudly to a collection of boards and nails with definite car potential. I set my suitcase beside a white wicker table that sagged under the weight of an assortment of houseplants growing carelessly out of their clay pots.

The screen door swung open and Rosie stepped out, red hair glinting in the afternoon sun.

Did her cheeks always rise above that hollow filled with shadow but no flesh? Was her skin always so pale, like eggshells, like paper? Or had I stored an ideal Rosie in my memory, the way I held onto a picture of a rambling, gleaming mansion instead of the worn but comfortable farmhouse this really was? Rosie and her careless curls and faded shirt and shorts was such a contrast to the finished women I saw every day, that was all.

But my sister's voice sounded strained, a little too bright. "Lee, it's great to have you home."

The shadow puppet from Djakarta, the raku vase from Kyoto, the scattering of objects I'd gathered on trips for the magazine, had defined home for some time. I'd come to think of Taconic Hills as the protective shell from which I'd hatched before I moved to the city.

"You look tired or something, Rosie. Are you all right?"

Her gaze wandered out toward the trees at the horizon line. "Good old country work's making me tired. If you're not careful, I'll Tom Sawyer you right into helping. Got the back of the house painted, that's partly what I've been doing. Making rugs and selling them, of course. Gardening, cooking, cleaning. I volunteer at the senior center twice a week and I help Andrew with his homework, nothing very demanding. *You're* the one who works too hard."

I stepped back, surprised at the challenge in her voice. "Whoa, level six, Rosie. I ask what's wrong, and you charge full speed to a level-six confrontation."

Rosie's face colored until her freckles nearly disappeared. "Sorry. I *am* tired, and there's this . . . I'll tell you later. Here comes Paul." She kissed the top of her son's head and then pointed at a car, a vividly colored toy on the ribbon of dirt road leading from town. Arms windmilling as though he were guiding the car home, Andrew ran down the steps. Rosie followed a few paces behind him, leaving me alone on the porch with my vague sense of unease.

With a spray of gravel scattering in its wake, a sleek red Triumph pulled up. I associated such cars with men who played stubborn games of squash and drank only single-malt Scotch. Dark hair curling at his collar, the driver fit the image, his bemused air evidence that he'd somehow learned to squeeze all the pleasure out of life. "Be good, Rosie," he shouted over the roar of the engine. Too bad—apparently this wasn't the time for me to find out what that curious half-smile meant.

Paul Cooper, tall, thin, rumpled after a day of trying to coax scores of fifteen-year-olds into understanding—and caring about—the workings of state and federal governments, straightened his long legs and let his canvas briefcase slip to the ground.

"Dad! Auntie Lee's here!" Andrew flung himself at his father. Laughing, my brother-in-law swung the little boy up in his arms.

A shiver of envy chased down my spine. This was real, this was solid, as far from the world of picture files and permission battles and people like Stewart McClaren as it was possible to get.

Paul planted a brotherly kiss on my cheek, then hugged Rosie. "First a shower, then I can observe the social amenities. Come on, Rosie, you listen to my watery baritone and soap my back and these two can get reacquainted. How about a barbecue? We'll eat by the light of the Japanese lanterns and for dessert . . ." He waggled his eyebrows and leaned down to whisper something to his son.

"We're going to go to Millerton to the Tastee-Freez! Yowza!" Andrew's cheer rang with delight.

Still laughing, arms twined around each others' waists, Paul and Rosie disappeared into the house.

I wouldn't trade places with my sister, certainly. Mike and I would never have chosen to do without cities and photography and the bracing irritation of professional challenges, but Rosie's life did have a sweetness about it that always appealed to me when I was right here in the middle of it. In a few days, I knew from experience, I'd see the sameness and the quiet stretching endlessly, and the twinge of envy that nipped at me now would fade entirely.

Andrew's warm little hand clasped mine as we strolled to the end of the ice cream line. Taconic Hills had been exactly the right choice—my shoulders were unknotting, my mind approaching that state of placid emptiness I'd hoped to achieve in Cozumel. Being with Rosie and her family was a bonus, all the more satisfying because I'd been able to skip the prolonged period of imagining and projection that colored so many of my visits. Stewart McClaren, bless his megomaniacal heart, might actually have done me a favor. . . .

"Look there." Rosie pointed at the sky. "The moon is waxing. Be full in a week."

I smiled; nobody in New York City ever used the word *waxing* unless they were talking about hair removal or furniture polish.

From the middle of the line, three restless, tow-headed boys called out to Andrew and scuffed pebbles with their shoes. Their mother, a pretty woman in a thin cotton dress and canvas espadrilles, tapped her fingers against her arms and watched their antics impassively. The pouch-bellied man looking off into the distant darkness was surely their father. New people, I thought, farmhands maybe.

Andrew shouted a greeting to the boys, then gestured to one of the picnic tables dotting the grass beside the Tastee-Freez. "There's Rick." He pointed reverently to an angular teenager dressed in a black T-shirt and jeans, his black hair cut short on the sides and long on top so that it fell in artful disarray over his forehead. "Rick Decker is his whole name. He stays with me sometimes when Mom and Dad go out. See that red and blue and purple thing on his wrist? It's called a friendship bracelet because a friend gives it to you and you never take it off except if it falls off. And then you're supposed to give it back to the person who gave it to you."

Rick returned Andrew's wave but the teenager tracked Rosie with an intense, searching expression. Oh, yes, that was a familiar glitter in those smoky, dark eyes—but why had he chosen a woman fifteen, sixteen years older? I wanted my sister to look right at that young man and send him the message that there was nothing secret between them, let him know she understood the invitation and was turning it down.

"Joseph's here too. He always honks the Jeep horn twice when I get mail. You know Joseph, don't you, Auntie Lee?"

"Joseph's still the mailman?" Joseph Farley—no one ever called him Joe or Joey—had worn the same red bow tie since he'd started on our rural route years ago. His face was still polished a smooth, glowing pink that made me think of a glass paperweight I'd seen once in a Venetian shop. A pear-shaped woman with sagging skin and wispy, no-color hair stood beside him. "Who's that?" I whispered, leaning close enough to Rosie to smell the milky perfume of her skin.

"Don't you recognize her? That's his aunt, the one who worked in the school cafeteria. Retired two years ago."

"Dolores Farley?" She looked as though she'd gained fifty pounds and aged a century since I'd last seen her.

"She's had a couple of hard years. Last summer Joseph was hit by a milk truck. Freak accident, the roads were really wet, one of those big-boomer storms. Dolores took care of him until he healed. And the year before, right around the end of school, he fell off a ladder when he was cleaning the roof gutters. Seems to be okay now but she's been nursing him and worrying since, I guess, June two years ago."

"Hey, Mom, look who's coming. Don! He's my friend, you know, Auntie Lee. We go on rides together. He must've met Dad in the parking lot." Andrew's words spilled out in an excited stream.

I recognized his friend at once: the driver of the red Triumph. Mike would have approved of the stirrings I felt, for the first time in months, as I watched Don walk toward us. He was solid, easy in his own body, moving with the shambling, quiet grace of a confident man. Paul, just under six feet tall, had to look up to talk to him.

"This is my Auntie Lee, Don."

Don and I exchanged the smiles of people who don't yet know

each other but intend to change that. We all fell into a friendly silence as Andrew bounced from one foot to the other. *"Everyone's* here tonight. Can I play with Timmy? Can I, Dad?"

"Okay, but don't go far. Vanilla with chocolate dip, right?" Paul's hand lay carelessly on his son's shoulder.

Andrew nodded, then raced away to the corner of the parking lot where the flaxen-haired brothers were playing an increasingly noisy game of tag. The oldest brother whistled shrilly and scurried into the shadows, and I turned at the sound of a rich but unfamiliar voice.

"Andrew's introduction left out a few important details. Like my name. I'm Don Ward. In the mornings, I teach music to the recalcitrants at Pine Plains High School, and in the afternoon I'm at Roe-Jan with the fifth and sixth grade."

Paul rolled his eyes. "Don's my driver, when I leave Rosie the car. He's a medium through which the soul of his saxophone speaks. But, really, he's a jazz band escapee."

"Escaping *from* or escaping *to?"* The man intrigued me, no doubt about it, but I felt myself slipping into an unaccustomed, almost adolescent shyness. A good enough reason not even to try to go home again, if visiting Taconic Hills doomed me to emotional states I thought I'd long outgrown.

Don explained that he'd given up city pressures—that is, if a New Yorker would deign to call Buffalo a city, he added with a mischievous twinkle—for the tranquility of country life.

Before I could ask why he'd chosen Taconic Hills, a flicker of movement drew my attention to the four-foot-high brick wall separating the parking lot from a corn field beyond.

Two figures, thin and fat, stood facing each other, hands on hips— the parents of the trio of boys with whom Andrew had gone off? The woman took a step back. The man pursued her, his bulk bulldozing toward her remorselessly, inevitably. My half-formed question was interrupted by the girl behind the counter.

"Next! Oh, hi, Mr. Cooper, Mizz Cooper. Mr. Ward. What can I get you?"

As Paul and Rosie and Don stepped up to the window, a snarl erupted from the parking lot. I felt myself being reeled toward the darkness, to the husband and wife and their anger. A sour taste rose to my throat. Horrified, I saw the larger figure kick out with his foot. The woman danced back, shrieking.

Didn't anyone else see this? Didn't they hear the sounds of fear and anger coming from the darkness? They were all going to stand around and pretend—the way all the people in that Memphis bar had pretended—that nothing was happening.

The woman broke away and darted deeper into the shadows.

"You come back!" The man ran after her, jammed her hard against the bricks, pinned her slender body to the wall.

I looked around wildly. Paul and Don, their hands full of ice cream cones, joked with the counter girl. Joseph Farley and his aunt stared at the flavor board. The high school students at the picnic table hooted and tossed a baseball cap from hand to hand.

What made him think he had the right to hurt her? And why did they all give him permission with their silence? I started to run.

"Lee! What are you doing?"

Rosie's shout drifted to me from some faraway place as I sprinted toward the wall. The smell of cheap wine and sweat hit me full in the face, and I gasped. I shoved at the man's shoulders. "Leave her alone! Stop," I panted.

He raised his thick arm. Struggling for air, I pushed against him again. So soft—that belly was warm, sloppy, like a full cow's udder, like a sack of undercooked oatmeal. Who had helped Mike? It would have been so easy for someone to be witness, to say *No, you can't do that!*

That was *my* voice crashing against the cool night air.

"Mind your own goddam business, lady." A growl rose from his throat. He swatted me away.

I stepped in front of the cowering woman as the man lurched closer, his jaw rigid with fury.

My hand curled into a fist. My arm stiffened. Then fingers closed around my wrist. Someone pulled me back.

"All right, Hank. Cool down. It's all over. Come on, Lee." It was Paul's voice, his hand on my elbow, guiding me toward the light.

I took in a huge, gulping breath. A ripple of pleasure coursed through me.

I had stopped him.

I had stopped his fists and his hotheaded rage while everyone else stood around pretending not to see or hear, eating their ice cream and ignoring what they didn't want to know.

Everyone's eyes fixed on me. Drumming filled my head. Rick Decker and the crowd of young men near the picnic table, Don Ward, Joseph and Dolores Farley: They all watched me with cold interest, peeling back my skin with their eyes. I was a specimen, an alien, and they looked at me with the special distaste they reserved for people who broke the rules . . . but I'd done it.

I raised my head and walked briskly to Andrew, who licked his ice cream and stared at his sneakers. Rosie stood behind him, her hands clutching his shoulders.

"People can't solve their problems by hurting each other," I said when I regained my voice. I knelt beside him and brushed an invisible hair from his forehead. "Sometimes they forget that."

He avoided my eyes. "And you were helping them remember, right, Auntie Lee?"

I nodded. A cold core of me knew that no such high-and-righteous thought had entered my head until the words fell out of my mouth, but I had no intention of taking them back.

I had stopped him. And I was glad.

9:30 a.m.

A pile of white cotton and yellow eyelet, grown tall to the point of nearly tilting into an unruly heap, lies on the floor beside the basket. I want to do more than simply remember; I want to get rid of that part of me that has been saturated with him.

"The waiting, that's what's making you upset. You're used to being able to charge in and make everything come out right, all the pictures matching the words, everything done on deadline. But this is hard. For me, too."

"That's what he's counting on, Rosie. He knows that about us. He knows that you're terrified of something happening to Andrew. He's done a good job of identifying our most vulnerable spots. He's playing to that."

"Our V spots?" Rosie starts giggling and I join her, and soon we're laughing so hard that tears leak from the corners of our eyes and our sides hurt.

Because we're laughing so loud and so hard, we're not sure we've really heard the telephone ringing. But the second ring echoes through the house. And then there's quiet.

"It's starting again." Rosie chokes out the words. I begin counting the silence under my breath as Rosie eyes the telephone, but I lose track somewhere after thirteen. "This is nuts. I'm going to unplug it." I jump up and move toward the table.

"No! What if something's happened to Andrew? You can't do that." Rosie puts herself between me and the telephone.

Of course she's right, and I back away, my hands open to her to show her I'm sorry. "Okay. I see your point, we won't unplug the phone."

I expect a smile but Rosie's features harden. "That was a ridiculous suggestion. There aren't any rules, are there, for how to behave in a situation like this? I was never afraid before all his damn black bows and all the other stuff. You know him so well, you say. You're so sure he isn't going to use Andrew? As a way of getting to me? To us. I hate that I can't see him, can't touch him. Move away from that phone and tell me again why you're so sure he's going to leave Andrew alone."

The only way I can convince her is to tell her everything I'm thinking but I want to put that off a little while longer. "Look, Rosie, at least we know that when the telephone's ringing, he's not here."

She shakes her head. "At least we *think* he's not here. There are all sorts of ways we could be wrong."

The telephone begins to shrill; Rosie's hands tremble. "I'm going to answer that. You stay here." She walks briskly to the table, then straightens her back, taller now and defiant as she reaches for the phone. "Hello?"

Rosie repeats her question, "Hello? Hello?" and holds the receiver in front of her, staring at it as though she might see the caller through the wires. "No one there."

She hangs up, and I'm suddenly cold with the meaning of the call. "Okay, now he knows for sure *we're* here."

Rosie is standing like a stick, like a lightning rod, in the middle of the room.

I reach in and pull a bulky red remnant from the basket. "Lord, I can't believe you still have this. Mom's old Christmas tablecloth. I haven't seen it in years. You remember that last Christmas we all lived here together?"

She lets her breath out in a sigh. "It was like we were on our best behavior, as though we knew somehow that by the next year

Grandma and Grandpa would both be gone and Mom and Dad would be packing up to move. There was a heavy snowfall, I remember, kind of a storybook holiday."

I have distracted her, as I'd intended. I want to give her a little more time, so I will continue this line of talk for a while; it's too painful to watch her being transformed by him even when he's not present.

"Are you kidding?" I'm still amazed that we participated in the same events and now use such dissimilar words to talk about the memories and feelings. "Horror story is more like it. Everything was so regimented. All those arguments, Mom insisting I had to be home for Christmas Eve dinner when I'd been invited to go caroling. I still wish I hadn't given in."

Now Rosie shakes her head. "Stop thinking of it as a restriction on your freedom. Maybe you could look at that Christmas Eve as an anchor Mom gave you to a stable world where everything isn't up for redefinition every minute."

"Forget it. It's one of the things we don't agree on. And we've figured out that we can survive without agreeing on everything." The rain patters down, a curtain of it, hazy and hypnotic, and I stalk the edges of the room and come back to the oval rug and sit beside my sister.

"If we do survive this," she says without expression, "then you're right."

I fold the tablecloth and put it on my lap, like a robe I'd wear sitting in a deck chair on a North Atlantic cruise in winter. "I guess I never thought about what happens to all this stuff. I use it for cleaning rags or give it away to the donation box on Second Avenue."

The steady rain drums noisily on the roof. Thunder rolls overhead. Rosie leans across the floor to touch the cloth on my lap. "How could you throw out something that connects you to your own past? Broken appliances, sure, but a Christmas tablecloth? A lifetime of memories for us, thirty-five years at least for Mom and Dad, and for the rest of the family."

"Exactly. That makes thirty-five years of nothing changing, of no one doing things differently. You remember what Mom told me when I offered to bring hors d'ouevres to Christmas that first year I was on my own?"

"You did make a point. I never told you, I guess I should have, but I admired you for doing that."

the *Seduction*

"You did? Then why did you let me go on believing I was alone, that I was the only one in the family who ever questioned those things? If I deviated even a little, it was like a message that I didn't love them, or respect them or something, I never knew what."

"Well, you understand, don't you, Mom tried. She thought she was being really progressive when she said you could bring the hors d'ouevres." Rosie's hands lie flat, splayed like tree roots on the rug.

I finger the tablecloth draped over my knees. "She said, I remember her words very clearly, they were, 'Honey, you can bring an appetizer as long as it's not something too exotic.' " My laughter bubbles up again.

"I probably should have told you then how impressed I was. It would have been reassuring, I can see that now. I guess triangles of peanut butter and jelly on white bread with the crust cut off was about as unexotic as you could get. I kept looking for the real tray, the one you were going to bring out after the joke."

I make statements, not jokes, I want to tell her, but a kind of unreality has set in again. Is the gun in my pocket a statement? Can it possibly be a joke?

The proof, either way, is upstairs in the closet under the eaves, but I can't go up to check. I think I know anyway; Rosie's face is evidence enough of what's going on. She peers out the rain-smeared window and shakes her head as if to tell me she sees nothing. I listen more intently to make up for what she doesn't see. "I'm afraid I'm not being very comforting right now," she says.

We both wander for a moment in our own thoughts, and we jump at the same time when the lights flicker and dim. But they brighten again and we exhale, relieved, letting go for just a moment of the need to see around corners and to hear whispers among the thunderclaps.

"I keep thinking there's something we should be doing." Her hands unable to be still, Rosie snips off a piece of thread, slips it through the eye of the needle in the pin cushion, knots it. She shakes her head as though she's clearing it of ugly images.

Now it's my turn to fidget and I stride the length of the room again; maybe I'll get somewhere else if my steps are big enough.

Rosie sets the needle in the fabric and rises, putting herself in my path. "You're letting yourself get too worked up. You have to get hold of yourself or you'll be unable to respond rationally."

"Rationally? I don't even know what's reasonable and what's over the edge any more. This isn't like coming up against a stubborn editor-in-chief or, I don't know, a door that's swelled shut from the humidity. I can't budge it with force, and I don't know what else to do."

Rosie puts her arms around me, containing me in an embrace, wrapping me in her own certainty. "Just get calm, Lee. We worked it out together. You'll know what to do when the time comes. Have faith in yourself."

Faith. I let myself sink into my sister's warmth, grateful that we're here together. I feel safe, and I pull away to look into Rosie's eyes. "Thanks for the pep talk. I'll be all right."

I'm aware that this is the second time in an hour that Rosie has used her physical body instead of words to change the course of things, and this new behavior makes me wonder what other surprises await me.

"You *will* be all right," she says softly. "I'll see to that. Will you turn on the lamp?"

As soon as she completes her request, the sound of shattering glass explodes from the back of the house.

3

My sleep was usually deep and dreamless, a long period each night of forgetting. But I tossed fitfully and awoke before sunrise, so disoriented that I struggled out of bed and made myself stand at the bedroom window a good, long time to be sure the summer-green leaves on the sugar maples at the edge of the meadow hadn't turned scarlet and fallen off the trees overnight.

The room felt tiny, the scent of the flowers Rosie had put in the china vase beside my bed oppressive. Mike's thoughtful face, looking back at me from the photograph I'd set on the shelf above the desk last night, seemed full of warnings. The incident at the ice cream stand lingered like a hangover.

I dressed quickly and tiptoed outside, wandered across the yard to the garden and opened the gate. My sneakers left shallow indentations in the soft earth. Rosie and Paul's shared passion for garden neatness always produced straight rows, and with so many plants coming in full, I expected to feel a calming, orderly peace as I stepped lightly between two ranks of lettuce. But when I knelt to examine the plants nearest me, my stomach knotted.

It was like hearing a favorite song with a phrase that had somehow slid sharp. Half a row of lettuce was ruined, the plants stunted and damaged. Stubs poked out of the straw mulch, uneven spikes turning black, the tender top growth eaten away. As I straightened, glittery black eyes peered at me through the peas.

A raccoon.

Relieved, almost laughing, I stamped my feet and yelled at him.

He stared at me, defiant. *I belong here too,* he seemed to be saying, *and I'll stay as long as I like. Unless you plan to do something about it.*

The brazen fellow paid me no mind. The pie-tin reflectors on the fence posts and the scarecrow—outfitted by Rosie in old jeans, a red plaid shirt with fray-cuffed sleeves, and a Mets cap—hadn't done their job. I threw a pebble in the direction of the peas.

Except for his searching eyes, the raccoon didn't move.

I tossed a handful of stones, but he just tilted his head and continued to watch me. Some country women, Rosie or Ruth Hoving, perhaps, would march to the bedroom closet, take down a hunting rifle, prove to the truculent creature just who was in charge, but I couldn't picture myself standing with feet planted wide apart to blast the interloper out of the garden, could only conjure a comical image of setting a cardboard carton over the fat body, leaving the black-ringed tail to point at me in accusation.

The raccoon craned to get a better look at me. Then he squeezed his round body through a hole in the fence and waddled disdainfully toward the stream behind the house. Having stared me down, he was off to celebrate his victory.

In my way of measuring, I was the victor. The raccoon was no longer in Rosie's garden.

Rosie stood beside the kitchen table, rubbing her face like a small child struggling to wake up. "I haven't slept this late in months."

"Then you didn't hear your visitor. Cheeky raccoon ate half your lettuce." I sipped the coffee she handed me. The rich, hot slide of liquid down my throat stung me into feeling like myself again. But Rosie was eyeing me with stern intensity, and from her expression I knew I was in for a lecture. Or maybe she was ready to talk about the ripple that was disturbing the placid waters of her life, that flash of a secret that had been interrupted by Paul's arrival yesterday. "What, Rosie? What's the matter?"

She set her mug on the table. "Nothing's the *matter*. I think you ought to know—the Steubens are going through a bad time. He's lost his job at the Agway and she's working at the market in Hillsdale. Peggy says he's a good man under a lot of pressure, and Hank, well, he gets so damn hangdog after an explosion. Not that this happens all the time. This is maybe the third time."

"The third time you know about. That man looked capable of anything last night. What if he'd hurt her?" The early morning strangeness licked at the edges of my consciousness again, like a toad's tongue searching for flies.

"It's not like that, honestly." She inhaled the curl of steam rising from her mug, then sipped the coffee. "I'm surprised you heard that raccoon and I didn't. He couldn't have been any noisier than all those sirens and garbage trucks you sleep through in the city."

"I guess it's all what you're used to. Nothing disturbs my sleep at home. Listen, you threw a switch but I'm still on the old track. Last night—I don't feel comfortable dismissing it by saying it's the Steubens' business. Whatever happened, I let myself go right past thinking to *doing*, and I don't like it. Anyway, yesterday, you started to tell me about . . ."

Rosie was stirring her coffee, making endless circuits around the bottom of the cup with her spoon with the concentration she usually reserved for the biographies she devoured by the pound from the library.

"So," I said, still searching for common ground, "we're having continental breakfast today?"

She fiddled with the lid of a jar of preserves. "Maybe that's what it is at your Parisian *pensions*. Us country folks still call it toast and coffee."

Before I could decide if we were engaged in a familiar dialectic about pretensions and simplicity, Andrew and Paul clattered down the stairs, squabbling cheerfully about whether the race car should be painted red or black. When he spotted me, a gorgeous smile broke across my nephew's face, as though he'd forgotten I was there and the surprise of it all added to his delight.

"You wanna have breakfast on the porch like we always do, Auntie Lee?" He leaned against me, and I nuzzled his cheek, breathing the smell of shampoo and soap. "There's a family of sparrows, you should see them, the babies got so big, and they all come if I throw them a piece of my toast."

"Sounds good to me. I never get to have breakfast on my porch at home." I handed him a piece of peanut butter toast and bit into my own, savoring the warm thickness.

"How come?" Andrew absently pressed his head against my arm and chewed while he waited for my answer.

"Don't have one." I grinned and refilled my cup, and we ambled outside.

Paul and Rosie trailed behind us. In the full morning light, the lilacs looked sadder, older. Rust tinged the edges of the few remaining flower clusters. Smoke belched from a tractor as it started in Ike Kronenburg's field across the road. Business as usual—the old Taconic Hills routines hadn't changed a bit. On cue, the sparrow and her speckled brood twittered and clamored for Andrew's crumbs.

Paul groaned and pointed to the road below. "Don'll be here in ten seconds. Hey, I forgot to tell you. He wants us to come hear him play at the Edgewood tonight. We'll all go—it'll be like the old days." He waited, his eyes measuring first Rosie's response and then mine.

Well, why not? I liked the thought of watching Rosie and Paul dance, holding each other close the way they used to when I spied on them from the top of the stairs when I was thirteen and my sister an ever-so-much older fifteen. And I wouldn't mind losing myself in the sad, sexy yearning of a well-played saxophone. "Love to," I said, almost too enthusiastically.

"Promise you'll hum in my ear?" Rosie fluttered her lashes, vamping as if for a camera, and squeezed Paul's hand.

"Off-key, just the way you like it, darlin'. I have to finish posting final grades. See you by, I guess, five." He handed Rosie his cup, grabbed his briefcase, and brushed her cheek with his lips.

Andrew lifted his face to his father's kiss, then scrambled to the porch rail and pressed his wiry body against Rosie's chest. Together, we watched Don's car roll down the road. Andrew's shoulders slumped; he muttered a reproachful "Dad" under his breath.

"Paul's supposed to wave now," Rosie explained softly. "Andrew likes the rituals. Me, too."

"It will be summer vacation soon," I told my nephew, "and then you can spend lots of time with your Dad, building that spaceship." Laughing, I pointed to the pile of boards on the porch.

the Seduction

"It's a *race car*, remember? Hey!" Andrew's voice was indignant. "Who put *that* there? What's—"

His little body tensed and he stared at the corner of the porch. I followed his gaze, my throat constricting.

This was why I had slept so poorly. This was what I had been waiting to find.

"Bus is coming, Andrew." The familiar growl of the old engine built to a whine as the bus struggled up the hill. Rosie spoke to her son in a slow, soothing voice. "Take your lunch box and go wait at the end of the drive, sweetie. I'll take care of it. Go on now."

Her hands firmly on his shoulders, she steered Andrew to the steps. He kept tossing confused looks back at the porch, until Rosie bent to him. "I'll throw them away," she whispered, "and clean off the wood. Don't forget to wave when you get to the road. Auntie Lee says she wants you to take her down to the stream, today or tomorrow, okay? Go on."

He took a tentative step toward the drive, then another, until finally he raced across the lawn. "Bye, Mama. Bye, Auntie Lee!"

"Bye, Andrew." We both raised our hands in farewell. Neither of us looked at the corner of the porch until the boy climbed the steps into the yellow bus and the doors closed after him with a hiss.

Then, the bus pulled away; Rosie spun around and dashed across the porch.

Someone had twisted the blossoms from a bundle of gray-green flower stems and wrapped them in a black satin ribbon two inches wide and tied in a perfect bow. The bizarre bouquet rested on the neatly stacked boards. A foul stink rose from the slime covering the decaying stalks.

"It's yarrow. Lacy leaves," Rosie whispered. "Black lace."

The stench made me queasy. "Looks like you've got a secret admirer," I said lightly. I thought of Rick Decker, Andrew's baby-sitter, his sharp face pointing toward us, his intense gaze following Rosie, delivering a secret message. Those dark-eyed boys always felt compelled to invent the romantic gesture.

"One of us does, anyway." Rosie reached for the rotting flower stems with two fingers, as though they might infect her if she touched them without the proper precautions. "Everyone was watching you last night."

So Rosie was blaming me for this silly prank. Perhaps I should have realized last night, before it was too late, that I was about to violate the rules of this tradition-steeped community. And then another thought pushed its way past my annoyance. Was it possible that I'd brought this strangeness with me from the city?

Where, the smallest voice demanded, *was Stewart McClaren right now?*

4

I was almost sucked into the dark, fibrous heart of the image: all that thick green slime glistening at the bottom of the blackened stalks, the leaves curling in on themselves wetly, as though trying to escape the rot. . . . It practically defined an absolute end of the spectrum, lushness gone too far into decay, and I had to get it on film, even though I knew it would never be part of the book. I knelt to get a closer look. The swollen mass had once been smooth, full of life, hadn't it, and it had passed in stages to this other—sickening—state. The smell drove me back.

"This is, as the mall rats say, righteously gross." To break the spell, I started to laugh at my own words but stopped; taking a deep breath was ill-advised.

"It's going right in the compost. I'm not going to smell that mess all day." Rosie's voice was soft but her words echoed in my head, abrupt, clipped short by impatience.

"Hold on, Rosie. It'll only take a second. I want to get a few pictures. It's a visual paradox, you know? A tainted offering, a gift of decay. I'll be right back."

I ran into the kitchen and grabbed my camera from the little desk where Rosie paid bills and wrote out recipes in her round, precise letters, then sprinted out to the porch.

"Light's wonderful." I spoke to Rosie's back. She was looking out across the lawn, her head tilted up as though she were checking the sky for birds of prey. "No glare. The detail will be sharp—"

I steadied myself against the stack of boards with one foot and leaned in for a closeup, advanced the film, turned the F-stop down a notch, shot another three, leaned back.

"Are you done?"

The ice in her voice was as clear and biting as it had been on those occasions—and there had been too many of them to suit either of us—when she'd walked into the kitchen to find Aunt Christa, head propped on hands, nattering away at me or when she'd found me deep in conversation with my current beau.

"Almost." I hoisted myself to stand on the porch rail so I could get a bird's-eye view. It wasn't like Rosie to let this prank—wasn't that pretty much required of high school seniors, a final irresponsible misdemeanor before adulthood?—ruffle her calm. I clicked off two more shots, then let the camera dangle from the strap as I searched her face for information. "All yours."

Wordlessly, she held the foul bouquet out in front of her by the bow, looking for all the world like one of those psychics who locate missing people by communing with their cherished objects. I shrugged and went into the kitchen; Rosie carried the bundle around to the back of the house. I watched from the window as she shook the flower stems out of the satiny bow onto the compost pile and then forked a layer of hay over the heap.

Her mouth was pinched with distaste. Her face shone with sweat; she lifted the hem of her shirt and wiped at her upper lip, a gesture so strange that my senses went on alert to monitor for other signs of this new Rosie, this sister moved to an unfamiliar coarseness by something I didn't wholly understand.

I pushed aside a stack of mail and set the camera back on the desk in the kitchen. By the time Rosie padded back into the kitchen her features were rearranged to their old, comfortable serenity. "We have to get going. I promised Sarah Hoving we'd stop by to say hello before she leaves to work on her Craryville hives. You think maybe some-one's trying to get your attention?"

"Like who? Nobody even knows I'm here."

Rosie quirked an eyebrow; I was grateful when she turned to the sink and started rinsing breakfast dishes, leaving me to scan my memory of all the faces at the Tastee-Freez, and to wonder again about that blue sedan on the Taconic State Parkway. After his display in my office—yesterday seemed so far away, so much had happened—and after his tricks cutting up magazines four years ago, Stewart McClaren seemed capable of anything.

At least I could track him down, using simple tools I worked with every day; all I needed was my voice and the telephone. It would give me something to do so that I didn't feel so without control. This wasn't going to get out of hand. I wouldn't let it.

"And that's the story. He hasn't checked into the hotel on Cozumel and the airline won't tell me whether he actually boarded the plane. There's no answer at his studio or at his apartment." Diner noises rattled around us and I stabbed at my pie, annoyed that the morning's intrusion was still the focus of conversation between me and my sister, even, by now, bored with the whole affair. "So. Who's this Don Ward?"

"My strawberry rhubarb pie is better than this." Rosie smiled broadly. "Isn't he something? He's a friend of Arnie Kincaid's, the principal, you know, at Roe-Jan. Arnie got together with the folks in Pine Plains and solved a budget crisis for both school districts by creating a shared music position. Don says he likes the freedom of the twenty-, thirty-minute drive in the middle of the day. Paul's been saying since Thanksgiving that you two would really hit it off." She paused for a breath and peered at me expectantly. "Say something, Lee."

"He's kind of cute." I grinned, and we broke up laughing, the way we did when we were children testing out the pleasures of gossip, learning to trust that absolutely no one else would ever hear the bits of truth and fantasy we traded in the dark before we fell asleep. "*Cute*," I said as the giggles subsided. "God, I haven't used that word in—"

"Is it really almost three o'clock?" Rosie asked, leaning forward to hear my answer above the thump and twang of the jukebox music. "Andrew will be getting off the bus at twenty after. How could I lose track of time?" She slid to the edge of the booth, fumbling through her purse as though the lost minutes might turn up at the bottom.

"This one's on me." I scooped up the check and laid a ten-dollar bill on the table, aware of the din and the bustle of the diner. Something had tuned my senses to high alert. Perhaps it was her sudden urgency or the feeling of intrusion I'd been trying to shake since the day before, but a sudden movement and a flash of color, tobacco brown, made my breath catch in my throat. "Was there . . . did some guy wearing a leather jacket just go into the men's room? Hang on a minute, okay? I think that was him."

I charged toward the rear of the diner, heart pounding, wondering if he'd seen me, wondering how long I'd wait before I asked someone to go in there and check. When Stewart McClaren came strolling through the door, I'd tell him exactly what I thought of him and what I'd do if he didn't leave me alone. I wouldn't sit still for his ugly games.

Rosie stood beside me, her foot tapping. "Can we go, please, Lee? I don't want Andrew to come back from school to an empty house. Not today."

Before I could respond, the door swung open and a squash-faced man with a receding hairline shoved his arms into his brown leather jacket and leered at us. "Help you gals with something?"

"I doubt it." I tugged Rosie out into the warm air, my face flaming with embarrassment. Had I wanted it to be Stewart? Was I going to see him everywhere now? Furious with him and with myself, I pulled the car door shut with a bang as Rosie turned the key.

We drove the entire twelve miles to the house in silence; Rosie, her foot heavier on the gas than usual, offered perfunctory waves to neighbors, Deeny Lambert, Joseph Farley, Peter Hoving, whoever we passed on the road, but said nothing to me. We stopped to retrieve a thick packet of envelopes and catalogs from the mailbox, and as we approached the house, I spotted a dented old sedan I didn't recognize, parked beneath the big sugar maple. My mind raced: Stewart Mc-Claren would never drive such a déclassé car.

Relief lifted the frown from Rosie's forehead as we got out of the car. "Rick's here. Baseball practice must've been canceled. Paul must've told him we need him to stay with Andrew tonight. Sometimes he comes for dinner when Paul and I are going out."

I pulled open the screen door to a ripple of male laughter, Andrew's little boy giggle and a teenage baritone chuckle, bursting from the kitchen. The sounds, so normal, so happy, drew us to the rear of the house. "Hey, guys, we're back," Rosie called as we approached the kitchen.

"Mom! Auntie Lee, you didn't tell me you were going to make a cake." Andrew stood on tiptoe, his nose almost touching the glossy icing of a chocolate cake.

Cake?

"I told Andy we'd have to wait for you, that maybe you were having a party or bringing it to someone's house or something." Rick, his hip slung against the door frame, sent Rosie a message that didn't have anything to do with cake. He fingered the colorful braid at his wrist as though his hands needed to be doing something to take his mind off his real thoughts.

"Now, where did that come from?"

Rosie walked past Rick, oblivious to the heat of his glance, and bent to give her son a hug. Concentrating the way she always has if she wants to avoid seeing something, especially someone's interested or inquisitive glance, she set her purse on the counter and examined the envelope on top of the sheaf of mail.

The cake sat on a plain white paper plate in the center of the table, the chocolate frosting laid on in tight swirls, a scarlet cherry marking the exact center. Neighbors weren't likely to bring a cake by, not all the way into the kitchen, not without a reason. If someone had noticed my arrival and brought a welcoming gift when we weren't home, they'd leave it on the porch, according to the rules of country hospitality. And it would be on a proper plate, china or cut glass, not this flimsy paper affair.

"Can I have some, Mom?" Andrew leaned his head against her thigh and looked up like an eager puppy, his arms at his sides and his dirt-smudged fingers already clutching the cake-cutter, which had belonged to our grandmother. "I can do it real good. Miss Kennard showed us how, and I can make real straight slices. We each had a turn last week at school, remember I told you. Can I, Mom? Auntie Lee, you get the first piece." As he stood with the knife poised over the cherry, his nose crinkled. "Eeeyew, there's an ant on the plate."

Rosie scooped the tiny speck into a paper napkin and tossed the napkin into the garbage. "Andrew, wait. Let me have that knife. Have some oatmeal cookies now. Let's save the cake for later so we don't spoil our dinner."

"Mom, look . . ." Andrew's brow furrowed and his mouth

twisted as though he were trying to solve a difficult math problem. "There's another one."

Rosie's gaze flickered from the cake plate to Rick. He laid a hand on Andrew's shoulder and nodded to Rosie, just once. I wondered how they'd come to such intimacy, to this silent, almost expressionless communication that passed between them.

"Come on, champ. Let's take those cookies and shoot a few hoops. I gotta go soon. I want to show you some pointers for making great lay-ups." Rick grabbed four cookies; Andrew followed him out the door.

"What's going on, Rosie? People do this when someone dies, when someone's sick. They leave food then, sure. But they leave it on the porch or on the steps or something, with a cover over it and a note saying who left it. And in real dishes, right?"

Rosie peered at the icing pooled at the bottom of the cake. "Looks suspiciously like the canned stuff I use when I'm in a hurry." She lifted the cake cutter, sliced into it.

First two, then four, then a swarm of black ants straggled out of the crumbly yellow cake. Heads jerking and legs slipping over the shiny icing, they scrambled frantically over the paper plate.

The sight made my teeth clench. I snatched the knife from Rosie's hand, sliced a straight line an inch away from the first cut, and fished out a small black satin bow with the tip of the cake knife. "Just like the flowers."

Her skin damp and white, Rosie choked out a hoarse whisper as she swept the plate, the cake, the ants, into a plastic trash bag and twisted a wire tie around the top. "Someone's trying to scare us," she said as she dropped the bag into the metal can beside the back steps.

Someone? Rick had been in the kitchen with Andrew when we arrived. I heard the edge of hardness in my voice. "Isn't it pretty obvious? You have to confront him, tell him he's got to stop this nonsense. Rick, I mean. Talk about trying to get someone's attention. . . . I'd bet that's what it is."

Rosie's face was oddly blank, her body stiff. Outside, under the big walnut tree, Andrew sat chattering at Rick's side on the fallen log that Paul had turned into a bench. Rick stared up at the kitchen window with such yearning that I withdrew guiltily.

I'd assumed all these years that my sister's life was a pleasant round of predictably ordinary events. Trouble came in the form of the car breaking down on the way to the grocery store, Andrew getting the flu the day before spring vacation, the water heater giving up the ghost just when guests arrive for a weekend—all manageable, everyday.

This was different.

Rick Decker. Black bows.

"You still haven't found out where that Stewart McClaren is." Rosie picked up the stack of mail, the cake apparently forgotten. Her movements were measured; her voice calm. "Maybe you should call the city, see if your friend, the one who's staying in your apartment, has heard from him."

Because I wasn't sure I could get Rosie to answer me about Rick and because Stewart *did* have a place of honor on the list of possibilities, I turned without comment and punched out my own telephone number. I pictured the ivory phone on my desk, the hammered brass jar with all my pencils and mat knives, the photographs of taxi drivers on the wall. *Come on, Maria, answer.* But the machine cut in on the fourth ring and I heard my own voice saying I'd be away, leave a message for me or Maria, call you back when I can. I pressed the retrieve-messages code and as the tape rewound, I smiled at the thought of Pinky tilting his head and squawking at the voices on the tape.

Two hang-ups. The third message, filled with static, seemed far away. The occasional sound of car tires slapping along a distant roadway provided an erratic backbeat.

Hello, Lee, the voice murmured. *Great paint job on the back of the house. Always did like soft colors. Much better than that acidy, glaring white. Aren't the cornfields looking healthy? I do wish the lilacs were just starting to flower instead of being so far past their prime. You'd look so beautiful surrounded by lilac flowers. . . .* And then a click. A cold, final click. Instead of a pile of mutilated magazines, Stewart was delivering his hateful message in brand new ways.

"He's here."

Rosie nodded and went on flipping through the mail, sorting envelopes into two neat piles on the desk. "What do you mean, he's here?"

"Stewart McClaren. He left a message on my answering machine. He's here, somewhere where he can see the lilacs and notice the paint on the back of the house."

"I guess it's time to start locking the doors. If I can find the keys." Rosie lay one hand on each stack of paper, her hands stark and red against the white of the envelopes. "You're going to laugh at me because I don't usually think this way, and that's all right. I don't really know who's leaving these things, Lee. I don't think it's Rick. You heard him, you saw his face when we came home. He was as surprised as we were. Maybe it's Stewart, maybe it's someone else, but whoever it is, they're giving us gifts. They're embarked on a . . . I don't know, it's a weird courtship of one of us."

"Or both of us."

Rosie's face had lost its vagueness. Her skin was pink, her eyes bright. "Don't say anything to Paul, all right? He's leaving tomorrow and I don't want him to worry while he's away."

I heard myself promise not to tell.

5

Strange, what soothes you when you find yourself on alien terrain demanding navigation skills no one's ever taught you. For me, that night, comfort was in the stars swimming in the black sea of fragrant summer air. They'd been there for eons, pinned to the velvet sky, glittering above celebrations and parties, above births and marriages, courtships and deaths. They'd been a friendly presence when I was shedding the skin of my childhood, and tonight I was grateful for their company.

Stewart McClaren and Rick Decker aside, I was determined to have a good time. I would drive down a quiet country road to the Edgewood, a boxy log cabin that had featured rock and roll in the 1970s, country music in the 1980s, and now, according to Paul, mixed it up so that in any month, anyone with the price of a beer could hear live music to suit any taste.

Rosie had convinced Paul to stay home—time alone, just the three of them, she said, a little shared quiet before he left on the senior trip. I didn't protest; I was relieved to know that Rick wouldn't be in the house and that Andrew would be reassured that all was truly right with his world.

Except for minor changes in their shapes and colors, the vehicles that crowded the Edgewood parking lot might have been left here from my last visit: pickup trucks, several older American cars, a station wagon or two. The bright red Triumph was the best evidence that fourteen years had passed.

Two people in jeans and white shirts, arms twined around each others' waists, stumbled laughing into a long rectangle of yellow light as the door opened. I walked past them into the brightly lit room. A swirl of sounds and smells—laughter, glasses clinking, voices shouting across tables, the pleasant mix of beer and wood polish and popcorn—greeted me.

Despite blasts of air-conditioning, the room was warming up. Jazz at the Edgewood had drawn a good-size crowd, and I made my way past amiable clusters of people to the empty stool at the corner of the bar. I ordered a Bud and prepared to let the memories wash over me. All the times I'd sat with a crowd of friends at the long table in the back, laughing, trying out a new gesture, striking an attitude of self-possession; the evenings of endless dancing, lost in the music, sweaty and not caring, only feeling good to be moving—I'd dip into them, for distraction and to measure the changes in my life.

"Any requests?"

That full, resonant voice was unmistakable. Don Ward, his shoulders straining the fabric of a brick-colored silk shirt, wriggled between two girls in black who stood behind me. He leaned against the bar, his legs crossed at the ankles and his arms folded, belt-high. I looked up past his mouth to his eyes; they were attentive, expectant, and I wanted to say something that would live up to their challenge.

"If you play 'Blue Monk,' I'll go home a happy woman."

He cocked his head like a retriever listening for a rabbit in the underbrush. "You're doing a good job," he said, smiling and nodding.

"A good job?"

Impatience flickered through the amusement on his face. "Impressing me. With your knowledge of jazz."

"Offering a backhand to your serve, that's all."

"If you're interested in games," he said with that smile still lurking at the corners of his mouth, "I should warn you—I always play to win."

"Then I'm at a disadvantage. I'm just in it for the good time." I raised my beer in a toast to the end of the opening gambit. "Do you realize this is one of the all-time great expressions of the incurably optimistic nature of man—moonlighting in a jazz band on weekends in Taconic Hills."

Don Ward offered a spirited defense of his self-described "practical" desire to keep music from becoming just an abstracted, academic exercise in his life. I fished a few kernels of popcorn from the plastic bowl on the bar and chewed until only a sweetish taste lingered in my mouth and a thin film of oil coated my palm. No napkin in sight; the bartender was down at the other end, talking intently across the scarred surface of the bar to a man with a mournful frown and graying muttonchops.

"Take notes, okay?" Don said gently. "I want a detailed critique at the end of the evening. We're thinking of going big time—Great Barrington, maybe, or Rhinebeck. Gotta go do it." He nodded toward the stage, where three men who might have been accountants or fellow teachers checked mikes and set up music stands.

"Good luck. Or is it break a leg?" I extended my hand, then withdrew it. "Popcorn oil," I explained.

Don Ward took hold of my wrist, turned my hand and raised it to his mouth. His lips, full and warm on the sensitive center of my palm, sent an unexpected rush of desire shuddering through me. "Salty," he said as he released me and walked to the stage.

He was testing or enticing me, I wasn't sure which. One thing I was certain of: Whatever had happened between me and Stewart McClaren in my office, I wanted this to be different.

The music started. The saxophone began a slow and sensuous meandering through the plaintive melody of "Green Dolphin Street," and for the next forty minutes, I let myself drown in the sounds. When the set was over, I delivered my report—the lyrical stuff was lovely, the swing numbers a little ragged—and then said good-bye. One piece of advice I'd valued from Aunt Christa was to leave a party when you're still having a good time.

Humming, I drove back to Rosie's, more relaxed, more alive, more fully awake than I'd felt in weeks.

Rosie and Paul snuggled side by side on the worn green sofa, open books in hand, the quiet broken only by the sounds of peepers and the distant yapping of a farm dog. I stopped in the doorway to take in the homey scene, and to enjoy the company—it was a lovely change to return to friendly faces, instead of the emptiness of my apartment.

"You both look like you haven't moved since I left." I plunked into the chair beside the fireplace.

Rosie smiled and slipped a curling strand of yellow yarn into her book to mark her place. "Not at all true. Why, Paul was off the sofa once for a whole thirty minutes. Made some phone calls and supervised Andrew's bath and then put him to bed."

"And you got up once, honey, remember. To call Sarah Hoving." Paul reached for her hand; it was one of those gestures that comes only with a deep comfort in another's presence, and after the passage of time.

"Twice," Rosie sniffed. "Once to answer the phone."

"I hope it wasn't a recording that tells you you've won a week in beautiful downtown Sheboygan and all you have to do is solve a puzzle and oh by the way include an entry fee of only ninety-nine ninety-nine. God, I hate that."

"In Taconic Hills? What I get is Sarah Hoving asking me to bring a green vegetable to the grange supper or Andrew's teacher wanting to know if I'll chaperone a trip to the post office. Or, in this case, Dolores Farley." Rosie tucked her legs under her. "Poor thing, I don't think she has anyone much to talk to since she retired. She went on and on about Joseph's accidents, how that milk truck almost killed him, how he would have died if the ambulance hadn't gotten there right away after he fell off the ladder."

I frowned; this little village was even more insulated than I'd remembered, even more dependent on weather and love affairs and illness to provide the story line of everyday life. "She calls *you* to talk about those things?"

"Rosie's the chief handholder around here." Paul patted her arm. "My wise, serene, available little Buddha."

Rosie slapped his hand away. "Are you trying to tell me I better start watching my waistline? Anyway, Dolores finally got around to her real point, which was that she had a box of fabric to bring me. Said she wanted to drop it by. I told her I'd call and let her know when's a good time. I get some of my best stuff from other people's attics."

"Let's do something outdoorsy, country tomorrow, okay?"

"Not so fast, Lee Montara. You haven't told us whether you liked the music." Paul's grin asked other questions.

I chose to answer only his words. "They'd do all right in the city, if they wanted to put up with the club scene."

"They do just fine right here." Rosie's tone said that some people stayed here because they preferred it, even if I didn't have the good sense to share their feelings.

"And Don?"

Paul had always treated me like the kid sister. I didn't mind his sweet, fraternal instincts, not really, as long as he restricted himself to *talk*.

"Interesting."

That word was enough to make him shake his head and laugh. "I waited up so I could tell you—I've left a message on his machine. I've asked him to keep an eye on things up here while I'm away."

I'm sure I frowned. In my initial confusion, I almost sputtered out something about being able to make my own choices thank you very much but the gravity of Paul's expression silenced me.

"I didn't feel comfortable knowing you and Rosie and Andrew were going to be alone with this weird stuff going on. Rosie told me about it . . . after Andrew showed me the stain on the boards. Personally, I agree with you that it's probably a senior prank. But just in case, I'll feel better knowing Don's going to be stopping by. I've also called Riley Hamm. I want the sheriff's department to make an extra pass or two up this way while I'm gone."

It was a *fait accompli,* and any protestations about this being the nineties, about women not needing to be taken care of, would surely start an interminable argument. Having Don Ward around a lot was intriguing, but the terms were less than ideal.

"I don't think we need to get carried away over this." Rosie's earlier distress was replaced now by a breezy nonchalance. "I mean, what do we have—a bunch of ugly dead flowers and a cake with ants in it, and two little black bows. Pretty strange, but so far, pretty tame."

So far. Did she think the joke hadn't played itself out? "Good, I'm glad you feel that way. We don't need to worry. With most of the seniors gone on this trip, it will probably stop. Maybe by the time you get back, Paul, it will be all over."

"If I find out it was any of my kids, they're dead meat. That's not even funny. Anyway, they're not all going, so it could be someone who stays behind. Some of them are too cool to piss in the woods. They'd much rather hang out and look unaffected, bore themselves silly."

That sounded like a pretty fair description of Rick Decker, but before I could say so, Paul stretched and pulled himself up from the sofa, kissed me on the cheek, and said, "See you in the morning."

Rosie stood too, and gathered up her reading glasses. "I'll be along in a second, honey," she said absently as he headed up the stairs.

"Even if I'm right and it's just a joke, I still think you should be careful around Rick. I don't like the way that kid looks at you, especially when he thinks nobody's watching. It's too . . . I don't know, too intense, as though he's burning a picture of you onto his brain."

Rosie fluffed a sofa pillow; her long hair cascaded toward her arms as she leaned forward. "He's young, he's starting to feel all those stirrings, and I'm, well, maybe not in your opinion but in his mind I'm mysterious and attractive. Older woman mystique, I didn't make it up. Anyway, he'll outgrow it real soon. I've known Rick all his life. He's stumbling toward adulthood, that's all. I just wanted to say that I saw that look on your face, Lee. I'm sorry, I shouldn't have asked you not to tell Paul about the flowers and the cake. I didn't mean for you to feel like a collaborator. Sorry I put you in that position."

She kissed me and padded upstairs. Anxious to be alone with my own thoughts, I followed, glad to close the bedroom door behind me.

The strip of narrow windows separating the gleaming hardwood floor from the sloped ceiling looked out onto darkness. Inside, the room was cheery, the bedside lamp throwing soft shadows against the far wall. I turned off the light, undressed quickly, peeled back the blue-and-white summer quilt on the four-poster, and stretched out in the darkness. Still able to see the faint outlines of the dried asters in the milk-glass pitcher on the dresser, I lay beneath the scented sheets and wondered about the secrets Rosie was still keeping.

6

My sister clasped her hands together and leaned against the sink, watching her husband eat his cornflakes. Those bags, she asked as though ticking off items on her mental checklist, would he be able to carry all that for the ten-mile hike in to the campsite? He said, yes, he'd done it for six years in a row, no reason he couldn't do it again this year. Did he have the extra flashlight batteries, his vitamin C—he knew how susceptible he was to colds when he forgot to take his C—and the journal she'd gotten for him at Oblong Books?

He indulged her. "I'll be fine, Rosie. I'll call you Tuesday night, around seven, okay? Meanwhile, you relax and enjoy your sister."

Andrew, his face a study in solemnity, paid close attention to their expressions and their talk, and I could see him absorbing lessons: what the father does, how the mother acts. I felt like one of those anthropologists whose very presence changes the behavior of the tribe they're observing.

"Will you take a picture of me and Mom and Dad?"

This was no casual request, I could tell from the thoughtful pursing of Andrew's mouth. In the face of his father's departure, he wanted to preserve his family intact, and he needed to change the subject.

"Sure. Let's go outside and wait for them," I said, searching for the black canvas camera case on the desk, on the kitchen counter, becoming more and more frustrated until finally Andrew tugged at my shirt.

"There it is, Auntie Lee. On that shelf." He was so proud that I wondered for a moment whether he'd hidden it atop Rosie's cookbooks so that he could be the one to find it. But surely that was entirely too premeditated an action for a six-year-old child; the misplaced camera was merely evidence of my own confused state of mind.

"How about if we try to take a picture of the birds? Bring some toast, why don't you? We have to be very quiet and not move or else we'll scare them away."

He trudged along beside me, head bent, and I sensed him reaching to find the grown-up place inside himself so that he could stand straight and wave his father on his way. It wasn't a bad thing to learn, as life lessons go, and I hoped that he'd end up pleased with his own performance.

"Toss them a little corner of the toast. What do you think they'll do, sweetie?" Immediately, I wanted to take back the endearment, so that he wouldn't feel so much like a little boy.

"I hope my Dad doesn't miss me too much. Ten days is too long. It's not fair." The toast dangled from his hand.

A familiar lament, but I wouldn't offer him the old retort: *Nobody ever said life was fair.* Because it might be, for him, and I didn't want to prejudice his thinking.

"Sure, go ahead. I don't mind being here alone for a while."

Andrew's chin dimpled with his effort not to cry. He turned away and shuffled across the lawn, intent on the grass beneath his feet. Suddenly, he dropped the toast, sprinted to the station wagon, pulled open the front door, and flung himself inside. Astonished, I watched him slam down the lock, first on the driver's side, then on the passenger door. He stared straight ahead, paying no attention to my shouts to open a door, any door. I walked around to the front of the car and made funny faces, trying to jolly him out of the car, feeling foolish and ineffective.

My sweet and stubborn six-year-old nephew would not upset me and would definitely not outmaneuver me. I stood still, held my breath, exhaled slowly . . . and noticed that the lock on one of the rear doors wasn't pressed down. I tried to appear nonchalant—Oh, Lord, what if he released the emergency brake—but Andrew followed my movements. I gave up on subtlety and yanked the door open. Too angry to speak, I leaned back against the seat, breathing hard.

The boy was stiff with resolve. "I'm going with Daddy to the bus stop. I am too."

Before I could say I thought that was a fine idea, he swiveled around. I turned, too, and saw the mail Jeep lumbering up the drive.

"He's early today," Andrew said flatly. "He usually comes just before lunch."

Joseph Farley's red bow tie blossomed against his pale blue shirt; he frowned as he peered through his windshield. Who could blame him? We must have looked odd, a little blond boy at the steering wheel, me sinking into the backseat. After a second, however, Joseph's face relaxed into a smile. He gave Andrew a two-finger salute, drove up to the mailbox, and deposited a thick stack of envelopes. Joseph executed a clean three-point turn and headed back down to the road, unaware that he'd come to my rescue by providing a well-timed diversion.

"I know how much you'll miss your Dad when he's away. It's hard, isn't it?" *Stop here*, I warned myself. *That's enough.*

A snuffle and a cough came from my little chauffeur. I gave him a second to collect himself, then leaned over the front seat and hugged him.

"I'm feeling better now." Andrew wriggled out of my arms. "You want to come with us to the bus, Auntie Lee?"

"Nope. *I'm* going for a walk. But thanks for asking."

Andrew pushed open the door and swung his feet to the gravel. "Dad! Daa-ad! You don't want to miss your bus!" he shouted as he ran toward the porch.

I was glad that I'd been able to tell the difference between what he needed and what he thought he wanted.

"Auntie Lee, you wanna go pick strawberries?"

Even if I'd promised Rosie that I'd spend the whole afternoon painting the side of the house instead of just the hour I'd volunteered, I couldn't resist the invitation in Andrew's eyes. I laid the paintbrush on the cover of the paint can. "Can we stop somewhere on the way so I can drop off my film to be developed?"

"Sure, Mom takes our pictures to the general store in Taconic Hills. They have one of those machines in the back and they have your pictures ready by the afternoon."

I could earn extra points with Andrew: strawberry picking and pictures of his Dad, with a bonus for the paint spatters dotting my arms. Mike would pitch a fit if he ever caught me taking film in to what he had once called the ruin-your-pictures-while-you-wait developers. But these were snapshots, not photographs; developing the film on this roll—Andrew, Paul, and Rosie loading the car and hugging and mugging for the camera, and the rotten flower stems—required speed rather than artistry.

I climbed from the ladder, rinsed off the brushes, and went into the cool kitchen to scrub the paint from my arms.

"Strawberry fields forever," Rosie sang cheerfully as we skipped down the porch steps to the station wagon. With the light behind her, her hair made a coppery nimbus around her face; she looked, somehow, contentedly aflame.

We dropped the film at the general store and sang Beatles songs all the way to Hudson. A grizzled old fellow with wiry eyebrows and cracked yellow fingernails wordlessly handed us baskets and we chose our spots along one of the paths between the rows of strawberry plants. The sun was strong and hot, as it should be for a proper berrypicking expedition, and in time-honored tradition, Andrew ate more than he tossed into the baskets, grinning at the sight of the reddish stains on his fingers as though they were a special achievement. He withdrew into pensive silence once or twice, but Rosie let him be, and his own natural good spirits won out.

I took four pictures of tiny berries glistening against the veined, furry surface of the tangle of leaves. Probably too corny for our book, but I shot them anyway, for my own pleasure.

We spent the afternoon making a strawberry-rhubarb pie, sipping iced tea in the shade, reading.

Around six, Don Ward staggered out of his car bearing two bottles of wine and a bowl of homemade pasta, a mesh bag of freshly picked basil dangling from one hand. I watched him move expertly around Rosie's kitchen, chopping tomatoes, mincing garlic . . . and I wondered how many other of his talents I'd have the chance to discover. We talked a lot about how to deal with raccoons, rabbits, and other garden interlopers, laughed, ate too much linguini, and drank entirely too much Chianti. I was concerned about him driving to the Edgewood and performing three sets without missing cues or forgetting a melody, but Don left us with cheerful assurances that he'd be careful, and that a cup of the bartender's industrial-strength coffee would set things right again.

"Porch time," I announced, aware that I'd gone straight past relaxed to sleepy; our day in the sun and an evening of drinking wine had pretty well done me in. Rosie shooed Andrew and me outside while she finished up the dishes. We didn't protest.

The sweep of the sky was a million shades of blue and shadows from the trees bordering the stream danced along the edge of the field. The beauty of it all was glorious and inspiring, even a little mystical in its variety and majesty, yet, perversely, my mind insisted on wandering along the narrow streets that twisted through Greenwich Village.

I watched Andrew, his head bent earnestly over a drawing pad; it was almost too dark to see but he kept at it until a low, red car with spoked wheels came to life on the page.

"Want to do your old aunt a favor?"

He nodded solemnly.

"Come sit on my lap for a few minutes." I patted my knees and he clambered up, his head reaching just to my chin, his hair smelling of child's sweat and herbal shampoo. I clasped my arms loosely around him, letting my fingers part as his chest rose and fell with his breath. His heart seemed so near the surface of his thin T-shirt. The bare skin of his arms was touched with the first chill of evening.

"Is it a few minutes yet?" Andrew peered up at me. When I nodded, he slid down and ran into the house.

A dog howled and I shivered. Feeling as though I'd lost all my country senses, I concentrated on the gentle rocking of the chair, but the motion felt studied, like something I was supposed to do because I was on a porch, and I stopped.

Riotous green, indeed. Taking pictures for our book was one way to be near Mike but it only postponed discovering what *I* wanted.

Part of me was relieved to admit that.

The rest of me longed to see the contours of Mike's face as he examined a lens filter. I wanted to stand beside him at the counter at Balducci's and order things we'd never eaten before to take home in little white containers. I longed to touch the curved line of his jaw, hear his voice in a darkened room.

Stewart McClaren's interest in me had been inspired by his desire to find a new home for his portfolio and by my availability since Mike's death. Just like Stewart to take advantage of a difficult personal situation. Talent aside, he lived by his tricks, had acquired a full repertoire of them. Old Stewart never went for what he wanted directly, if he could be manipulative about it. It was the chase, the game that gave him pleasure.

My reverie was broken by Rosie, bearing a tray with two coffee cups and a plate of chocolate chip cookies.

"Andrew's in bed. Some days he goes from full tilt to fast asleep in ten seconds." She handed me a cookie, and sat in the rocker to my left.

"Did you ever think that power, not money, is really the root of evil? I mean, the photographer I told you about—if it's him, what he's doing may be his way of gaining power over me, a tactic to get what he wants."

It was barely light enough for me to see Rosie's frown. "I don't understand."

"Maybe I've had too much wine to say it clearly but. . . . Okay, try this. Let's say Stewart's threatened by women who can make decisions about him. Professionally. Personally. I don't know, both maybe. And the only way he can handle it is to feel like he's the one in control so he—"

"You're doing it again." Rosie's voice was firm, annoyed. "You turn everything into a test, Lee. You try to squeeze other people's behavior to a shape that fits your view. Everyone else does not see things that way."

"Not everything. Not everyone. You're putting words in my mouth. But some of what happens between certain people *is* a struggle for power. You can't deny that and. . . . It's late, Rosie. Maybe we should have this discussion another time." I was too tired and too tipsy, we both were, to argue the metaphysics of perception and reality, and the psychology of power. "We're going out antiquing tomorrow, aren't we?"

"No, Lee, don't change the subject. Have the courage to go on with what you started."

I sighed, hoping that somewhere in my alcoholic torpor I could find the logical thread to explain my point. "Okay, what about this: Some people don't have much confidence in themselves, so they only deal with others they think are less powerful. Then they try to shift the balance, they poke around until they find their opponent's weak spot and—"

"I knew you were going to say something like that. You just can't leave things alone, can you?" she cried sharply.

Instantly alert, I sat upright, holding on to the armrests of the rocker, ready to hear whatever she'd been avoiding telling me from the moment I'd arrived, knowing that she'd controlled the conversation because she couldn't talk about it any other way.

She got to her feet and moved to the edge of the porch. "I've been getting phone calls. . . . Two rings and then silence. Thirty seconds later, the same thing. It goes on for eight or nine minutes and then stops. It's happened six times in the past two weeks. When Paul is in school." Her voice was hoarse, the way it sounded when she was trying to keep herself from crying. "You had to keep pushing, didn't you, Lee? First all that stuff happens with the flowers and the cake. . . . I don't have any idea who's doing these things. I don't know, now I think it was wrong not to tell Paul about the phone calls. I just didn't want to ruin this trip completely for him. He'd either stay home or worry the whole time he was away. When you told me about Stewart McClaren, I thought maybe you'd feel I was trying to edge you out of the spotlight or something, give your situation less significance, I don't know."

I wanted desperately not to have had four glasses of wine. I wanted to see Rosie's face but the blanket of darkness had settled over everything. She sounded like she believed we were engaged in a competition: Whose problem was the most commanding, the most compelling, the most insistent?

"I look out there in the night and I wonder if he's hiding in the trees and watching me, maybe sitting home with a beer can on his chest watching *America's Most Wanted*, or I don't know, I can't think what someone who would make those calls would actually *do*. You can't imagine, can you? Otherwise, you wouldn't have—"

"It must be awful." Impulsively, I stood and held out my arms to hug her. But Rosie ran past me, ignoring me. Why? What had I done to make her shut me out?

The screen door banged and she ran up the stairs, the sound of her steps fading into the bleak silence.

Your move, Rosie, I thought as I sat back down in the rocker and defied the darkness to frighten me. *I tried to make it right between us, but you were determined to maintain control. Now it's up to you.*

7

I lay in the bed I'd slept in as a child and listened to the birds and to the sounds of the morning kitchen, Rosie talking to Andrew, making coffee, running water to wash last night's pots. Last night . . . if I could only go back and live it again, minus at least three of those glasses of wine . . . if only Rosie had told me earlier about those phone calls, had accepted my overture of comfort before she ran to the shelter of her own bedroom. My confusion kept me company in the shower as the hot water pounded onto my shoulders. Clouds of steam penetrated the haze in my brain, and I realized I wasn't angry at Rosie. I was only uncertain about what I'd find when I went downstairs, how things would be between us.

I'd be returning to New York City in a week and I wanted to get it all in, all the laughter and the games with Andrew, and all the talking that Rosie and I still hadn't done, if she'd allow it.

Rosie looked radiant, Andrew pensive when I entered the room. I poured myself coffee and sat between them, watching Andrew push a piece of toast around the edges of his plate.

"What's up, Doc?" I rested my chin on my hands.

Andrew didn't even try to smile. "Mom says she had a dream about Daddy. I wish I had one."

"Your daddy knows you love him even though you didn't dream about him. He loves you too and he'll be home in a week. You gonna show me the beaver dam later?" I stole a glance at Rosie; her glow hadn't dimmed, but she hadn't yet made eye contact with me.

Andrew wriggled impatiently in his chair. "Sure. After our picnic. Mom says we're going to hike up Vixen Hill and have a picnic. I'm going to go feed the birds now, okay, Mom?"

"Go ahead, honey." Even her voice was light, floating through the silken air without a thought about what Andrew might find when he pushed open the door and stepped onto the porch. I wondered if he felt the same shiver I did whenever I went outside, if he checked the pile of boards with a feeling of dread.

Rosie stretched out her legs and sighed. "That dream was so real, it was almost as though Paul had come to visit during the night. Did you ever have anything like that, I mean with Mike or someone you were close to but they were far away?"

My stomach clenched at the sound of his name. Mike's only appearances these days were in my nightmares. "Nope," I said evenly. "The picnic sounds perfectly wonderful to me. You already asked Sarah Hoving about going up Vixen Hill?"

The lovely, sleepy mist of Rosie's lingering dream evaporated and her eyes, wistful only a moment before, clouded. "Actually, I called her last night about bringing you up there sometime. You know Sarah —said I was silly to think I had to ask."

Then why had her name changed Rosie's mood instantly? "Sarah always was one of my favorite people in Taconic Hills," I said. "Peter, too."

"She asked me about the flowers and the cake and the black bows. Said her mother-in-law was worried about us. I swear, Ruth Hoving really does know everything, practically before it happens."

"Well, that's what you get for living in a small town. Everyone knows your secrets. Riley must have told Ruth that Paul called about the stuff with the black bows. Listen, can we stop and get my film before our picnic?"

"No problem. General store's open at ten on Sunday. We'll have a lovely day, relax a little in the sun. We can both use that."

So this was Rosie's way of telling me that she, too, didn't want last night to affect our time together. "If you start getting the food ready, I'll grab the picnic basket. You still keep it in the garden shed?"

"Same old nail in the same old shed." Rosie squeezed my arm, and brushed my cheek with her lips. "I'm glad we're doing this today."

I doused the last, fleeting resentment over my rejected hug last night, and kissed her.

Outside, a breeze fluttered the leaves of the oak tree, shaking little flakes of sunlight onto the porch. Andrew stood engrossed in the comings and goings of the sparrows. Suddenly energized, I walked briskly past the flowering quince beside the cellar door and across the path to the garden shed. A shiny gleam in the gravel caught my attention, and I knelt to see what it was. My spare lens cover—how had it gotten here? It must have fallen out of my camera case on the way back from the strawberry orgy. I stuck it in my pocket, grabbed the wicker basket from the shed, and headed for the house.

Taconic Hills, a town so small that all its commercial buildings—a general store, a café, a weekly newspaper office—would barely fill half a block along Sixth Avenue, was nearly deserted. The June heat had sent everyone to outdoor pursuits, I suspected; even the normally crowded general store was experiencing a lull.

Rosie and Andrew waited in the car while I ran inside. On impulse, I tossed a bar of imported chocolate studded with hazelnuts into the shopping basket while Deeny Lambert retrieved three new rolls of film and the packet of photographs from the back room for me.

Ten minutes later we parked beside Vixen Hill Lodge, next to Sarah Hoving's pickup truck. Andrew raced ahead to the spillway at the end of the pond, slowed as he crossed the log bridge, and then sprinted toward our destination, the clearing at the top of the hill. Rosie and I scrambled more sedately over outcrops of rock and skirted the bushes that kept the deer fed well into the fall.

The path disappeared into a thicket of berry bushes; I followed Andrew's golden head, picking my way through the brambles. "I remember now. You can't see the pond again until you get clear to the top."

Fifty yards later, Rosie huffing behind me, I marched the final steps to the crest of the hill. The pond appeared, blue and sparkling in the sunlight. The lodge, the farms below, and the hills stretching beyond spread out in a breathtaking vista.

"This is paradise, you know? I forget about places like this some-times." Sighing, I plopped down on the grass, and the packet of pho-tographs slid out of the bag I was carrying.

"Can I look, Auntie Lee? I want to see the pictures of my Dad."

"Just a second, sweetie. Let me find them for you." He didn't need to be reminded of our dead bouquet. Much better for him not to look at images that brought back that other, more disturbing morning.

After I exclaimed over the silly faces they'd all managed for one of the shots, I handed him four photos. Andrew took himself and the pictures off to a flat rock, where he sat and stared and stared, as though looking hard would help him remember every word and ev-ery bit of feeling from the hour before his father's departure.

The shots of the yarrow stems were good, almost too good, and I shivered as I stuck them in my pocket. I worked my way casually through the rest of the roll, seven or eight pictures of the cake, and of Andrew mugging with happy abandon, until I came to an unfamiliar image.

I've always believed that one evidence of intelligence is the ability to take elements out of context and make the necessary leap to appre-hend their meaning.

By that measure, I was struck doubly dumb. I couldn't understand what I was seeing. Even if I knew what words to say, I'd lost my ability to speak. The photograph dropped from my fingers; Rosie cocked her head and frowned.

Swallowing hard, I reached for the snapshot and forced myself to look at it.

A figure lay propped against a huge boulder that rose up among the weeds in an abandoned orchard.

His arms were flung out as though in welcome, the sleeves of his leather jacket undone at the wrists. Stewart McClaren lay, eyes closed, in the shade of an old apple tree.

Watching me intently, Rosie turned ghostly white.

"Stewart McClaren," I said when I could manage speech. "I don't understand. Lord, I know he's bold, but to come into your house, take my camera, take this picture, and then return the camera. . . . All without our knowing about it?" I recalled the search for the camera when Paul was leaving, how Andrew found it atop Rosie's cook-books. And my spare lens cover on the garden path, near the quince that leaned toward the cellar door—had Stewart dropped it there? It was possible, anything was possible.

Color flooded back into Rosie's face. Her fingers pinched at spikes of grass until the green blades were torn and ragged. "If he's trying to scare you, he's doing a good job of it. Me, too."

"I'm sure Stewart took the picture himself, with a timer." My mind was racing now, fueled by my anger that Stewart had devised this scheme as retribution for my turning him down. "You have any idea where this boulder is?"

Rosie nodded. "Just up East Taconic Road, past the abandoned iron mine, in the old Koslowski apple orchard."

Stewart McClaren had gone too far, but I was about to rein him in. As soon as we got back to Rosie's, I'd call Riley Hamm, get him to track down Stewart's car, keep an eye out for him, talk him into quitting his ugly game. Riley wasn't the hulking, beefy type, but the menace in his voice when he was angry was enough to convince anyone not to make the sheriff's deputy say something twice.

"I refuse to let some self-centered photographer spoil our picnic," I declared, and I proceeded to think about nothing else for the next hour, my frustration growing and swelling. With every bite of my sandwich, I tasted only my own anger.

On the way home, I tried to follow Andrew's rambling story about his entry in the school science fair but an ugly refrain kept pushing everything else away: *Stewart McClaren was in Taconic Hills.*

"Wait a minute. Pull over, Rosie." I blinked the scene into focus. Some part of me must have been keeping track of where we were while the rest of my mind was wandering among the bizarre artifacts of the past few days. We were on East Taconic Road, near what used to be the Koslowski chicken farm, across from the old apple orchard. "I want to take a picture, honey," I said to Andrew, needing to explain myself aloud to someone. "I'll be right back."

Rosie started to say something, then shook her head wordlessly. I got out of the car and climbed over a sagging post-and-rail fence into the prickers and whiplike branches of the underbrush. I had to see the apple orchard and the boulder for myself, see if they told me anything about Stewart McClaren.

Grateful for the chance to *do* something, I charged into the sultry afternoon heat, crossing a stream, choosing the right rock to step on to reach the other side without getting my sneakers wet, skirting the hardened mounds of meadow muffins.

The ancient gnarled trees ahead sprouted sucker branches at odd angles, as though a blind man had pasted them on helter-skelter; I thought about Stewart McClaren, eyes closed, framed in the photograph by two trees.

The boulder, stippled with glinting jewels of light, sat among the tall grass, as it had in the photograph.

I crept around the big rock, my hands cold despite the heat.

Nothing there. Relieved, I laughed aloud; the sound ricocheted back to me from the sharp granite surfaces of the boulder. No Stewart, no leather jacket. No black bow. Only a rock, hard and mute, where Stewart's head had lain.

10:00 a.m.

"String of lights blew down. That's what made that awful noise." Rosie points with her head at the dangling Japanese lanterns as they're lifted by another gust of wind to smash into the stone barbecue.

I start breathing again, but I'm not at all calm or focused. "I can't concentrate on this stuff any more. God, all these old blouses, tea towels, whatever, it's like turning your life into a museum piece, something to be remembered instead of lived."

Rosie pushes back out of the deep chair she's let herself sink into. "Nobody's forcing you to go through the basket. I find it soothing, that's all, to keep my hands busy."

At the mention of busy hands, my fingers sneak back to my pocket. The gun is cold to my touch, and because it would deny me—a woman—power, I resist the phallic comparison I've heard so often, as I have resisted all my life the defamation of the sex act, life-affirming, pleasure-giving, into a curse word. At this moment, it is clear to me in more than an abstract way, that killing someone's spirit is the real obscenity.

"You know, Rosie, in a way, I *do* feel a little sorry for him."

Her anger cuts me. "Don't do that to me. I have to think about me and you and Andrew. Get hold of yourself, Lee. Don't go drifting off. Isn't that what you said to me, not half an hour ago? Well, take some of your own good advice, okay?"

I hate that she's turning this into another contest of who's right, who's behaving properly. I thought we were past that.

And maybe we are and it's only me, persisting in an outmoded pattern of thought, the way some people go on wearing sweater sets or saddle shoes. Rosie folds the last piece of fabric, an old pajama top with blue-shirted cowboys and green cactus against a brown background, and then reaches for my hand. "You used to be such a tomboy, Lee. Kids Andrew's age, they aren't tomboys anymore. Now, they're just active, athletic little girls. Some things really have changed."

"I never even thought about what that word meant. Tom*boy*. I just needed to put distance between Aunt Christa and me. I guess it was my inclination anyway, to be active and impulsive, so I played up that part of myself. Until my hormones took over." I'm not sure what to say now, and before I can think of something, I hear the tinkle of breaking glass as another bulb in the string of lanterns bounces against the barbecue.

After she peers outside, perhaps to satisfy herself that the noise was made by the wind, she turns to me again. Rosie's face is lovely, clear, like a porcelain doll's head with two circles of color to mark the cheeks, glass-green eyes brushed by long lashes. "I think I'll put up some water for tea."

She is gliding, not walking, toward the kitchen, and I follow, glancing left, right, over my shoulder to see what's around me. As I pass a window I inspect the landscape beyond the fogged glass, rubbing a fist-size viewing circle at each stop. On the road below the driveway, a milk truck lumbers through the intersection, headlights cutting the gray with a blade of light, but mostly the road is deserted.

I hurry through the dark hallway. When I step into the kitchen, Rosie spins around. She nearly knocks the teakettle from the stove.

"Whoa, it's only me." I force a smile.

Rosie is even paler in this room, washed to ghostliness by the white walls and the bright lights. I watch her pull the teapot and a perforated metal tea ball down from the closet, busy, taking care of things, just like always. Above the piercing whistle of the kettle and the clanking of spoons against pottery mugs, her voice is clear and firm. "Sugar?"

"Sure. No milk, just sugar." The rain cascades down the window, and I'm freezing, even though I'm sure it's at least seventy degrees in here. I rub my hands along my bare arms, but that doesn't help much.

"You should put on a sweater," Rosie says distractedly as she passes a white ceramic mug across the kitchen table to me and sits in one of the high-back chairs. "Drink the tea. It will be good, make you feel more alert and less, I don't know, you look so dreamy."

If I appear dreamy to her, then perhaps we are mirrors. Perhaps we always have been. "I'm sure it wasn't random, the way he chose his target."

"Right now, does it matter?" Rosie blows across the surface of her tea and sips noisily, her eyes narrowed against the steam. "However this came to be, we are going to do something about it. We decided we're in this together. We did decide that, didn't we? Tell me if I've got something wrong."

I wrap my hands around the mug, trying to absorb as much heat as I can. I peer into the amber liquid and breathe its perfume. "Earl Grey. Thank you. No, you've got it right."

Rosie runs her finger along a tiny chip at the edge of her mug. "You remember, Mom used to make this when we were sick. Earl Grey, two sugars, and a piece of dry toast. Then, if that stayed down, we graduated to ginger ale and Jell-O."

"I hated sitting in bed with that old metal tray on my lap. I always managed to spill something, and then Mom would make that face, the one where she tries not to show how disappointed she is." When Rosie was sick, I would be allowed to tiptoe in and bring her a glass of water. How I envied her; she seemed so peaceful, contented with her shoe box full of crayons. Stillness has always been one of her talents.

Rosie is back in the present before I am, I can tell from her eyes, checking the window, looking at the clock in that darting, excited way that makes her pupils huge, dark openings into which any movement, any change of the light will fall. She turns to the sink, pretending to rinse the cups and the teapot, but I know she's really reading the landscape for signs of disturbance.

I'm working at keeping all the realities going at once: the waiting; the ordinary rainy day that will mark the end of my vacation; the knowledge that I am already a different person than I was last week; the uncertainty of how long, how deep the transformation will prove to be, how much of my core has been saturated with the colorings of this time. I am changed in many ways, I know. For Rosie, will the answers be the same?

"Will you go back to the city?" she asks, as though idle conversation will stop the chatter in her mind.

"Yes, tomorrow, Rosie. That's where I want to be. My work is there, my friends. And I love the city for the fun of it."

"Fun? That's not how I think of—" Her words are choked off and her mouth hangs open. "I saw something. In the bushes, a movement, I don't know, it looked like a black slicker, the kind fishermen wear, only not yellow."

I jump up from my chair and stand beside her, the warmth of our touching shoulders not enough to stop my shiver. For the first time, I think that maybe we were mistaken to give up on trying to convince Riley Hamm of what we believe. No—I can't dwell on that—I can't undo it.

Rain lashes at the window. I can't see details but I can make out distorted shapes, colors. Drenched and faded, the scarecrow in Rosie's garden droops, as though he's admitting he's once again failed to keep out an intruder. I cover the scene in quadrants, the way Mike taught me to do when I'm blocking a shot for compositional interest.

Upper left, the garden. Unless he's slithering on his belly beneath the peas, he's not there. Lower left, the lilacs, the tarp covering the paint cans and ladder and the folded drop cloths. The lilacs are a possibility. But I see nothing out of the ordinary. Lower right, the barbecue, the picnic table, the dangling string of Japanese lanterns. Nothing there. Upper right. The log bench and Rosie's flowers and Andrew's swing set.

I study the moving swing, hold my hands tight to the edge of the sink, cold and damp, and the swaying stops.

Rosie graces me with a smile. "I saw him. I mean, I saw something and I hope it's him. It's going to be soon, he knows it all has to be over in the next few hours. He's going to try one, two more enticements, I know it, to be sure he's got us in the right frame of mind. And then he'll make his move."

I realize, finally, that Rosie really has been thinking of this all along as a seduction. He's planned it out, generated a mood, delivered his little gifts with the intention of creating a yearning in us, a longing for something we, like all of the uninitiated, don't even know how to describe because we haven't yet experienced it.

But somehow, my sister has been able to keep herself on that fine edge of knowing and not knowing, being drawn irresistibly closer, giving off the right scent, so that he will persist. And when he has nearly achieved his end, she'll be the one who will win, like the old joke about the man who chases the object of his affections until she catches him.

I'm in awe of her power and suddenly afraid. She's not the old Rosie. But then, as I have already realized, I'm not the old Lee.

"Do you think you'll be able to do it?" She nods her head toward my pocket and I understand her question.

I nod back.

"How do you know?"

How can I possibly answer her? Who knows until the moment arrives? I've been considering my own capacities, what I can do, what I can't do. And maybe that's the part he hasn't counted on, how having the opportunity to examine myself has changed what I'm capable of doing, what lines I will cross. If he hadn't lingered in this sick, extended tease, I might not have had the chance to think about my response in such detail. I don't know if Rosie's going to like my answer, but I know I have to protect both of us.

And I will. I will do whatever it takes.

An explosion of thunder directly above us rattles the cups on the table and the stink of ozone kicks me back into the present. And then I feel another disturbance, perhaps of someone standing at the front door trying to turn the knob. I run into the living room, but I see no movement. The rain-swept porch is deserted.

When I return to the kitchen Rosie has pressed her nose against the back door glass, like a child longing for something that's just out of reach.

I hate him for what he has done to her, and for a moment I believe that I will be the one to give him exactly what he wants.

8

"Listen," Rosie said, "you have to tell Riley Hamm about Stewart's plans to go to Cozumel. Riley's going to figure it out anyway, so you might as well beat him to it. I'm sure he remembers how the guys have always flocked around you ever since you were, what, fourteen? If not for your peace of mind, tell him so that it's on the record. For your own protection," she said after we'd returned home.

Rosie was only applying her standards to my life with as even a hand as she did to her own.

When she was nine, she longed to have a horse. She cut out pictures lovingly from Grandpa Montara's old farm magazines—proud stallions; mares and foals; handsome chestnuts—and stuck them under the maple frame of the mirror in our bedroom. She read *Black Beauty*, *Flicka*, every horse story she could drag home from the school library.

For Halloween, Mom dug up an old red blazer, and Aunt Christa wrestled Rosie's unruly hair into a low ponytail. Rosie tied a bright red scarf at her throat; when Mom asked about it, my sister said she'd borrowed it from her friend Susie. At the school party, Rosie announced grandly that she was an equestrian.

Weeks later, I overheard a muffled discussion, punctuated by my sister's very clear sobs. Fragments of sound drifted up the stairs: my sister, blurting out that the red scarf had been stolen from Delson's by Susie; Mom, saying softly that because of the lie, Rosie wouldn't be getting her horse for Christmas; Dad, offering the compromise that since Rosie had finally told the truth, maybe she'd get the horse for her birthday in April.

My sister seldom had to learn a lesson twice.

"You *have to* tell Riley," she argued as his car pulled into the drive. "If you try to hide what happened in your office, Lee, it'll be worse when they do find out. And they will, and it will make them more suspicious and make you less . . . less innocent. Riley or someone else is sure to ferret out that this McClaren fellow had reservations on the same flight to Cozumel, that you were booked into the same hotel. He'll probably even find out about Stewart's reservations at the restaurant."

"I don't want to *hide* anything," I said, trying to convince myself I meant it. But, in fact, I was, wasn't I, trying to hide Stewart's strange vehemence, his declaration of obsession.

If it became necessary, I'd make Cindy an ally, however reluctant; surely whatever she might feel about Stewart, the receptionist would describe how I'd tossed my tickets on her desk, tell about my anger when I asked how Stewart found out I was going to Cozumel. The truth would speak for itself.

The deputy's stiff-gaited approach as he walked up the steps convinced me that Rosie was probably right. He would be businesslike, competent, objective—that was his job.

Riley Hamm no longer smelled of Old Spice.

That was the first thing I thought when he walked into Rosie's living room. Looking at his face, I expected that familiar scent to follow, but in the six years since I'd seen him, he'd switched aftershaves. Yet he still looked like he'd been pressed in a vise, and his narrow face bore the same grave, unblinking expression I remembered.

"Sorry it took me so long to get out here, Mizz Cooper. Mizz Montara. Been another fire, a bad one, up at the Henleys' farm. Number sixty-four in what, seven, eight years now. Damn, I want that guy." He squeezed his bony hands into fists, demonstrating what he'd do if he caught the elusive Copake arsonist. "Anyway, can't stay long.

Another state expert's coming down"—he checked the watch on his hairy wrist—"before long. What's this about a picture?"

I passed him the photograph.

This being Taconic Hills and not New York City, I expected a show of concern, maybe even surprise that Rosie and I were the obscure objects of someone's desire to communicate a message neither of us understood. But if Riley felt anything, he didn't let on, even when I explained that I had no idea how Stewart had gotten hold of my camera. Riley listened to my account of finding the boulder, of examining the surrounding area, and then he asked, "And, so what's the problem here, exactly?"

"Maybe it will make more sense if I tell you something about this man, and what he did a few days ago," I began. "I'll make it as quick as I can."

While Rosie perched on the edge of the sofa and watched me, I told Riley about Stewart's magazine mutilations four years ago. I described the confrontation in my office, giving Cindy my tickets, the rotten flower stems and the cake and the black bows, about thinking I'd misplaced my camera, my shock when I went through the photographs, the impulsive visit to the orchard and the rock.

But from the very start, I was fighting two battles as I spoke. My words brought back the insult of Stewart's body pressed against mine. And when I looked at Riley's face, I knew it would take all my will and a lot of verbal fancy dancing to overcome the taciturn officer's assumptions about men and women and assure him that, no, I hadn't flirted, teased, courted, or otherwise sent signals of invitation to Stewart McClaren.

"Tell me this," he said, his back not touching the chair, his fingers clutching his sharp knees. "You knew the person in this picture from your job, is that what you said? I'm not clear whether you were dating him or not."

"Listen, Riley, you *are* clear. I said it twice at least. Stewart is a freelance photographer and that's all. He wanted to sell my magazine some pictures and I turned him down. Like I said, he's pulled tricks before when his work was rejected. He told me he was staying at the same resort I was, so I didn't go. Then this picture I didn't take turned up in this roll of film. No, I was not dating the man." My temper was beginning to fray: I knew Rosie recognized the danger signs from the way her eyes held mine.

"Then tell me why he'd make plans to go to the same hotel as you," Riley Hamm persisted.

I leapt from my chair and marched to the window, but I couldn't hold back the torrent of words, and I couldn't stop moving, pacing the length of the sunny room. "You ever read in the papers about men who become obsessed, how they become fixated on revenge? He's got a history . . . that *must* be what's going on. You're wasting my time and yours by putting me through this again. He's out there somewhere, and he's been in this house twice—more, because he had to take my camera, bring it back, deliver that cake. That's not counting that god-awful bouquet on the porch. So while you're asking me to justify his actions, he's out there scheming. I think you'd better—"

"That's enough. Don't tell me what I'd better." Riley's voice was mild but his gaze bore into me. "Far as I can see, there's nothing for the police to do around here. Some New York City photographer is interested in you is all."

So, Riley Hamm had sat in Rosie's living room, declining her offer of coffee, refusing even to change expressions, for thirty minutes, while I told my story twice and answered each of his questions, and as far as he was concerned, his duty was done.

He pushed back from his seat and stood behind the chair, his large-knuckled fingers curled onto the back rest. "Anything you're leaving out? Nothing else unusual, no verbal threats, no strange cars on the road near the house, nothing?"

I shook my head and glanced over at Rosie; she brushed a damp strand of hair from her forehead and said, "No strange cars."

But she didn't say anything about the telephone calls, and before I could mention them, Riley was sidling toward the door.

"I have to tell you, Mizz Cooper. I don't get this, none of it. When your husband called and told me about the dead flowers and asked me to keep an eye on you two, it sounded like someone was playing a joke. Still feels that way to me."

Just like that, I was dismissed. He had addressed Rosie as though I hadn't spent all this time telling him about Stewart McClaren. I exploded. "And that's the end of it? Don't you think you should get someone out there to look at the rock, check the orchard area?"

For the first time, his features rearranged themselves into what I grudgingly conceded was a smile. "Mizz Montara, you understand a lot about pictures, am I right? And I know an awful lot about policing. Now if you excuse me, I got a meeting. This firebug's on one of his sprees, he's gonna make it a long week. If you think of anything you might have forgotten, give me a call, hear?"

I watched his car pull away. Riley had blown through like a dry, impersonal wind over a drought-parched land, promising the possibility of relief and delivering nothing, not even a shower. I wanted a storm, a crashing, pounding deluge that would sweep away the menace and leave Rosie and Andrew and me in peace.

Riley's blithe dismissal of my concern was one straw too many. Accustomed to pounding away my frustrations on long walks over hard city pavement, I was unfit company, and I left Rosie and Andrew to press lettuce seeds into the good earth of the garden. I stomped through the waist-high corn in the field across the road, barely aware of the sharp-edged leaves scratching at my legs. I marched along a tractor road that cut through the woods behind the field, vainly trying to subdue the waves of anger that crashed over me when I stopped to take a breath.

The sun was high and hot, but I tramped on, knowing that if I walked long enough and hard enough eventually the dust would settle and the air—and my thoughts—would clear.

When they did, finally, one thought emerged from the haze: I didn't like being the slate on which Stewart wrote his insinuating messages.

It was Sunday. That would slow me down a little, but it wouldn't stop me, and neither would Stewart McClaren. Reversing my steps, I followed my own footprints in the crumbly soil of the path I'd taken through the field. I climbed upstairs without bothering to announce my return to Rosie and dug through my purse for my address book. The shadow-filled hall was cool and quiet; I spread a pad and my address book on the telephone table and dialed Stewart's home number, tapping my fingers in double-time to the unanswered rings.

The sound of his silky voice on his outgoing message grated against my barely controlled fury, and a torrent of words spilled out of me.

"Stewart, this is Lee Montara. Listen carefully. I'm on to what you're doing, and I'm not going to put up with it. Stay away from me, from my camera, and especially from my sister's house and her family. Whatever your problem is, keep it to yourself. You've gone too far, and I'm very angry. My friends in the magazine business will be interested to hear what you've been up to. If you want to think of this as a warning, then maybe you're smarter than I thought."

the *Seduction*

I slammed down the receiver, reconsidered, and left a similar message on his studio machine. Then I dialed my home phone.

"Honey pie, what's happened to you?" Maria said, with no more than my hello to prompt her. "You sound like you could tear apart the cables on the Brooklyn Bridge with your teeth. This what happens when you go on vacation? My God, girl, you better come right back home and go to work."

Still tight with tension, I explained about Stewart McClaren and asked if she'd gotten any calls from him.

"He's the one who left that message about the paint and the lilacs? Nope. Everyone seems to know you're away. No calls. Pinky misses you, though. He let me sleep until seven-thirty this morning so I didn't have to strangle him." I pictured the fine brown skin around the corners of her eyes creasing as she narrowed her eyes. "Aren't you afraid of someone like that, of what he might do? I want you to be careful, *chica*."

Her words rekindled my anger. "I can handle him. Don't worry about me, Maria. Just, if he phones, tell him to check his answering machine. And don't tell anyone where I am or what's going on, all right?"

She sighed, but I knew I could trust her. "When you coming home?"

"Not until Sunday, like I planned. He's not going to chase me away from here, too. Listen, I have a few more calls to make. You kiss Pinky for me and take care."

"Parrot lips? No way, *chiquita*. I'll stroke his wing feathers, that's as far as I go." She laughed and hung up.

I riffled through my book. The travel editor at *On the Road*, three free-lance photographers, the photo editor of *Weekend*—they'd all ask questions I didn't want to answer if I called on Sunday to chat about Stewart McClaren. Tomorrow was time enough.

A little calmer, I went downstairs. Andrew was dropping ice cubes one by one into a pitcher, his face screwed into a scowl as the level of the liquid rose perilously close to flood stage. When I touched his arm, he jerked his head up as though he'd been caught at something naughty. He lifted his arm and threw a final ice cube into the pitcher, ducking out of the way of the noisy splash. "Don's here," he said, avoiding my eyes. "He's in the garden, talking to Mom."

I glanced out the window; I had been so busy delivering my tirade to Stewart's answering machine and to Maria that I hadn't even heard a car pull up. Rosie was on her knees, pulling weeds from between the stake-and-string rows of newly sprouted chard. Don Ward, dressed in a blue workshirt and well-worn jeans, leaned a muscular forearm against a garden post and gestured to the top of Rosie's bent head.

My sister smiled up at him, straightened, and pressed her hand against the small of her back, a gardener's unconscious signal that stooping over dirt is not a natural human posture.

"Look!" Andrew abandoned the tea pitcher and ran to the door. "A kitten!"

9

An orange-and-white mound lay curled in the crook of Don's arm, its skinny tail falling like a question mark toward his wrist. Andrew flew out the door and sprinted toward the garden, nearly tripping over the cellar steps in his excitement.

Mesmerized at first by Don's long, graceful fingers stroking the kitten's ears, I shook myself free and followed Andrew.

"It can't be more than four, five weeks old." Rosie took hold of the kitten's back legs, peering intently between them. "*He* can't be. Where'd you get him?"

Don knelt, and Andrew moved nearer to get a better look. Like a hungry baby bird that had fallen from its nest, the tiny kitten wriggled and made a plaintive noise. "Some kid at the Millerton Super. You know how they stand outside to give away litters of kittens? Well, this one had Andrew's name on it."

With a skeptical frown, my nephew examined the kitten's fur. "No, it doesn't. How could it?"

We all laughed. "What I mean is," Don told Andrew gravely, "I thought this little fellow looked like he'd enjoy hanging out with you."

"Is he for me? Really?" Andrew stretched out a tentative hand; Don cradled the kitten as my nephew ruffled the fur on its neck. "Maybe we can get a doll-baby bottle and give him milk."

"He's big enough to drink on his own. Honey, go inside and bring out a clean saucer and the container of milk." Rosie nodded at her son; flushed with excitement, he streaked into the kitchen.

"Every guy needs something to cuddle." Don grinned and rubbed the cat's belly.

"It's really very sweet of you to think of him. He could use something to distract him until Paul gets back." Rosie seemed unaware of Don's double entendre and I was disinclined to respond to it.

It wasn't even tied with a black bow, I thought as Don set the kitten on the ground. Smiling, we watched it stagger, like a clown feigning drunkenness, in the ankle-high grass.

"I know what his name is." Andrew bounded down the steps, skidded to a stop in front of the kitten, and splashed milk into the saucer. "It's Leonardo. Like the turtle."

"Turtle?" Belatedly, I remembered the cartoon characters, warrior turtles who brandished swords and wore headbands that lent an antic fierceness to their unlikely grace.

"Leonardo, it is. Here, let's put this where Leonardo can get at it easily." Don moved saucer and kitten to the path beside the kitchen steps and set both down gently.

Andrew plunked himself on his stomach in the grass. He watched intently as the kitten first dipped one speculative paw into the milk, then shook it and licked at the drops clinging to the soft pad of skin.

"Try again, Leonardo. Drink the milk," Andrew coaxed. The kitten edged closer. Its tiny pink tongue nipped toward the saucer experimentally, then lapped the milk greedily.

Don's attention seemed more drawn to Andrew than to the kitten; he watched the boy appraisingly, then tapped me on the shoulder. He whispered, "Come for a walk with me. Let's leave this sweet domestic trio alone."

"We'll be back in a little while, Rosie," I said, and my sister nodded without looking up. They did look like a picture—if only I were working on a collection of family portraits instead of a nature book, this pretty backyard scene would have been perfect.

Don and I strolled past the lilac bushes to the front yard in comfortable silence, stopping as though by shared signal to watch a screeching blue jay leap from limb to limb of a maple tree.

"My mother gave me a cat when I was six." Don kicked at a stone. "I really wanted a dog, but she said she wouldn't take responsibility for some creature who barked and disturbed the neighbors and who needed to be walked twice a day. I loved that cat. Treated me with typical feline aloofness, only sat on my lap when it suited him. Sometimes, though, he chose exactly the right time. When I was sad or if I had a cold, he'd curl up right on my chest. Slugger, I called him, because he was always batting things around."

We walked on past the cornfield, to the stone wall that separated Ike Kronenburg's alfalfa field from his lawn. Don turned to the narrow path, found a shaded spot on a large, flat rock, and sat down.

I sat beside him. "Andrew's been a little droopy since Paul left. It was perfect, you coming by right then with the kitten."

"Well, I'm a musician. Can't get along without good timing."

"It's okay to admit you're a nice person, Don Ward." A breeze carried the scent of him, crisp and tangy, to me.

"Well, now, for a woman unaccustomed to handing out compliments, that was high praise."

"How do you know about the frequency of my compliments? We've only known each other a few days, and not under the best of circumstances, either."

"You want to talk about it?" Suddenly serious, he stretched out his long legs. "It's more than those flowers and the bows, isn't it?"

Perhaps, a hundred miles from my ordinary setting, I'd sloughed off my protective coloring, allowing him to see me clearly. But if I was suddenly more transparent than usual, I'd also acquired the facility to see a new presence lurking, shapeless and threatening, in the corners of my life.

The story of the photograph and the disturbing response from Riley Hamm spilled out, complete with the details of Stewart's behavior that day in my office. "The whole thing took me by surprise. I'd seen him around before, at the magazine, parties, that kind of thing, but I must have missed something, or maybe he decided to try a new tactic. The, I don't know, the *shock* of it caught me off guard—and then all this black ribbon stuff happened. I don't understand what he wants and why he's bringing it all the way up here. It makes me furious that he's dragged Rosie and her family into it. And Riley just made it sound like I was leading him on. Stewart, I mean."

"He sounds like a man out of control." Don's expression was thoughtful. "Stewart, not Riley. But it's not so hard to understand why he chose you."

"What does that mean? I'm not fishing for compliments—I'm just not good at seeing myself. I don't think anyone is."

He looked at me a long time, as though he were measuring my capacity for the truth. "You sure you want to hear this?"

Even if it was hard to take, I needed to hear what he had to say. I nodded.

"The first time I met you, at the Tastee-Freez, I thought, well, here's a pretty woman who understands sadness too well. Your eyes, that's how I knew. You were keeping something deep inside you, protecting yourself in some way. I've seen people on the bitter side of a love affair and that wasn't it, it was a deeper thing, a loss that you were holding close."

"You're right, exactly. I guess I'm a little amazed that it was so easy for you to see. And here I thought I'd done such a great job of hiding it. Did Paul or Rosie tell you . . . ?"

Don shook his head. "Paul only talks about your work, where you're going on assignment, things like that. Rosie talks mostly about how much she misses you."

"The man I was living with was stabbed to death four months ago." Saying it didn't make me choke on my own words now; either I'd passed some milestone or talking about it to Don made it easier.

He tugged a blade of grass loose. "I'm sorry," he said softly.

"I'm trying not to let it take over my life. That kind of control sometimes backfires. I never realized I was walking around looking so damaged."

"Not damaged, no. Something simpler. Hurting. And angry. You reacted to Hank Steuben as though it was you he was pushing around that night."

Shadows of leaves and branches played in shifting patterns across the planes of his face. "I guess I was still full of adrenaline from that confrontation with Stewart. Six, seven hours isn't enough time for some insults to lose their sting. You're very perceptive."

He grinned. "For a man."

I laughed then, and started to get up. "For anyone. I've had enough analysis for a while. Let's get back."

His hand kept me from rising. "Just one more thing, Lee—I want you to know something. I was attracted to you right away, but the signals you sent confused me. I wrestled with trying to stay cool and uninvolved but," he shrugged, "cool only plays well for certain tunes. It's not natural for me."

Don Ward got up. I watched him unfurl slowly to a full stretch. I stood, too, drawn by his smile into the circle of his arms. His big body felt strong and comforting against mine, and I took his face in my hands. His kiss was sweet, gentle, and then I let him go.

"You're absolutely right." Smiling, I stepped back onto the path. "Natural is good."

Leonardo slept all through dinner and the lazy, peaceful evening that followed, nestled like a fuzzy little confection in the safety of his owner's lap. Taking care of the kitten seemed to renew Andrew's good humor; it gave us all something to focus on for a while. Don left around nine and, pleasantly tired, Rosie and Andrew and I went to bed not long after.

Some time past three, I awoke, restless and hot. I stumbled into the bathroom, splashed my face, sipped cool water from my cupped hand.

On my way back to bed, I noticed a trickle of light seeping under Andrew's door. I tiptoed down the hall and pushed the door open, cringing as the hinges squealed. He lay sprawled motionless atop a rumpled sheet. One leg was flung over the edge of the bed; a dangling hand reached for the soft, sleeping kitten at his side.

Andrew mumbled and rolled over; still asleep, he groped the air restlessly and frowned, becoming quiet only when his fingers found the kitten again.

How nice to seek comfort, and find it so easily. I returned to my room weary but too awake and full of questions to sleep. I couldn't concentrate well enough to read, but at least I could flip pages in a magazine. I rummaged through the pile Rosie had put on the shelf of the bedside table, my attention caught every once in a while by the familiar style of photographers whose work I knew—a woman who loved to wash out colors and blur everything into soft edges, like the cover of a romance novel; a young black whiz whose vignettes of city life and hard times might one day earn him the awards and the recognition he deserved.

And then I realized that I'd missed something. I'd spent my working hours looking at photographs and understanding the sensibility behind the camera; surely the skills I'd acquired might help me figure out how Stewart McClaren thought, what he believed about the world, and why he might be doing these awful and disturbing things. Excited, I found a copy of *Vanity Fair* and scanned the contents, then flipped to the story about Cape Cod.

Stewart had a better eye than his Milan portfolio indicated; he had eschewed the predictable sand dunes and grizzled fishermen for an essay on Provincetown theaters. In a series of high-contrast, grainy shots, he followed the transformation of a stage from bare wood platform to squalid prison cell flanked by what appeared to be an interrogation room. The bleakness, the dehumanized harshness came to eerie and disquieting life as two dewy-faced stagehands added each element: a grimy bare bulb hanging over the rickety table; a rusty can that held mere stubs of pencils; the crusted and soiled bucket in the corner of the cell.

That play was the last thing I'd pay money to see. I tossed the magazine back on the shelf and pulled out another. He'd done a story for *Esquire* on Disneyland, and it had been a hot topic at one of the parties in the fall. I couldn't remember what had been said, but that hardly mattered. The story spoke for itself.

Whatever was grotesque—excessive kitsch, endless banks of controls required to operate some of the rides, the tangle of bloated adult fun seekers lining up for ice cream cones—he'd managed to capture in his dark, loving embrace. Stewart McClaren clearly loved the dreamworld shadows; his photographs caressed the illusions until they became full-blown deceptions.

I grabbed the pad from the bedside table and began to scribble. I wrote down everything I knew about McClaren, from his leather jacket to his marketing tactics to the kinds of photographs he took. And then it struck me: I'd become his partner in obsession. I'd been thinking about nothing else, had been lured into dancing with him. Stewart McClaren was leading and I was following, taking stumbling steps according to his nasty whim.

I'd allowed him to dictate my movements, but I didn't have to remain in his thrall.

I flipped the pad closed but left the magazine lying open on the table to remind myself of the nature of the enemy. When I tried to bring up Stewart's face and his voice in my memory, he was all mixed up with the faces in his photographs. The only clear image that stayed with me was Don Ward's square jaw and his amused, warm eyes.

the $Seduction$

For a large man, he lingered airily in my thoughts, a song I was trying to catch in a container. Then I glanced at the desk. Mike's face looked down at me. The day I'd taken that picture the light had been hazy and the streets black with rain.

His eyes sparkled, telling me to reach, to stretch, to enjoy myself. I thought again, as I had at the Tastee-Freez, that Mike would approve of the tentative connections I was making with Don. And he'd understand my feelings about Stewart, too.

Mike had dismissed him as superficial; he'd missed Stewart's darkness, but I saw it clearly now.

It was even possible that all the events of the past week were simply one big photo opportunity for Stewart, a setup, to put me off balance and draw me into a murky pit so that he could take pictures of my descent while he hovered out of sight, camera held up to his eye, shooting me in my distress.

Shooting me. . . . No, that wasn't the way it was going to work, but the words, once planted in my mind, wouldn't go away. *Shooting me.* The refrain wouldn't stop, not even in my sleep.

10

"Leonardo spent the night in my room, and he made me have that bad dream," Andrew reported as he clutched a glass of orange juice.

Rosie puttered at the counter, filling his lunch box with foil-wrapped packets and a Ninja Turtle thermos. "What do you mean, honey?"

Andrew pushed the glass away. "My car, the one Dad and me are building? Me and Leonardo were in it and I couldn't get it to stop and it went faster and down the hill, you know, the one behind school, and I couldn't find the brakes and it just kept going."

Rosie pulled up the chair beside him; she rubbed the blond down on his arm so that it glinted in the morning light, and said, "But when you woke up you were safe in your own bed, right? It was just a dream, honey."

Andrew's attention was on the kitten. "Why does he sleep so much? That means he's sick, right? That's what I do when I'm sick. I think I better stay home and take care of Leonardo."

Rosie pointed out that any kitten who consumes a full saucer of milk is perfectly healthy. "Besides, Leonardo needs to sleep so he can grow. All babies do," she assured her frowning son. "Let's get moving, kiddo. I'll walk you to the bus stop."

I let them go, hand in hand, across the lawn. They needed their time together—and I had calls to make. From the window at the end of the upstairs hall, I watched Rosie, her hands absently stroking his golden hair, as she waited with Andrew for the bus.

I grabbed my telephone directory from my purse and flipped pages, looking for inspiration, finding it finally in the listing for *Old Home*.

I dialed the magazine number. "Victoria Landow, please. This is Lee Montara calling."

After what felt like an interminable silence, Vicky's voice rasped: "Montara! I thought you were in Cozumel."

"Listen, I need to get in touch with Stewart McClaren. Do you have any idea if he's available for work like now, tomorrow, today?"

"Whoa! You sound like a woman possessed. Stewart McClaren? I didn't think he was your type."

Annoyed, I said, "He's not. Can you just tell me where he is, Vicky?"

"You're not going to tell me what this is about? Has our persistent young photographer been up to his old tricks again?"

Any note of exasperation in my voice would prompt more questions I didn't want to answer. "Business," I said.

"Umm hmm," she giggled into the phone. "As for Stewart's schedule, believe me, I'd like to know the same thing. He was supposed to do a big shoot for me Friday, some scrumptious brownstone renovation project in Brooklyn. Never showed up, never called, nothing. Not like Stewart to blow such a big one. Stunts are one thing, but a no-show . . . believe me, he'll never work for me again. I had to call twelve different—"

"Vicky, I'm sorry to cut you short, but I've got, well, things to deal with here. Lunch next Wednesday, right? See you then." Before she could say anything more, I hung up.

End of my most promising line—this wasn't what I wanted to hear but it was exactly what I'd expected.

"Let's make a plan, Lee," Rosie said when I came downstairs. "We both need to do something to get our minds off all this stuff. Didn't we say we were going to find some fabulous antiques at fantastic bargain prices? Let's poke around Kendall's, see what the old fellow has today."

My choice would have been to drive under the baking sun in search of the perfect, lush green spot by a stream or in the middle of a meadow, and shoot a couple of rolls of film, but Stewart McClaren had managed to spoil the very notion of a bucolic idyll. Besides, Rosie seemed to need something else.

I laughed. "Now Kendall's is an antiques shop? Everyone's coming up in the world, I guess. That place has been a junk store ever since I was ten and as far as I'm concerned it always will be. Genteel junk, maybe, I'll grant the old guy that much."

Small-paned windows filled with plants and a jumble of chipped but cheerful figurines formed part of the east wall of Kendall's, admitting a stream of sunlight to the open front room. Properly dim and musty, the back room was divided into narrow aisles of ornamental wood objects, larger pieces of oak and maple furniture, and glass and pottery bric-a-brac. I examined ducks, wreaths elaborately carved and gilded, picture frames of burnished cherry wood, and finally spotted a butter churn. The wood was golden oak, the handle worn smooth from use.

"What do you think, Rosie? No plants sitting on it, no lamps coming out of the handle, no glass tabletop. Just a plain old churn standing there in the corner of my bedroom to remind me of Taconic Hills."

Rosie nodded. "But don't act like a tourist. Make old man Kendall work for his price. Funny, I never think of you coveting butter churns."

"It does look more like it belongs in your house than mine, doesn't it? Sometimes," I said, enjoying the slippery feel of the satin edging of a Drunkard's Path quilt draped over the foot of a sleigh bed, "I picture you in a house with kerosene lamps lighting the family sing-alongs. You know—Saturday night baths in tin basins, jars of spiced apple rings and sauerkraut lining a cellar wall."

She whooped and hugged me, and I stumbled, catching myself before I knocked over a display of medicine bottles. I stored away a memory of the look on her face, mouth relaxed, eyes sparkling with pleasure.

"That's a lovely picture," she said. "Not quite accurate, but sweet. I don't mind that you associate me with all those nice things. *I* see *you* rushing around from glamorous city to glamorous city, gorgeous men trailing after you, your closet filled with chic but tailored little beige and black numbers that cost more than Paul makes in a month."

My eyes widened. "You really think that? That's wonderful. And how do I pay for all this on my modest photo editor's salary?"

"We're not talking reality, either one of us. Oh, no—" Rosie tugged at my sleeve and motioned me behind a tall, scarred wardrobe that smelled of mothballs and cloves. "There's Dolores Farley. Rats—I never called her to arrange to get her fabric."

I peeked around the corner. Dolores Farley looked like a hodgepodge of leftover parts, almost-delicate torso resting on the massive and shapeless pedestal of her bottom. She was bent over a music box, entranced by the intricate carving of flowers and vines on the lid.

"Remember when we bought the ballerina music box for Aunt Christa?" Rosie spoke in a whisper, her body pressed against the wardrobe. "She barely looked at it, never mind thanking us. God, she could be mean. Especially when she'd been drinking."

Another childhood observation confirmed; at least I hadn't imagined that boozy belligerence. But Rosie—how long had she known? "You knew that then? About her drinking?"

"Shh," Rosie warned, and she dipped her head in the direction of the music box aisle. "I don't want Dolores to scold me."

I shook my head; ducking a friendly neighbor might keep us trapped all afternoon. "We can't hide here forever, Rosie," I whispered. "Besides, don't you think she's recognized your car? Just tell her you meant to call her."

Rosie grimaced, then squared her shoulders. "You're right. Let's face the music."

We stepped into the aisle and Dolores looked up. Her pale gray eyes narrowed when she saw us. "Rosie Cooper," she said in her little girl's high voice, "you get younger every time I see you. I was just thinking about calling you to see if you was going to be around later this afternoon. So I can drop off that box of goods. And what's this I hear about black bows and flowers?"

The grapevine had even more tendrils than I'd remembered.

"This is one of my days at the senior center. Tomorrow's better, Dolores. Say, eleven in the morning?" Rosie turned to me, smiling, ignoring Dolores's question. "You remember my sister, Lee, don't you?"

"Sure, sure I do, you won that Veteran's Day poster contest when you were in fifth grade. Visiting the old stomping grounds, are you?" Dolores shifted her bulk from one foot to another, as though she were trying hard to maintain her balance. "You in Taconic Hills for good?" Her colorless eyes studied me.

"Just for a week. Then I have to get back to my job. How's Joseph? Rosie tells me he's had a bad time of it lately." Standing in a second-hand store listening sympathetically to a sad and lonely old woman go through the litany of her problems wasn't high on my list of vacation activities, but Dolores had been nice to me—to all the kids in school—and I could give her a few seconds of my time.

"Well, I guess you heard about his accidents from Rosie here. He walks with a little limp sometimes when it rains. Where his leg was broke, I think it hurts him more than he lets on. It pains me just like he was my own child to see him hurting. But at least he's still out there working just like always." She glanced down at her watch. "Heavens, I have to get going. See you with that fabric. Around eleven tomorrow, all right?"

Rosie nodded. "Thanks, Dolores. I appreciate it."

Dolores Farley nodded and waddled away, puffing a little as she pushed the door open.

"You're such a good person," I said, deliberately passing the butter churn without a glance. "I don't have so much patience for martyrs."

"Dolores, a martyr? I don't know, Lee. She wasn't fishing for praise or sympathy. You remember looking forward to lunch when we were kids, because Dolores would always have a compliment to dish out along with the mashed potatoes? She treated us all as if we were her very own children. I wouldn't call that being a martyr." Rosie pushed open the door and we stepped outside.

I blinked back the glaring sunlight; Rosie's generosity was certainly more universal than mine.

"Come help me make space for Dolores's boxes. In my sewing room."

Rosie tossed a bundle of mail on her desk in the kitchen and pushed open the door to the small, low-ceilinged room. When we were kids, it had been a pantry, crammed with bins of flour and rice and cornmeal, the shelves stocked with soup and cereal and jars of tomatoes and jam. Over the years, as the household shrank from seven and then reassembled at three, Rosie pulled down half the shelves, set up her sewing machine and her ironing board, and rigged an old painted door on two sawhorses to serve as a work surface. Charts of herbs and wildflowers and pictures of quilt patterns cut from magazines covered the limited wall space.

She could manage rearranging the boxes to make room for Dolores's contribution without me; that wasn't the point of her asking. Glad for the excuse to spend more time together, I followed her inside. She was balancing on a three-legged stool, reaching for a cardboard carton from the top shelf when a series of loud knocks rang through the house.

"Be right back," Rosie said, hopping down from the stool.

In the company of my sister's heathery blue and pink fabric collection and those pictures of delicate plants on the walls, all expressions of Rosie's serene imagination, I became restless. I sauntered toward the front door, half-expecting to hear Riley's thin, nasal drone. Instead, I heard Rosie, her voice pitched high with annoyance. A hulking shadow blocked the light beyond the screen.

"There you are, Lee. I was just about to call you. Hank here wants to talk to you." Rosie turned and smiled as though graciousness, or at least, good manners, would deflect some of his barely concealed hostility.

"What can I do for you, Mr. Steuben?" The sight of Hank Steuben irritated me. His lumpy presence brought back the scene in the Tastee-Freez parking lot in too-vivid detail.

"Sorry to disturb you, ma'am." The man bent his unkempt head as though he were ducking to see under an obstacle. He coughed, and I shuddered at the wet, sloppy sound. "I wanted to tell you that you better . . . you better be the good Christian I think you are, because I need to ask your forgiveness. I didn't mean to yell at you that way the other night. I'm real sorry. That's all. I just wanted to say that."

The tension in Rosie's shoulders eased a little, but I wasn't ready to be off my guard. This wasn't a man who made apologies because he felt genuine regret about hurting someone. He was saying a quick Hail Mary to clear the slate of his sins until next time, I was sure of it.

"Okay, Mr. Steuben. Thank you for telling me." I stepped up to the screen door and touched Rosie's arm to signal that, as far as I was concerned, the interview had ended. "Is there anything else?"

Hank Steuben snapped to attention as though he'd been slapped.

He muttered something I couldn't hear, then coughed into the crumpled handkerchief he pulled from his pocket.

"What did you say? I'm sorry, I didn't hear you." I *did* hear the annoyance in my own voice. That kind of intimidation might work with his wife, but I wasn't willing to play his nasty game.

"I just wondered to myself whatever happened to the idea of charity. It says in the Bible that—"

"Mr. Steuben, I'm sorry to interrupt, but we've got things to do now. I accepted your apology. I don't mean to be rude, but I don't want a lecture on the Bible. Come on, Rosie. Let's take care of our chores."

At last, Rosie responded to the pressure on her arm. She turned with me away from the door.

I headed for the kitchen, but I heard very clearly the word *bitch* as Hank Steuben stood fuming on the porch. I ignored it. People on subways had called me worse for accidentally bumping into them during rush hour.

"You forget, Lee, this is a small town and I choose to live in it. You could have at least been civil to him," Rosie scolded.

"And you could have told Riley about your telephone calls," I snapped back. Rick Decker's hot glare danced into my memory. "You protecting someone, Rosie?"

Her face flushed with color. "Don't make foolish accusations, Lee. Don't let your imagination carry you away. Reality is difficult enough already."

11

"So, what do you think about Don?"

Still awash in anger over Hank Steuben's visit, I was startled by Rosie's question. She had seemed lost in her own musings, her mind on the afternoon's activities at the senior center or her book, instead of being on the porch with me and the buttery sunshine. She pulled open the drawer of the white wicker table between us and laid her book inside, waiting for my answer.

"He's certainly not someone I expected to meet in Taconic Hills. He's been around since September—what do *you* know about him?" I reached into the bowl on the table, snapped the end off a pea, and ran my thumb along the split pod, letting the peas plink into the metal bowl in my lap. The kitten clawed at my bare ankle, and I dangled a peapod in front of him. He batted at it, fell over onto his back, then scrambled upright.

"Know, as in history? Well," and I heard the smile in my sister's voice without actually having to see her face, "he's from Buffalo, got divorced eight years ago when his wife decided she liked the prospects of a Lake Forest doctor better than a Buffalo music teacher and sometime jazz musician. He has no children, cooks great asparagus-and-bacon omelettes, and disappears every summer on a trek to find the new jazz sounds in the cities of America." She extended her hand; I passed a shiny pod to her. "I like him. He doesn't seem to want anything in return for his friendship, if you know what I mean. He doesn't ask for anything, just enjoys the company. He's started to seem like . . . I don't know how else to say it . . . like a brother."

I heard something new in Rosie's voice, a trill of excitement or admiration that I didn't understand. "Rosie, do you have a crush on Don?"

She tipped her head back, amusement dancing in her eyes. "God, Lee, you're so thick. I'd never dream of getting into *that* kind of sibling rivalry with you. You've always given off some kind of magical perfume that turns men into mush."

"Rosie, do you have any idea how hard it is to have a relationship with mush?" I'd tried for years to get my sister to understand that even if I *could* attract the men I was interested in by simply exuding an exotic scent, there was absolutely no guarantee we could make something satisfying out of the connection.

She crunched the peapod thoughtfully. "It looks like you two might be interested in each other and I'd love to see something happen, that's all. Not that I'm trying to play matchmaker. But someone like Don, sort of settled but still a little unpredictable, would be good for you."

Good for me? She made Don Ward sound like medicine. "If these things were decided by my brain, you might be right. But I'm not looking for someone who will be, as you put it, good for me. I *am* attracted to him. I just don't know yet if I *like* him."

Rosie held the stringy end of the pod daintily between two fingers. "You don't have to be sure about anything right now. It's only four months since Mike's death. And you're extra sensitive, we both are, because of those black bows and the picture of your friend, that's all."

"*Friend!* How can you say that? I explained to you about—Oh, hell, Rosie, not you, too. McClaren's not a friend. He's some egomaniacal photographer who claimed he had this thing for me. I'd rather go back to your first question. What am I going to do about Don?"

"What do you want to do?" Rosie said simply.

the *Seduction*

I wanted to be on Cozumel lying in the sun on the hot sand, as I'd planned.

"Nothing," I said truthfully. "I'm going to wait and see what happens. I'm not going to charge into anything. I'm not going to have any expectations."

"And what if he does? Have expectations, I mean?"

"That's his problem, isn't it?" It sounded colder than I'd intended.

The reproachful frown that crossed Rosie's face melted away. "I have to go. My little group at the senior center gets anxious if I'm late. I told Rick he didn't have to come by to stay with Andrew after school today because you'll be here."

As though she could only break away from the house by plunging off the porch, Rosie gathered her purse and a box of folded remnants and ran down the steps to her car.

"I wish Mom could come with us." Andrew's downcast eyes brightened. "I know! We'll show her later. We'll take a walk so she can see our dam. It's terrific!"

Such trust and optimism still fed the springs of his young enthusiasm. "How do you know? We haven't even built it yet."

"Cause I do know. It's *gonna* be terrific. Cause we're gonna make it that way."

After seeing him subdued by bad dreams and sleeplessness, this transformation was wonderful to watch. His compact body seemed to buzz with excitement; I wished I could harness that energy and dole it out, bit by bit, on those days when I wanted to do nothing more than pull the covers up to my chin and watch the world spin around.

I tousled his fine, pale hair. "You ready, champ?"

Andrew grinned up at me. "That's what Rick calls me."

Even hearing the young man's name made me uncomfortable. "I'm going to bring my camera. Remember that book I told you I was working on? I want to have pictures from Taconic Hills in it. What else do you think we should bring along on this dam-building expedition?"

"Juice. Crackers but without peanut butter." He leaned his round cheek against his fist. "And a hammer."

I laughed. "What's the hammer for?"

He raised his eyebrows; the question seemed to have taken him by surprise. "Well, when you build things you always need a hammer, right? And then if the bad guy comes, we can bonk him with it."

This time, I caught myself before my laugh escaped to embarrass and confuse both of us. My amusement crumbled at the realization that he was still afraid. In the past three days his world had changed; now, he saw demons lurking in the thickets and shadows. I wouldn't lie to him. Telling him I would take care of everything was even worse than a lie; it was an empty promise I couldn't fulfill. "I don't think we're going to run into any bad guys down by the stream. Ready to go?"

Andrew thought that over and then nodded. "Okay, here's the crackers. I'll carry the juice." He said nothing more about a hammer.

Heat waves rippled the still air. As we strolled along the edge of the field of corn, we talked about how it would be when we were cooled by the stream, the shade of the leafy canopy above our heads. We stopped to look at a fallen bird's nest and to examine what appeared to be raccoon tracks, five curved and jointed toes above an oval pad, in the damp, sandy dirt at the water's edge. Andrew chattered about the nature book his class was writing in school, about baby animals and how they learn to take care of themselves, about Leonardo.

At some point, I stopped being acutely aware that I was trying to distract an uneasy child, and we fell into the simple comfort of each others' company. By the time we reached the stream, I was no longer startled every time a twig snapped beneath our feet, and Andrew listened with wide-eyed wonder as I described the dams and bridges I'd seen in my travels.

We gathered rocks in a mound, stepped into the cool water and began to build our shore-to-shore dam. "Don't we need to have cement or something, to plug up the spaces?" Andrew asked when our necklace of stones reached halfway across the stream.

"We're going to stuff some twigs in the big spaces. Even though there are still little spaces, the water can't go through as fast as it wants to. You'll see, this dam will make a terrific pool."

Andrew nodded and laid another stone in place. Soon we were sitting in the promised pool, eating crackers and watching a squadron of bees inspect the blossoms of the pink-veined wood sorrel beneath the trees. Then Andrew discovered a tiny forest of wild watercress sprouting among a cluster of rocks along the bank. "There, Auntie Lee. Take a picture of *that*."

the Seduction

How wonderful: He'd understood completely what I was looking for and he'd found the perfect image for the book. I pointed the camera at the green shoots bending to the force of the rushing water. Andrew watched intently, then became absorbed with the way the stream distorted things, wriggling his half-submerged fingers and delighting in the watery illusion, so fascinated that he wasn't aware he'd become the camera's subject.

I had a fleeting wish to stay here forever, to linger in the peaceful shade, but Andrew's restlessness and my own subdued anxiety gradually swam to the surface, bubbling up from the pool of quiet like sharp-toothed fish slipping from shadow to shadow.

"Time to go back, kiddo. We'll get out of our wet clothes and make some iced tea for when your mom comes home."

We grabbed the cracker box and the juice container, slung our sneakers over our shoulders, and navigated through the high grass toward the cornfield and the garden beyond, the scarecrow's Mets cap our Polaris.

"Let's do remembering," Andrew said brightly.

I was instantly transported to bedtime, and all the nights years ago that my father would come in and sit on my bed or Rosie's and conduct sessions he called "remembering." Each of us had to come up with one good memory, something that had happened during the previous twenty-four hours. "It can be as little as finding a lost sock or seeing a flower that you really loved, but it has to be real," my father said, explaining the rules to me and Rosie. "No making things up." For a while, it became a habit to go through my day looking for what I was going to tell at night. I saved up good things and tried to figure out which would be the best. And then it became a contest with Rosie, who was forever bringing nature memories, when all I could manage to hold on to were achievements—sliding safe into second base or being the only one to solve a rebus. I was glad that Rosie had continued the exercise with her son.

"Okay, you first." I smiled down at him, at the pinched and worried look that scrunched his features—so like his mother's—into a frown. I'd always believed that people move instinctively toward happiness, however clumsily—he had asked to do remembering because he needed to ward off a bad feeling with a good one.

"No, you. And it has to be today."

"That's easy," I said, my heart full with the pleasure of being with him. We emerged from the sunny cornfield, and the house sprang up in front of us, the backyard looking like an advertisement for country living, stone barbecue, walnut tree, garden, scarecrow and all. "I really liked it just now, when we were sitting in the stream. It was very quiet, and it felt friendly and cool, and I was glad to be with you. It was a *peaceful* happy, you know what I mean? I usually have more excited happy times. I really liked it."

"My turn." Andrew trudged ahead, kicking up tiny clouds of dust as he scuffled along the dirt path. "I know! I liked going out this morning for breakfast and seeing the birds. They were busy getting worms, just like always. That's what I liked."

I nodded; we each have our ways of convincing ourselves that the world is the familiar place we want it to be.

As we approached the house, I noticed a light flickering in the kitchen window, as though a small flame burned inside, teased by the gentle breeze. I knew at once that I had to go in first, had to make sure Andrew was engaged in some activity that would keep him outside without arousing his fear or suspicion.

"Before you come in, will you pick a lot of lettuce for our salad? The greenest leaves you can find, okay, sweetie?" I took the empty cracker box from him, and wiped a smudge of dirt from his cheek. "We're going to make a special dinner for your mom."

"Okay. I like helping." His eagerness was delicious, almost heartbreaking.

"Remember, make sure the lettuce is absolutely the greenest in the garden." I smiled despite the tightness in my throat, watched while he pushed open the wood-framed garden gate, and then I sprinted to the steps.

I had left the screen door open and the kitchen door unlocked, hadn't I? I'd made it so *easy* for him that I practically invited him in.

With one final look to check the garden and Andrew, bending over the lettuce, I hurried inside.

On the counter, seven squat candles blazed brightly in thick glasses. A black ribbon tied in a precise bow circled each glass. The dancing flames cast crimson spatters on the white walls. I licked my thumb and forefinger and pinched them out. Trying to touch as little of the surface as I could, I wrapped each glass in a paper towel and stuffed them into an empty grocery bag.

I jumped when the screen door banged shut.

the $Seduction$

"These ones are the greenest," Andrew announced proudly. "Peeyew—What smells like burning?"

I shoved the paper bag under the sink and turned. "Oh," I said, "I just lit a match because the pilot light went out on the stove. That's all that was burning here."

It was amazing how easily the lie came.

12

I stepped backward, pushed the cabinet door shut, and leaned against the sink.

"We're going to have pasta primavera tonight. You ever have that before? This is a secret recipe I got from a man who can whistle one tune at the same time he hums another. He runs a little restaurant in Italy, in a city called Florence, and he puts broccoli and carrots and zucchini in the sauce just a few minutes before he serves it so that they're crunchy but not raw. That's called *al dente.*"

I rinsed tomatoes and babbled on about the recipe and Signore Caporelli while Andrew poked a finger into the handle of the sugar bowl.

"I don't like that kind of spaghetti. I like meatballs." Restlessly, he pushed away from the table and headed for the back door. "I'm going to go find Leonardo."

With Andrew outside, I could move the candles so that he wouldn't discover them when he was helping with dishes or looking for one of the mysterious items little boys are forever declaring they absolutely *must* have. Riley would come by to pick them up, and the candles and the black bows would be gone from the house. I left the lettuce on the counter, grabbed the bag from under the sink, and raced up the stairs to my bedroom.

A realization jolted me as I set the bag on the high closet shelf: Stewart McClaren really was brazen enough to come into the house while Andrew and I were a couple of hundred yards away at the stream. This time, though, I wouldn't be the one to blink first, as I had been when I'd given away my tickets to Cozumel.

There were laws against what Stewart McClaren was doing—harassment, breaking and entering—even a citation for a broken headlight or spitting on the sidewalk would let him know he was being watched, and that might be enough to stop him. I'd make sure Riley knew about the blue car that had shadowed me on the parkway on Thursday, and this time I would see to it that he followed up.

Downstairs, the kitchen screen door slammed.

"Auntie Lee, where are you? Leonardo knows his name. Watch this!"

By the time I came down to see the performance, Andrew was outside, sitting on the back step, leaning forward and dangling a multicolored braided strip in front of the kitten.

"Look," he said, his eyes bright. "Come, Leonardo." As he said the kitten's name, he moved the thong, and Leonardo, cleverest of creatures, quirked his orange-and-white head.

"Pretty smart cat you've got there." I batted at the braid. "What's this?"

But before I heard his answer, I knew: it was Rick Decker's friendship bracelet. That day the cake made its mysterious appearance, he'd stood in the kitchen. Talking basketball. Watching Rosie. Fingering a strip of braided cotton thread. A lovelorn teenager—perfect. Exactly what we needed right now, another unwanted, anonymously delivered item. "Where'd you get this?"

"Leonarrr-do." Andrew bounced the colorful bracelet up and down, intent on the kitten and its antics. My question curled up into the air like a wisp of smoke and drifted away, unnoticed.

I knelt and let my hands rest on his shoulders. My face was level with his now, so close I could see the downy fuzz along the line of his jaw. As long as Andrew and Rosie insisted on protecting Rick, I wasn't likely to get either of them to answer my questions. "Andrew, I asked you something. Where'd you get the bracelet, honey?"

But he went on with his game as though he and the kitten were alone in the yard, looking up only when he heard a car rumble up the drive. Not Rosie's clattery station wagon, not the hum of Don's little Triumph, the sound was nonetheless familiar. When I walked around the side of the house, I saw the seal on the door of a Jeep nearing the mailbox. Like the cavalry troops cresting the horizon just in the nick of time, I'd been saved once again, the impasse with Andrew broken by the U.S. mail.

"Let's see what Joseph has for us," I called, but Andrew didn't look up. Thoroughly frustrated and glad for the diversion, I jogged down to the mailbox.

Joseph Farley waved an envelope. "Missed this one. Found it at the bottom of the pile. Don't know how it got there."

"Thanks." The thick envelope he handed me appeared to be nothing more urgent than a bank statement. "How's it going, Joseph?"

"Oh, fine." One thick-knuckled hand gripped the steering wheel; the other moved deliberately to the gear shift as he revved the engine.

But I didn't want him to go, not yet. He spent all day on the roads of Taconic Hills. Maybe he'd noticed someone hanging around near the house while Andrew and I were at the stream. While he was making his appointed rounds, Joseph Farley might even have seen Stewart's car.

"Joseph, you didn't happen to see anyone around here before when you were delivering the mail, did you?"

"You mean today?" He tipped his chin up and looked straight ahead through the bug-smeared windshield.

Didn't I speak the same language as everyone else? "Yes, today."

Slowly, his head swiveled in my direction. A gentle crease ridged the fleshy space between his fair, sparse eyebrows. "Not before. When I left the mail, there were no other cars here. Not then."

"How about any time in the last few days?"

"You mean, except for Mizz Cooper's and that one there?" He pointed to my rented car.

"Right, Joseph. Except for those." Thoroughly regretting that I'd even bothered to ask, I began to edge away from the Jeep.

"Only that little red Triumph that teacher drives, the one who brings Mr. Cooper home. Seems like I remember the Steuben car, Hank's." He backed up into a turn, pulled forward, and stuck his head out the open window. "Oh, and that old beat-up Plymouth. The Decker kid's."

Of course. Come to pay a call on Rosie under the guise of helping out with Andrew. But, for the moment, I didn't care about Rick Decker. I was more interested in someone else. "You see a strange blue car, dark blue, anywhere around town in the past few days?"

The red bow tie bobbed as Joseph shook his head. "Strange? You mean one I didn't recognize? No, not a blue one. Not that I recall. I have to get going." The Jeep bolted down the driveway, and I carried the bank statement to the house, trying to sort out fact from conjecture, concluding finally that the only thing I knew for sure was that I wanted the games to stop.

"Andrew won't talk to me, either. He's never done this before. Honestly, Lee, I've read about the stages kids go through but he's always been so open, so easygoing. I don't like what's happening to him. You're sure he didn't see those candles?" The dark circles under Rosie's eyes, badges of worry, gave her the look of a wild, injured creature.

"I'm certain. If Riley ever returns our calls, I'm going to ask him to find Stewart. God, if this doesn't convince him. . . . The dispatcher said he was out on that arson investigation. She promised he'd check in with us when he got back."

"Well, I hope it's soon, and I hope he actually *does* something this time. This Stewart . . . he sounds like the kind of person who would go to extremes to get himself noticed."

"Especially if the payoff is big enough." Stewart McClaren certainly was capable of creating an elaborate drama, trick by evil trick, that would culminate in a Grand Guignol finale.

Rosie cleaned the kitchen counter with long, unenthusiastic swipes of her sponge. "Andrew's so sensitive to my feelings, he's getting upset just because *I* am. There've been too many strange things . . ."

I wondered if Rosie included Rick Decker on the list of things that made her uncomfortable.

"Why don't you tell Rick straight that Andrew found his friendship bracelet? He's a bright kid, he'll figure out that you don't want him slinking around here if you give him half a clue. And maybe then he'll stop looking at you like that."

Rosie didn't raise her voice and she didn't scowl at me. She tossed the sponge into the sink, wiped her hands on a towel, and said evenly,

"I can't just tell him to stop coming around. It would feel like an accusation to Rick, I know it."

It *was* exactly that, and no matter what words she used, it was bound to sound that way. "And if you don't, aren't you encouraging him?"

And then I remembered what Andrew had said at the Tastee-Freez when he pointed Rick out to me the first night of my visit. "Rosie, *you're* not the one who gave him the friendship bracelet, are you? His dropping it conveniently in the yard, that's not his way of giving it back to you, is it?"

"I don't believe you!" A dark flush crept up from Rosie's neck and stained her cheeks. "Here we are practically under siege by some lunatic friend of yours and you take the opportunity to lecture *me* about how I should respond to a silly adolescent crush? If you're so interested in who gave Rick the bracelet, why don't you ask him yourself?"

Mike used to say that my impatience came from a quirk in my wiring. My electrical circuits required complete and speedy closure, he'd tease. And now I was bombarded with memories: the hungry look in Rick's eyes when he watched Rosie; the message of his hip-slung slouch.

"Okay, if that's the way you want it." I grabbed the telephone book from the shelf above Rosie's desk. Eight Deckers listed in the southern part of Columbia County, but only two of them in Taconic Hills. "Is his father's name Frank or—no, this must be it. Richard Decker, Senior. Up on Snyder Road. That's right, isn't it, Rosie?"

But she wouldn't answer. Like her son, she wouldn't even look at me.

Once again, according to Rosie, I was the one in the wrong. I slammed the phone book shut. "I want to ask him, face to face, about the bracelet. I want to see his eyes when I tell him we found it. I shouldn't be gone long. You sure you don't want to do this? It might be better that way."

Rosie's back was all the answer I was going to get.

I pivoted and raced to my car, pulled on my sunglasses, and headed for Snyder Road.

All around me, the unmistakable signs of early summer burst across the landscape. Fields of mustard plants the color of ripe bananas alternated with the new green of young alfalfa; bright dame's rocket raced along the peaks of rock gardens; brilliant white sheets flapped on laundry lines. But I couldn't keep my mind on the scenery. How could Rosie deny what was so very obvious? What lies did she tell herself that would justify Rick Decker's insolent stares, his blatant invitations?

Whatever it was, I wasn't under the same spell. I almost drove past the mailbox, but I braked hard and pulled in beside a faded white saltbox with a green shingle roof and a peeling red door. The lawn was nothing more than a weedy jungle growing right up to the foundation.

Hood raised, the battered black Plymouth sat in the driveway. Rick leaned against the fender, one foot resting on the chrome bumper as he wiped a wrench with an oil-stained rag, a watch on his right wrist . . . and nothing on his left. He tossed the rag on the ground and set the wrench in a rusty toolbox as I walked toward him.

"Hi. Working on your car?" I shaded my eyes against the glare.

When he nodded, his raven black hair fell toward his eyes; it didn't seem to bother him nearly as much as it did me. He wasn't going to make this any easier, and neither was pretending that I was here on a social call.

"I stopped by to ask you a question."

He treated me to his cynical, tough-guy smile. "Anything you want to know, all you gotta do is ask."

"I see you're not wearing your bracelet today."

The smile became a frown as he brushed the hair off his forehead. "My bracelet? You came here to talk about my bracelet? What's it your business?"

"Andrew found it. Near the house. You were wearing it the last time you were over, right? On Friday. That *is* the last time you were at my sister's house, isn't it?"

Snorting with impatience, he closed the distance between us until the tips of his boots almost touched my toes. I'd never realized until that moment how exposed I could feel in sandals.

"Look, lady, you trying to say something? You don't like me, that's your business, but you sound like you're trying to say I did something wrong. I haven't been near your sister's house. Maybe it is my bracelet. It must have come off when Andrew and I were playing basketball. So what?"

I shrugged, trying to smile and succeeding only in a grimace. "Just asking. No problem."

As I turned and walked back to my car, I felt his eyes on me, the
ory heat in them generated by anger.

Regret set in on the drive back to Rosie's. I should never have
erfered; how self-righteous, how holier-than-thou I'd been. I for-
ive myself only a little on the grounds that Stewart McClaren had
rned my world into a bad dream that colored even the daylight
urs with a lingering darkness, and I steeled myself to admit to my
er that I'd made a mistake.

osie was in the sewing room when I returned, sorting fabric into
according to color.

houldn't have gone out there, Rosie. It was patronizing to you
Rick, and I'm sorry," I said softly, ready for whatever anger she
eap on me.

y surprise, she tossed a blue wool square into a box and said,
ou an apology, too. In a way I'm glad you did it. I realized
were gone what my problem was. Rick was a leftover fan-
y high school days, but the trouble is that only one of us is
He *has* been making me uncomfortable. I know how he
but I was hoping it was something he'd outgrow. I've
. I shouldn't have let you go through with that confron-
ld have talked to him a long time ago."

tears stung my eyes. "Oh, Rosie, I *am* sorry. I hate
of this week. I wanted us to have a peaceful, happy
ll this. . . . Why don't we spend the evening to-
ree of us? We can all use a little quiet. I'll call Don
stop by."

t that?" Her smile brightened and the dark and
er eyes turned almost playful.

e now. It'll do him good to have someone say no.
nyway."

her sorting and went into the kitchen to call Don. He
second ring, and the sound of his voice almost over-
. Before I could change my mind, I told him that it
if he didn't stop by for dinner. Rosie and Andrew and
time alone, I said.

a mandate from a friend—"

on. I know you promised Paul you'd look after us. We'll
the phone tucked between my cheek and my shoulder
circles on the window glass.

questioning your competence, Lee. I'd like to see you.

the Seduction

You're leaving in less than a week, and after that my trusty Triumph and I are taking off for parts west."

The picture of Don and his little red car whizzing down the ba roads of middle America in search of the next musical high made m smile. "Send postcards," I said.

The silence on the other end went on for so long I wondered there was something wrong with the telephone. But finally he sai "I'm terrible at reading maps. I get lost all the time. Just last summer meant to go to Chicago, but I ended up in Atlanta because I had t map turned the wrong way."

"Try a Greyhound," I offered, "or don't worry about reaching particular destination. Just let the roads carry you."

He laughed softly. "I was rather hoping you'd offer to be my na gator."

"I'm a map dyslexic myself. I should hire tour guides when I anywhere outside of Manhattan. Thanks for the invitation, thoug you find yourself in New Orleans in August, last two weeks of month, I'll show you the best gumbo place in town. Or come to York, any other time."

"But don't come for dinner tonight, right?"

"Not unless you're hungry for rejection. Seriously, Don, we're up here, just the two of us." Usually, telephone flirtations were but this was only frustrating; I didn't mean what I was saying was certain he heard my ambivalence.

"Three," he said.

Andrew. "Of course, that's what I meant. Rosie, Andrew, and

He sighed. "You're going to miss me, Lee Montara."

"I look forward to that," I said.

"Good, fine, but I'm not giving up. Okay, I'll stay home to you meet me in an hour on the road that cuts across from Ancr to Copake Lake. In the shadow of Old Croken. Will you do want to show you something."

Before I could say no, he added, "My car will be parked old fire road. See you then."

Why not? Maybe Rosie could coax Andrew out of his mo then we'd have our quiet evening together. And I wouldn't pretend that I didn't want to see Don Ward.

13

The afternoon had turned suffocatingly hot. The valley steamed beneath a lid of humidity that sealed it off from any vagrant, cooling breezes. In the last few years before I moved to New York City, I'd hated the damp lassitude of summer because it had limited activity to essential chores, punctuated only by an occasional trip to the kitchen in search of an iced drink. Now, the amiable stupor offered unexpected promises.

Promises, though, had lately turned into threats. Those flickering candles in the kitchen, those precise black bows, even Rosie's odd telephone calls and Rick's friendship bracelet insisted on leaping into the jumble, turning my mind soupy.

I pointed my car toward the hill and pushed my hair off my neck, humming along with an Annie Lennox tape, the music a fitting minor-key accompaniment to the melancholy that crept over me. As the song wound down, the road curved sharply to the right; when it unfurled again into a straightaway, I spotted the low-slung red car.

Don Ward sat in the dirt of the turnout, leaning against the side of the Triumph with his arms clasped around his knees, a meditative look softening his craggy face. Such a big man with such a small car—odd that they seemed to belong together. I pulled in behind him, turned off the engine, and climbed out of my car into the still, dead heat of the day.

"Sight-seeing?" I asked, shielding my eyes against the sun.

Straight-faced, Don drawled a melodious "Nope."

"Ambushed again, then." I hunkered down beside him. "Am I interrupting some vital communion with nature? Or are you waiting for a sign from the universe?"

"I just got it." His gaze flicked over my shoulders. "Want to go for a walk?"

I wriggled my toes and pointed at my sandals. "I'm not dressed for hiking."

His laugh was pleasant, indulgent. "I didn't say do you want to go for a hike."

He stood, extending a hand to help me. But I pushed up the way dancers do, my legs strong and my back straight. He held out his hand again; this time I took it. We wound between pricker bushes toward a cluster of pine trees along a narrow ribbon of pressed-down grasses that I suspected was a deer run in the fall. A sagelike scent rose as we crushed the greenery underfoot.

"Where are we going?" I asked.

But Don said nothing. We kept a steady pace until we came to a stream, barely more than a trickle of water that even Andrew could step over. A sudden thought sent a chill through me: I was following docilely, lamb to some unknown slaughter, as a man I hardly knew led me to a place of his choosing.

"Don, I want to know where we're going." I stopped in my tracks and almost fell forward because he maintained his firm grasp on my hand. I yanked my wrist away, ready to turn back to the car.

Concern welled in his eyes. "I frightened you."

My jaw tightened, but I was determined not to let him see me flinch. "Between the heat and what's been going on at Rosie's, this isn't exactly a good time for guessing games."

"I really am sorry, Lee. That was thoughtless of me. I understand completely." A grace note of warmth brightened his rich voice.

"Listen, Don, I'm sorry. I'm afraid I'm not very good company right now. Let's take this walk some other time. Before I leave, okay?"

He grinned. "Okay, but I don't know if I can wait to give you my little gift."

"Gift?" *Wrapped in a black bow?* "It's not my birthday."

Disappointment darkened his amber eyes. "I know it's not. One of the things you don't know about me—and there are lots of things you don't know about me yet—is that I hardly ever give birthday gifts. I give gifts when the spirit moves me. I saw this yesterday, it made me think of you, and the spirit moved me."

If I'd met him on my trip to Cozumel, would I have been so wary? Or would I go along with the adventure of the game and play until it was time to return to my real life? Mike used to tell me that my impulsiveness would help me professionally when I remembered to take pictures the way I lived. "Look with your heart," he'd said. "Embrace the things that move you."

Had I'd simply forgotten what it was like to be with a man who acted spontaneously, who didn't have a calculated plan for everything including sex and laughter, who knew his own boundaries and valued his freedom?

"I don't need gifts," I said quietly.

"Okay, let's not do *that* one to death. How 'bout we talk about the weather?" His hand was cool and dry, his voice light. "When it gets like this, there's nothing to do but give in to it, let the heat make everything soft and blurry, forget about work and responsibility. People who live near the equator shouldn't be expected to compete with hardy northern types, don't you think? Geography is destiny, and here we are."

We had reached the shade of the circle of pines, and my arms and neck, damp from perspiration, were cold. Don Ward stepped close, wrapped his arms around me, and kissed me. I pushed away the memory of Stewart in my office; this was different. I had given Don signals, and he had interpreted them correctly.

I leaned into the kiss, conscious of all the places where our bodies met, enjoying the shock of awareness.

But then he stepped away and held up his hand, telling me to stop. "Wait," he said, his voice no different than when he was talking about the heat. "I want to look at you."

A slender columbine bent in a breath of wind, and a pleasant excitement rippled through me. Don traced my face, my throat, the lines of my body with his eyes. It might as well have been his hands on me, for the effect that steady gaze had.

"Turn around," he said hoarsely.

"Don, what in the world—"

"Please, Lee. Turn around."

And I did, my self-consciousness and my impatience growing as I imagined his eyes on the curve of my back, pictured his face as he continued to look at me. "Don, this is—"

His lips brushed the nape of my neck. "Now, don't move. Five more seconds. That's all."

From behind me, I heard the sound of tearing paper. Time stretched on; a swarm of thoughts assaulted me.

I might be out here in the woods, my back turned on a madman.

I mustn't behave like a foolish child. The black bows were not an excuse not to let someone I found attractive near me.

I should run to my car and drive straight back to Rosie's.

I should wait and let this heightened anticipation play itself out.

I almost laughed. A teacher. I was feeling all these things about a high school music teacher. And a friend of Rosie and Paul's. I was about to turn around when the air rustled behind me and Don stepped closer. His hand reached across my shoulder toward my throat.

My mouth was so dry I could hardly swallow. Fine, dark hairs swirled along his arm toward his wrist. And from his graceful fingers, a string of pearls dangled.

He let the pearls drop down until they bumped along my breast. Little by little, he pulled the strand of beads up, each one passing over my erect nipple, each one sending a wave of heat through me.

"Wait," he whispered. "Stay this way."

With a single, deft movement, he secured the clasp around my neck.

"Now you can turn around." He touched my shoulders with gentle, insistent pressure, and when I turned, his eyes, hooded in shadow, were fixed on the necklace. "Perfect," he pronounced.

"Don, what is this?"

His smile was charming, indulgent. "For someone who reads the *New York Times Magazine* regularly, you sure ask funny questions, Lee Montara. You can take this string of pearls and try to invest it with meaning beyond its intention. That's your privilege. But I'm simply giving you a gift because I want to. Because you are a classic—elegant, even in your jeans and well-washed T-shirt. I'm not asking you to make a lifetime commitment to me, although I may later, and I don't want anything in return, although I hope you're at least a little intrigued. I just want you to have this. And, no, I didn't steal it, and I'm not plundering a family inheritance, and also, no, this isn't something I do all the time. I don't know why you moved me to do this, but you did, and I'm grateful to be feeling such strong emotions after a long time of, how should I say it, being asleep."

His speech was nice, but I'd had too many unexpected presents lately. I felt dizzy from the heat of the day and the chill of the pine forest, and from the unexpected turn this outing had taken. I reached behind me to feel for the clasp so I could undo it. "Don—I wish I could accept this gift in the spirit you're offering it. There's so much I don't understand in my life right now. I just can't add one more thing." My fingers found the clasp and I worked it open, then let the strand slide off my neck into my hand. "Here. Please understand. I just can't take these now."

Except for the rise and fall of our breathing and the drumming of a woodpecker in a far-off tree, there was only silence. "Listen, Don. I like you, I like your music, I like your conversation, and I like your kisses. So far, all good signs. But I can't take these from you right now."

Why couldn't I simply let it be? Silently, I cursed Stewart McClaren for making my life feel more complicated than it should have.

"I understand," Don said evenly. His fingers closed around the pearls. "I can wait."

11:00 a.m.

I prowl the kitchen, wishing I could do something to speed time, wishing too that I might find a way to make the future stretch endlessly into the distance ahead. The rain pounds down but the thunder and the lightning have stopped; in their place a wind has come up, gathering force and scouring the valley from north to south.

At least he's not having an easy time of it. At least he's soaked through his clothes to his skin, rain is blurring his vision, the mud is sucking at his feet.

"You remember old Mr. Roth?" Rosie is pointed toward the big window as though there's a movie playing that only she can see. "How he used to come to mow the lawn with that old push mower and his pants were always falling down lower and lower and lower and we'd hide upstairs and peek behind the shade waiting for the big event to happen?"

"So you feel a little like you've done this before, is that what you mean?"

But she goes on as if my question has never been spoken. "I caught him once in the house. Upstairs, in Aunt Christa's bedroom. Nobody else was home."

This doesn't sound like a story I want to hear now; I'm suddenly more afraid for the young Rosie than I am for the woman sitting across from me, and I can barely get out the words to prompt her to tell me what happened. "What was he doing?"

"Going through Aunt Christa's drawer. Touching her things, and making this weird snorty sound, like he was having trouble breathing. He didn't see me, and I backed down the stairs as quietly as I could and ran to the tree house and hid. He came out in a couple of minutes." She's talking so softly now I can hardly hear her and I lean forward to catch her next words. "At least it felt that way to me, but it could have been much longer. When Aunt Christa came home, she accused me of messing with her stuff. Which, as you remember, was strictly off-limits to us."

Why has she never told me this before? I wait for the story to come to some satisfying end, like her telling about Mr. Roth and Dad firing him, or Mother mediating and getting Aunt Christa to believe whatever Rosie says, because she is such an honest child, so good, so perfect. But Rosie says nothing, and I wonder what ending she has written in her own mind.

"You know what she did?" Rosie smiles and hugs herself. "I was ten, and I thought the only thing I'd care about ever in my life was horses. I guess a lot of little girls go through that, but I was enchanted by them. And she knew it. She gave me her old jodhpurs, said that if I wanted something of hers I should have said so, said she'd been planning to give them to me all along and had forgotten."

For a moment, I am stung by this unexpected ending, wishing in a childish way that it had happened to me, and that Aunt Christa had given me more than the burden of her unhappy musings and a trio of silk scarves when I graduated from college. But I understand what that gift meant to Rosie.

"It was terrible. I had seen Mr. Roth in her room, and I didn't know how to tell her. And then I had the jodhpurs, which I adored, but I'd gotten them under false pretenses. It was so mixed up. I finally did say something about Mr. Roth but she didn't believe me. In the end, the only thing I could think of was to thank her, and then I put the riding pants in the back of my closet. I never wore them."

I reach across the table for her hand. The delicate bones that run down from her fingers to her wrist feel so thin, as though they might snap if I pressed too hard.

"One more time," I say. "Let's go over what we know once more to see if all the pieces still make sense. I keep thinking there's something we should be doing—"

Her hands incapable of stillness, Rosie pulls away from me. She snips off another length of thread, slips it through the eye of a needle, knots it at the bottom. "All right. We know," she says as she begins a fine line of running stitches to join a folded piece of cotton, "that this terrible event happened when he was seven."

Fingers poised above the fabric, she shakes her head. She has said that she won't let herself feel sorry for him but I don't think she can avoid it. I must keep the confusion and the sympathy from my voice when I talk to her about him, and I try to sound neutral. "And this charade is really an invitation for us to be there with him."

Before Rosie can take her part again in the catechism of horror, another crash outside breaks the silence, and I leap up. Hot tea sloshes over my cup onto my thigh; it stings, but I ignore it as I make a dash to the window, right behind my sister.

She peers out, then sighs deeply. "I have to fix that. We won't be able to hear him if the damn wind keeps slamming those lights into the stone."

I nod. "I'm going with you."

Rosie doesn't answer; she is already pushing her arms through the sleeves of the oilskin mackintosh that hangs on a peg beside the back door. She tugs a rain hat onto her head and tosses a yellow poncho to me, then opens the door.

The rain falls in sheets; it is warmer out here than I thought it would be. A newly formed river is snaking its way, brown and muddy, between the flagstones. Beyond the trees a faint silvery light makes me think the storm will be over in two or three hours at most.

"Turn off the power!" Rosie shouts through the battering rain as she points to a tangle of wires near the barbecue. "That line's hot. Just flip the red circuit breaker, the biggest one in the box. At the foot of the cellar stairs. You remember."

I stand for a moment with rain streaming into my eyes, considering my prospects—opening the door, going into the empty house, and then descending to the cellar alone—and then, happily, I'm moving forward, fueled by anger and resolve.

Rosie comes up behind me, her wet face pink with effort. She speaks with the crisp authority of a country woman accustomed to dealing with small crises. "I have to get the wire cutters from the shed, Lee. After you kill the power, grab the electrical tape from the kitchen and bring it out to me."

My feet move automatically, and I try first to make my mind quiet so I can hear. Then, I concentrate on seeing everything around me. I can do it all—cut the circuit, grab the tape—and be back outside in less than five minutes. Nothing will happen to Rosie in that time. Nothing will happen to me, either.

Without incident, I run back inside, dripping rain onto Rosie's clean floor. I pull open the door to the cellar. The pungent odor of damp earth greets me.

If I had a flashlight I'd feel much better about going down there.

No, Rosie is outside, I don't remember where she keeps the flash-lights, I do know where the circuit breakers are, I'm going down there. Fourteen steps, that's all. The box is to the left of the last step.

Why didn't anyone ever put in a railing? But I take the first step, then two more. I keep moving forward. The string of lanterns slams against the barbecue again. Through a narrow, cobweb-crusted win-dow, I see the bright crackle of a spark as the live wire touches some-thing. Three more steps to go.

At the next-to-last step, I stop, listening beyond the wind for the sound of Rosie, something that will tell me everything is all right. But I hear only the rain, steady, beating, beating on the wooden cellar door.

What a funny time to think of Edgar Allen Poe. The cadence of my own thoughts somehow has suggested "The Raven" to me. Now I can't get the word out of my head. *Nevermore. Nevermore.*

When I step onto the dirt floor, I nearly lose my balance, but I grit my teeth and quickly regain control. One step, then reach out to the left. The cold metallic door of the circuit breaker box rewards me. I pull it open, squint in the darkness, my nose almost touching the switches.

Something bumps against my foot.

I scream and jump away from it, but I have enough presence to avoid slamming backward into the stairs, and I realize even before I hear its frightened mewing that it's the kitten. It tries to hook itself onto my jeans.

Shaking with relief, I reach over, feel for the biggest switch and flip it down. I gather the damp and shivering kitten in my hands and climb back up to the kitchen, comforted by the small creature, some-how soothed into believing that everything will be fine. I set him down beside the stove, then scrabble through the drawer until I find the roll of electrical tape. Leonardo is trembling; his eyes shine like beacons as he tracks my movements. Rosie will need scissors, too—I run to the living room and collect the pair she's been using to cut fabric.

Outside, the rain is still fierce. I shout an okay to my sister, who is bent over the Japanese lanterns, kneeling on the wet flagstones and holding the cutters poised over the wires. In one clean motion, she snips the line from which the lanterns used to hang. Then, she sets the clippers down and wraps the exposed end of the electrical wire, no longer hot because I've done my job, in heavy black tape. She tapes the dangling wire to the corner of the house and sticks the wire cutters in her pocket.

Rain pours down her face, and I run ahead of her, fling open the door, hand her a towel.

"You did a great job. That was wonderful." I sit heavily in the kitchen chair, the seat still warm from the heat of my body.

Rosie presses the towel to her face, mumbles something I don't understand, then lets her arms drop to her sides. "I'm very tired, Lee. I'm so tired. Why is it so dark in here?"

Rosie's lapse unsettles me. We both have to stay alert. "I just flipped the main circuit. The power has to be switched back on." I push my chair back to start for the cellar. But she's already up and walking toward the hall.

The kitten claws at my leg and cries, and I lift him into my arms. I let my sister go about her business. Rosie is so familiar with this house, it will only take her a second to find the right switch. Soon, we'll have light again.

I rub my cheek against the kitten's side, feel the tiny little ribs, the sensual softness of his fur. All this contact is so hypnotic that I lose my sense of time passing; when the kitten stretches and digs his thin, sharp nails into my palm I feel as though I'm waking from a trance. And I realize that Rosie hasn't come back to the kitchen.

I set the kitten gently on the braided rug.

I walk down the hall, trying not to think.

The cellar door opens to a gaping, dark recess, and from the void I hear Rosie, talking.

And then I hear his voice. I can't make out what he's saying. I can't even tell the state of his emotions, whether he's angry or triumphant or afraid. I know only that he's down there with my sister.

My head is clear. I will call the sheriff's department and alert them, get someone out here in a hurry. The phone is on the wall, not ten feet from me, and I try not to make noise as I tiptoe, so quietly, so carefully across the floor. God bless little children and first-grade teachers— Andrew has made a list of important telephone numbers and it's pinned to the wall beside the phone. Relieved, I lift the receiver.

But there's no dial tone. The phone is dead.

14

"You were right. We all needed to do nothing and go to bed early. I feel much better, don't you?"

Rosie held a freshly washed, still-damp pillowcase to her face and took a long breath, then smiled into the morning sunshine.

"I *am* glad we kept it simple." Glad, too, that we hadn't spoken about Rick Decker and his bracelet, or why, even after three more phone calls yesterday, Riley Hamm hadn't bothered to come by about the candles our intruder had left. Nor had I told Rosie about Don and the pearls, trivial by comparison, a topic that generated contradictory feelings in me, as separate and chaotic as weeds threatening to take over an untended garden.

Rosie reached into the canvas bag hanging from the clothesline. She pulled out a wooden peg, the old kind without springs, like the ones we'd spent endless winter days painting faces onto. Somehow, she had always managed to make her clothespins look cheerful. "You find out anything about Stewart?"

Now she was on a first name basis with him. I handed her one corner of a sheet and walked it along the line until it was taut. "Nothing that I didn't already know. The New York magazine community is small and almost, well, incestuous. If I ask a lot of questions, people will want to know why and I don't want to give him the satisfaction of being the topic of so much conversation. Besides, I'm supposed to be on vacation in Cozumel and everyone knows it . . . unless Cindy made a public fuss about my not going."

Only Rosie's eyes, emerald and amused, smiled at me over the top of the sheet. "Impetuous, impulsive, and impatient Lee Montara? No one who knows you would think twice about that."

"Now, if you'd said impertinent, impassioned, and imperious then certainly they'd know it was me." I snapped a cornflower blue towel to shake out the wrinkles, pinned it to the line. The task, repetitious and deadening if I had to do it every week, every summer, had taken on its own soothing rhythm. "Let's get those last few pieces on the line and then I'm driving you into Millerton. We need a pizza break."

"In the middle of the day? On a Tuesday? You're a terrible influence, Lee. Sounds wonderful."

We hurried through the job, emptying the laundry basket in record time, and while Rosie settled in with her book in the shade of the porch, I went upstairs to wash my face and change into a clean T-shirt.

"You ready?" I sat in the rocker beside her and peered over at her book. She hated to stop in the middle of a chapter, I knew, and she held up a finger to signal that she'd be another second.

"One more—oh, Lord, I forgot. Good timing, Dolores," she muttered as an old green car, its rear fender patched with white Bondo, pulled up under the maple tree. Dolores Farley hauled herself out, then bent to retrieve a large carton from the trunk.

Rosie stuck her yellow yarn marker in the book and set it back in the drawer of the wicker table. Sighing, she rose and stood at the porch steps, waiting to greet Dolores and usher her inside. I sent Dolores mental messages to hurry her visit along as I followed them through the hall to the sewing room.

Dolores looked around the room from corner to countertop as though she'd been expecting to find something and was surprised that it wasn't there. Being invited into the hidden rooms of a neighbor's house was one of the special pleasures of small town living, and Dolores was taking advantage of the entertainment.

"Nice print, Dolores." The top piece of fabric in the carton, a finely detailed cabbage rose pattern that brightened a square of beige cotton, was the only one I'd even think of using in a rug; the rest were either too garish or completely washed out. "Looks like you've brought enough fabric for a whole roomful of rugs."

"This is terrific. The folks at the senior center have just started a quilting project and they'll be thrilled." Ever gracious, my sister folded the flaps over her neighbor's contribution and patted the box.

Dolores beamed and twirled a strand of thin hair around her index finger. She pushed the hair behind her ear. Her lumpy hips bulged against the shapeless black skirt as she turned her smile on me. "You enjoying yourself in our little village?"

"I always do."

She smiled her approval. Her gaze skittered across shelves and pictures, coming to rest briefly on the open ironing board and the loops of brilliant colors, rainbow skeins of embroidery thread, hanging on cup hooks beneath one of the shelves.

"Gotta get back. Today's bread day. Joseph likes homemade." She smoothed imaginary wrinkles from her skirt with fleshy hands. Still, she made no move toward the door.

"He's feeling all right?" Even as she stepped into the hall and edged Dolores toward the front of the house, Rosie offered sympathy and concern.

"Tired out by all the heat, but at least his leg don't bother him." Thighs quivering, Dolores trundled after my sister.

"Thanks again for bringing the fabric by." Rosie leaned against the open screen door and moved aside to let Dolores pass.

"Glad someone's going to get pleasure from it. I surely don't, not once things have been around a while. Can't always have it but I like new." Dolores waddled down the porch stairs like a toddler learning to walk, one swollen leg moving to a lower step, the other catching up.

"Take care, Dolores," I offered, the words rattling in my head. *Take care that you don't eat too much? Take care that you don't put so much energy into other people that you forget about yourself?* Chagrined at how harshly I'd judged a woman whose life was so different from mine, I turned toward Rosie. "Now, can we get that pizza?"

"I'd forgotten how they gawk."

A steady stream of out-of-town cars clogged Main Street, the precious shops and inns just across the border in Connecticut luring tourists from the city. We might have been lions and elephants in a drive-through wild animal park, a species new and fascinating enough to provide the sightseers with a day's diversion from real life.

"You forget. To them, we're just part of the scenery. You know—colorful natives, English country gardens, billowing fields of corn, all those red barns." Rosie's wave took in the town, the hills and fields beyond, probably everything for miles in either direction. "October is the worst. Leaves and all that. But the tourists are good for the economy so we don't complain, at least not out loud."

"For sure, they won't be stopping here for pizza. Not quaint enough." A blast of heat from the ovens along the back wall rushed at us as I pushed open the door to the red-and-white dining room. Framed posters of Venice and Rome covered the walls. A Shop-Rite calendar, still turned to March, hung beside the cash register. Wonderful yeasty, garlicky smells made my stomach rumble with anticipation.

A girl who looked too young to drink the beer she balanced on her tray handed us slightly sticky menus. Her ebony hair and long-lashed eyes seemed familiar; I was sure I'd never met her before, but I couldn't shake the feeling that I should have known who she was. "In here or outside?" she asked brightly.

This was Rosie's party. "Your pleasure, madam," I offered.

"Outside, definitely. We'll take our chances with the tourists instead of the heat."

We followed the young woman and her bobbing earrings, a school of silvery fish swimming on curved wires, to the small wood-floored patio. A jaunty red-and-white-striped umbrella above the only empty table provided welcome shade.

"Diet cola for me." I glanced at the menu but it was only for show; I'd been thinking pepperoni pizza and a house salad since I was attacked by the aromas in the dining room.

"I'd like a lemonade, Debbie," Rosie said, squinting up at the girl. "Rick get that construction job?"

And then I realized: the eyes, the inky hair that slid down carelessly over her forehead, even the provocative stance, all ran in the family. Rick's sister.

"I, uh, I don't know." She glanced at her pad, suddenly flustered. "He, uh . . ."

"Something wrong, Debbie?" Sympathetic and concerned, Rosie

had slipped on her wise-counselor cloak, and Debbie Decker's worries tumbled out in a rush of words and jangling earrings.

"He took off in his car yesterday, last night, and hasn't come home. He's done this before, once, remember? Last year when he failed English? He was scared of what Dad would say so he stayed away four whole days. It drives Mom nuts. Nobody knows where he is."

Beneath her freckles, Rosie paled. "I'm sure he'll be back in a day or two. Give your Mom my regards, will you, and tell her not to worry."

Nodding morosely, Debbie hovered at our table as though Rick might appear if she waited long enough. I hid my glimmer of relief at the thought of Rick Decker's absence by rattling off my order; Rosie, her color returning, said she'd have a salad and a plain pizza. When Debbie disappeared inside, Rosie's expression moved from anger to confusion, finally settling into a tentative and tight-lipped resignation.

"Rosie, you can't—"

"Don't tell me what I can't, Lee. He was upset because of your visit. That's why he ran off. You insulted him. I shouldn't have let you go out there. I should have done it myself." She folded her napkin in half, began pleating it like a fan, her fingers moving constantly, betraying her distress as they worked the paper. "I need to apologize to him—"

"You don't even know why he ran away. Maybe he had a fight with his girlfriend. Maybe he failed another subject at school. He's done this before. Another day or two, he'll be back."

Rosie smoothed the napkin. "Did I tell you about the Sclafani twins? About their trip to Mexico?"

We talked about old school buddies, shoving Rick Decker's disappearance into a dark corner until our order arrived. Rosie smiled up at the dark-haired girl. "When Rick gets back, tell him I said hello, okay?"

Debbie flicked her hair back over her shoulder. "It's the heat makes him do that kind of stuff. In the nineties last year, too, when he did this. Seems like the weather's getting to everyone around here. Hank Steuben really lit into Peggy last night. Sitting right at this table, right where you are now. Made an incredible mess, he did." She swiveled between two chairs and started clearing dirty dishes and glasses from another table.

"Maybe when his wife decides she's tired of being knocked

around, *she'll* disappear." I peeled the paper from my plastic straw; my words lay adrift in the vacuum between us. Rosie let them hover unanswered, and I searched for another topic to fill the void. "What are you going to do Thursday? With your seniors, I mean?"

"What? My seniors—I don't know. Probably just take them out to the community garden. Unless it rains." She searched the cloudless sky as though checking for signs of a change in the weather. "I wonder what he does out there, where he goes. He didn't talk about it at all last year. He just showed up again four days later as though nothing had happened. Do you really think I've missed something, Lee? About Rick, I mean. I never realized his crush was so serious. I mean, I never thought of him as so . . . I don't know, so *smitten*."

I stepped gingerly onto this delicate ground. "You said it yourself, it's his biological state, he's a teenager dealing with raging hormones. He'll be all right."

"I hope he comes back soon, I really do. It feels like the whole world's gone weird—Rick and Hank and all these . . . things happening." Rosie stabbed at a fat black olive, then set the fork on her salad plate, stared at the line of cars idling in the afternoon sunshine.

"Taken one thing at a time," I said, groping for comprehension, "this stuff might not seem so odd."

Except for the black bows and the unsettling offerings that had been left at Rosie's house. Except for the photo of Stewart McClaren. Except for Rosie's anonymous telephone calls.

Not one of these things, even as an isolated occurrence, was remotely ordinary. Together, they had charged my visit with such tension that I wanted to grab Rosie's hand and run down the highway, hair flying recklessly in the wind as we left the eerie and cloistered world of Taconic Hills behind.

If I couldn't do that, I could try again to salvage the rest of my time here. "We've let ourselves get sidetracked these past couple of days. Why don't we take Andrew to the beach at Stissing Lake after school?"

Rosie's eyes focused absently on mine. "That's a great idea. He loves the water. He did real well at swimming lessons last year. Not that I let him swim out to the raft alone yet. Maybe by the end of summer. . . ." She toyed with her pizza crust, her face softening to a smile. "Why don't you go just the two of you? He'd like that. I'll run back into town and do one of my major grocery raids. And then after supper we can collect fireflies."

I laughed aloud. "I can leave the big city but I can't get away from the bright lights, can I?"

And Rosie laughed with me.

15

With only a dozen cars huddled near the cinderblock bathhouse, the Stissing Lake parking lot looked empty. I rolled up beside the cozy cluster of vehicles, glad, somehow, for the company of cars and pickup trucks. Andrew had jiggled his foot against the seat all through the fifteen minute ride from home, offering one-word responses to my questions about school. Still subdued, he yanked the blanket from the backseat of the car and started across the blacktop to the path while I gathered towels, my book, my camera. We both pulled off our sneakers and walked barefoot on the soft carpet of grass past the deserted volleyball court and an empty picnic table.

Andrew's nose wrinkled. "Watch out for all the goose stuff. . . . What do you call it?" He pointed to a squishy pile in the grass. "My Dad says it's not nice to say *shit*."

"Thanks for the warning." I smiled at the notion that *stuff* might become the term of choice.

A cluster of long-limbed girls sat atop a picnic table. Wearing barely filled halters and skimpy bottoms that rested precariously on undefined hips, they pointedly ignored the trio of boys on the raft anchored fifty feet from shore. Children frolicked at the waterline under watchful adult attention.

The scene might have been a page from a photo-essay on the timelessness of small towns. The introduction would contend that VCRs and microwaves hadn't changed the way rural America lives; those conveniences, the text would conclude, provided the locals with more time to be who they already were. *Here is Dolores Farley*, a caption might read, *still taking care of other people. This is Rick Decker*, another would say, *unburdened by chores on the family farm, brooding more intensely.* Even Hank Steuben and his wife would share a placard explaining that they'd perfected their roles, one bitter and blustery, the other long suffering and defeated.

Andrew scampered ahead, sliding into a sandy spot near a pile of jeans, belts, and running shoes heaped in the shadow of the lifeguard chair. "Right here," he said matter-of-factly. "Let's sit here."

The warm sand beneath my feet made me think of faraway beaches—Kaanapali, the Lido, my abandoned Cozumel. "Okay, but remember what we said in the car. You can go in the water only as far as the elastic of your bathing suit. When I come in, then you can be over your head. Got it?"

"But I told you. I can swim, I can too." Andrew's voice grated with a petulant whine. He kicked at the blanket with his bare foot.

"Those are your mother's rules, and they're mine, too. We had a deal, remember?" I wondered whether all parents felt a tug of regret when they had to say no to a child; maybe practice made the imperfect system less trying.

He peeled off his yellow-and-gray-striped shirt and his jeans and sprawled on the blanket. I could count his little ribs, could see the bumps of his spine, and his nearly naked vulnerability made me want to turn him around and shake him. *And tell him I was making rules for his own good?* I couldn't believe that every adult who'd ever said that really didn't have her own convenience in mind. I was learning all kinds of things this week.

"Tell you what," I said. "I'll come in with you in ten minutes, after I've had a chance to get a little crispy."

His chin lifted and his back straightened, good signs, but I still wanted confirmation. "That okay with you? One nod for yes, two for no."

Perhaps he'd learned from Rosie, as Rosie and I had learned from

Grandma Montara, to count to five—if you waited for ten, she said, you might give up counting—when you were angry. When he finally flopped over to face me, a smile crept into the corners of his mouth. Still, the smudges under his eyes worried me.

"All right, kiddo, we've got a deal. Give me five."

He raised his hand, we slapped to seal our agreement, and he ran off toward the other children playing at the water's edge.

Drops of water pearled on his wiry body when he emerged from his dunk in the glassy lake. He shook his head like a spaniel, the way the young men on the raft did. I squinted and shaded my eyes, checking to see if I recognized the haircut, the diffident tilt of his hips, the anything-but-casual Rick Decker. No—two of the boys were too short; the third appeared to be a ponytailed blond.

Dripping water from his hair and his bathing suit, Andrew raced back to our blanket. "I'm going to swim out to the raft, okay?"

"You asking if I'm coming in now? We had a deal, right?"

He plunked down face first onto the blanket and buried his face in his arm. Maybe he was afraid that the children at the shoreline would think he was a baby. Perhaps he was just plain angry. In any case, I'd made him wait long enough to save face for both of us.

"You ready for that swim now, champ?" I stood, braced for a clamor of enthusiasm and a running dive into the sparkling lake. "Race you to the water."

But he lay there motionless.

"All right, stay here if you want to, but I'm going in. The sun made me hot and I'm going to get cooled off. If you change your mind, I'll be happy to swim with you."

Without looking at him, I walked across the pebbly sand to the water's edge. The feel of the slippery lake bottom made me recoil, as it had when I was Andrew's age, but I took four long steps into the water, then dipped my body up to my shoulders. The cold water raised goosebumps all over me—involuntarily, I thought about Don Ward and the pearls—then I kicked off and swam out toward the whooping, splashing teenagers on the raft.

Recovered by now from his pout, Andrew was probably waiting for me on the sand, ready for his swim. I treaded water, shook the drops out of my eyes, and turned toward the shore.

But he wasn't there, and he wasn't on the blanket. My heart beat wildly as I scanned the shore, checked the kids playing at the edge of the grass, looked around me in the water.

the Seduction

No Andrew.

The skin on my arms prickled uncomfortably and the sun suddenly seemed cruel. Surely I was just not looking in the right place. Maybe that wasn't our blanket. . . . I swam for shore, kicking out behind me, stopping once to look back at the raft, and when I staggered up onto the sand, I saw that Andrew's clothes were gone. The little bundle he'd tossed onto the corner of the blanket wasn't there, his sneakers weren't there, *he* wasn't anywhere in sight.

Frantic, I forced myself to stand very still. I faced the water and swept the entire beach with my eyes. The scene was so peaceful. So normal. Mothers chatting, their arms and legs glistening with lotion, while their children dug in the damp sand. Young men showing off on the raft for the benefit of the young women who pretended not to notice. A clump of trees on the left, a cluster of houses on the right— he might be anywhere. *Anywhere but in the lake.*

"Annn-drew!" I shouted, and heads turned toward me. I started for the woods, hoping to spot a catlike flash of yellow and gray stripes, a little blond glimmer in the bushes. If only a saucer of milk was enough to lure him to me. . . . The notion made my heart twist in panic.

I plunged into the woods and followed a narrow path that twisted through the thick underbrush. Again, I called out his name. With the sound of my voice echoing from the dense trees, I headed back. When I was eleven, I'd run away; hiding in the crook of a maple limb seemed great fun then, but my nephew wasn't crouched on a low branch, at least not where I could see him.

My fragile composure shattered all at once. By the time I reached the blanket, I noticed, as though I were assessing a stranger, that I was in the throes of panic—wild, irregular pulse; clammy skin; confused thoughts—and I gulped down a deep breath.

I pulled on my jeans and shirt and scooped up the rest of our things. I would unlock the car in case he came back and couldn't find me, and then I'd check the woods again. Surely—

When my feet hit the blacktop, I jumped back, startled. I'd forgotten how hot it got, forgotten the acrid smell of softening tar, the rough surface grabbing at the soles of my feet like sharp little claws. Hopping while I tried to pull on a sneaker, I turned one more time to check the beach. How would I tell Rosie?

And there he was, sitting with his back against the cinderblock wall of the bathhouse, his arms hugging his legs and his chin resting on his knees. A noisy barrage pounded at my temples—relief and anger, gratitude and fury. *Be the adult*, I reminded myself. *He's only six years old.*

"Andrew! What are you doing there?" I shouted.

"I thought I saw Rick. I wanted to tell him about Leonardo." His mouth barely opened when he spoke, and he stubbornly refused to look at me.

"What did he say?" No old black car, no slouching, angry teenager in the parking lot: Where the hell was Rick Decker hiding?

Andrew merely shook his head. I couldn't keep up with all this, and I didn't want to try. I was wet and uncomfortable, still frightened by his disappearance and annoyed by his pouting. "Why didn't you tell him about the kitten, Andrew?"

"He drove away too fast."

Enough—I didn't have any patience left for guessing games. "Then why didn't you come back to the blanket? I was worried about you."

His mouth set in a stiff slash, the way I knew mine used to whenever Mom interrupted me to say it was time to do my chores. I could always squeeze out five more minutes on my bicycle, if I pretended not to hear her. And now my nephew had decided he wasn't ready to talk to me, and there was nothing I could do about it.

"We're going home," I said curtly. "If you won't answer me, then I don't feel very good about staying here. I'd be too worried about you. Let's go." I headed for the car, listening for his footsteps behind me, hearing nothing. When I turned, he was still sitting with his spine pressed against the bathhouse, his bare legs stretched out in front of him on the blacktop. I strode back and stood over him. "Get up now, please," I said through my teeth.

He made me repeat it before he lifted his head and shot me a defiant glare. "I don't like you anymore," he mumbled. But he got to his feet.

Right then, I wasn't sure I liked either of us. Andrew had behaved badly and I'd responded in kind. I felt a pang of guilt. If I could change everything with an apology, the way Hank Steuben thought he could fix things by saying he was sorry, I would have.

Andrew shrugged my hand away and ran ahead of me to the car. By the time I reached him, his cheeks were wet; huge tears shone in his eyes.

the Seduction

"I didn't mean that. I don't feel too good," he said, and he leaned over and clutched his stomach.

I knelt beside him, scared and waiting, my own sadness nearly overwhelming me. The tremor that seized him seemed to pass, and he let me fold him into my arms.

"And I didn't mean to shout like that," I murmured into his hair. "I was really worried when I couldn't find you, and I guess I took it out on you by yelling at you that way. I'm sorry, sweetie. And I do love you. I love you very much."

He wrapped his arms around my neck and held on as though he were grateful that I'd forgiven him. I clung to his small, limp body as if to prove to myself that we were both safe.

16

On the drive home, Andrew stared out the side window and I
concentrated on the road, occasionally stealing a glance at him to see
whether he'd shucked his sullen mood for the voluble enthusiasm I so
loved. Unaccustomed to the patience small children demand and relieved that I'd be able to turn him over to Rosie soon, I swung onto the
winding dirt road that led to the old house. Alone in the quiet of the
bedroom beneath the eaves, I would make sense of the disorder of my
thoughts.

But the driveway was empty. Andrew took his time getting out of
the car while I gathered up the sandy blanket and the beach gear. Just
how long could a woman shopping for three ordinary people spend in
a supermarket, anyway? I looked back down the hill, hoping to see
her car as I walked toward the house—and bumped into Andrew.
He'd stopped midstride, halfway down the path, his attention fixed
on the front of the house.

A cluster of balloons bobbed against the porch rail.

Even before I saw it, I knew they'd be tied with a black bow.

the Seduction

"Andrew, wait! Let's go in the other way." I stole another look at the balloons—four red, three blue, one big black satin bow—as I tried to hustle him around to the backyard, but he wouldn't budge.

Frozen, he stared at the strange, brightly colored blossoms held together with that shiny bow. The whole bouquet tilted oddly as though it were weighted with sand. "They're so ugly. I don't like them." His voice was hardly more than a whisper.

I steered him gently forward. "You think Leonardo would like some water? I bet he's hot and thirsty. You know, baby cats can't store a whole lot of food and water at one time so they have to eat and drink more often, especially when it's hot like this."

Reluctantly, he shuffled along, tossing anxious looks over his shoulder even after we reached the back door. I prattled on, blathering about kittens and cats and the differences between them, using the barrage of words to push back fantasies of Stewart McClaren and revenge. Those thoughts would keep, I'd make sure of that, but I had to do something about the balloons right away, before Andrew became too curious or even more frightened.

"How about if you put some water in Leonardo's saucer? You know how to fill it. Partway, right?"

His only answer was a nod. The kitten scampered out from under the table to greet him, and to my relief, Andrew became engrossed in its antics. He carried the water dish to the counter, chattering to the kitten as he dragged a chair over to the sink.

"I'll be right back, sweetie."

Stopping only to grab the scissors from the sewing basket, I ran out to the porch. Andrew was right—the balloons *were* ugly. I started to cut them free of their mooring but I turned at the sound of a car coming up the drive.

A sharp noise startled me—much later, I realized I'd punctured a balloon; I assumed for a long, slow-motion moment that the popping sound that had jolted me was the car backfiring—and then a wet spray hit my face.

Reflexively, I wiped my eyes and my cheek, cut the balloons free, looked down at the black bow in my hand. After several horrified seconds, it registered that the scarlet smears on my fingers were blood.

The car screeched to a halt and Rosie flew out. "Lee!" she shouted as she ran toward me.

"It's okay, Rosie." But it wasn't. I felt soiled, consumed by the need to get the blood off me. Still clutching the balloons, I fled up the stairs to the second-floor bathroom and dropped them into the sink.

I intended to wash my face and my hands without looking in the mirror, but I was riveted by my reflection in the silvered glass. Blood dabbed my chin and forehead, a swath of it marking my cheek where I'd wiped at my face, spatters dotting my nose. An uneasy laugh broke loose. I finally had freckles.

Shuddering, I turned the hot water on full in the shower and kicked off my sneakers, then quickly stripped off the rest of my clothes. I was standing naked on the fluffy white rug when Rosie appeared in the doorway.

She gasped when she spotted the black bow and the red and blue balloons, resting on their sides like beached whales in the sink. The one I'd pricked lay flaccid and bloody against the white porcelain. "My God, Lee, what—?" At the sight of my face, she drew back. Then, white faced and calm, my sister knelt and gathered up the heap of clothes I'd flung to the floor.

"Andrew's in the kitchen," I said. The rising steam had obscured my sickening reflection in the mirror.

"I know. I got him settled cutting out pictures for a school project. Go ahead, take your shower. I'll be downstairs. I'm going to call Riley Hamm right this minute."

No more. This wouldn't happen to me or anyone else ever again. My blood-smeared hands shook with anger. If Riley was too busy with his damn arsonist, I'd see to it on my own. Tomorrow when Rosie went out to the store or on some other errand, I'd drive my car down the road so that he'd think we were all away. I'd pull off into a tractor road and walk back. I would watch the watcher, and I would catch him. On film. With my camera. And then, whatever Riley Hamm thought about it, the proof would be there, damning and irrefutable.

I stepped into the tub. I didn't look down at the swirl of bloody water as it gurgled down the drain.

"Riley's out on a call somewhere with Harris Del Santo. Everyone else in the sheriff's office is working overtime on the arsonist thing. The dispatcher said Riley would call as soon as he could get to it." Arms folded under her breasts, Rosie shrugged her shoulders and sighed. "I'm not surprised at anything, not after this week. Those balloons—" She hugged herself tighter. "It's such a *boy* thing to do, you know what I mean? You remember how Jimmy Fritz used to drop water balloons out of trees, what was that, fourth grade?"

"No little boy did this, Rosie." In the shower, it had all come together, and now I said urgently, "It really is a kind of sick courtship, all these presents. And it's consistent with how Stewart McClaren operates, how he acted in my office the day I came up here." Industry gossip be damned—I would track him down and make sure he understood that I was willing to do what ever it took to stop him. "How's Andrew?"

Rosie stuffed the last of the groceries, a roll of paper towels, into the cabinet under the sink. She folded the empty bag. "He said he wasn't feeling well. He took Leonardo and went upstairs to his room. It's more than those balloons. . . . Did something happen at the lake, Lee? He seems upset."

"He thought he saw Rick and he walked off while I was swimming. I still don't know if it was Rick. Andrew said whoever it was took off before he caught up with him. And then, instead of coming back to the beach, Andrew hid out near the bathhouse. When I finally found him, I yelled at him. I feel terrible, but I—"

"Ssh, I know. It's awful, thinking a child is lost. And I *hate* when I lose my temper with him." She put her arms around me. "Give it a little time. He'll forgive you. Things will settle down and you'll see. . . ."

In the quiet summer kitchen, I longed to sweep away the confusion I'd brought into my sister's life. But before I could say so, Rosie released me and ran to the window.

"It's a Bronco. Looks like the dispatcher finally got through to our very busy sheriff's deputy."

17

Today Riley moved with purpose, undeflected, his hat pulled down so that the peak made a curved shadow over his eyes and across the bridge of his nose.

Ever mindful of propriety, Rosie went to the door to greet him. "I'm glad you got here so quickly, Riley. When I called, the dispatcher said you were out in the field."

He strode past her, frowning. His business clearly was with me.

"You've found him, right?" Just as I'd known all along—Stewart McClaren wasn't so very clever after all. He'd been so intent on pressing his bizarre suit he'd overlooked something important. He'd made a mistake, and he'd been caught.

"In a manner of speaking," Riley said blandly. Still standing between Rosie and me, he pulled a notepad from his pocket and flipped it open. "What did you say your photographer's name is?"

My photographer—Mike. But that's not what you mean, I know. "Stewart McClaren."

"You can describe him?"

"Will you tell me what this is about? Where did you find him?" I'd already given Riley more than enough information to positively identify Stewart, especially in Taconic Hills; he would stand out among the farmers and shopkeepers and even the regular weekenders, who forsook their city uniforms for easy country garb.

"Will you please describe the man for me?"

Exasperated, I repeated what I'd told him two days earlier. "He's about five feet maybe ten, eleven inches tall, slender. Brown hair combed straight back, brown eyes set close together. Thinks he's a sharp dresser. His leather jacket, the ads call it 'distressed.' That means they charge extra because someone hits a perfectly good piece of leather with a mallet until it looks old and beat-up."

"Did he have a small mole along his jaw?"

I closed my eyes to conjure up Stewart's face; the exercise made me angry, bringing up the curve of his jawline where it angled from his chin toward his ear, that oily smile on a mouth meant for bragging or sneering. Yes, a mole, light colored and small but definitely there, on the left side.

"That's right. And manicured nails that he kept—" *Did.* Riley said *Did* he have a mole. Confused, I felt my anger give way to momentary relief. *No more black bows.*

"You okay?" Rosie put her arm around me, drawing me close.

"I'll be fine. Riley, you're going to tell me why you're asking all these questions."

He sighed and flipped the pad shut. "We've found a body. Now, based on what we already know and what you've just told me, there's a fair chance it's your friend. . . ."

My friend? No, that wasn't right. A body—the meaning of Riley's words shook me. I hated Stewart McClaren's tricks with all my heart, but surely death was too harsh a punishment for bad manners and weird high jinks.

"We need a little more information. The manicured nails, that helps. You know anything about body markings?"

"I already told you. I don't know anything at all about Stewart's body. I only knew the man as a business acquaintance. If he's your corpse, I'm sorry he's dead. But, really, I don't have any idea about—"

"The dead man didn't have any identification on him?" Rosie kept her arm around me as she spoke, her hand firm and warm on my shoulder.

"Yes, sure. A wallet, says it's who I thought it was. But that's not enough. I needed that mole."

"You have the photograph I gave you, right? That should help." The world had stopped spinning, finally, and I was thinking again.

"Picture wasn't enough to go on." Riley took out a handkerchief and wiped his upper lip.

I'd given Riley a decent three-quarter shot of a man lying with his eyes closed; his entire body, his shoes, yes, even his face were all clear and visible. It wouldn't take an expert to verify that Stewart McClaren was the subject of that photograph. "What do you mean?"

He stuck the handkerchief back in his pocket, then cleared his throat. "Part of his face is—it's gone. He was run over. Tractor was making a turn, up one of the corners in Ike Kronenburg's back field, Ike heard this thump, and when he got out, he found this . . . body. The right side of his face is pretty well torn up."

"That's horrible." My stomach knotted as the image of Stewart's mangled face sprang up in my mind. "Have you notified his family?"

"Not yet. The police in New York City, they're checking his apartment and trying to find out as much as they can. Thought *you* might know about his family."

"No, I only know a few mutual business contacts. Maybe one of them can help you out."

"I was hoping for more. Man was dead couple days before he got chewed up by the blades, maybe early Friday, according to the coroner's first guess."

Riley had the good grace to look away while I sorted out what he was saying. Friday—the morning Rosie and I found the flowers on the porch; the cake appeared in the kitchen that afternoon. Friday night, I went to the Edgewood to hear Don play. The candles were left in the kitchen *Monday*, the balloons *today*. Black bows. Stewart McClaren had nothing to do with them. The realization stunned me.

And then I understood where this was all going. Stewart hadn't simply wandered into a field and stopped breathing and then been run over by a tractor. Riley was involved because there was a good chance Stewart had been murdered.

"Mizz Montara, I have some questions about where you were Friday."

"Friday?" I reached up and pulled Rosie closer to me. My thoughts jangled; I couldn't put the pieces together.

"She spent the whole day with me." My sister's damp hand clung to mine and her unblinking gaze fixed on Riley Hamm.

If the sheriff's deputy said anything in response, I didn't hear it. I was too busy trying out the notion of my new status, all my thoughts crashing against Riley's insinuations. "You can't really believe I had anything to do with this. Don't think you can railroad me to cover up your inaction after I gave you that photograph."

A tiny muscle twitched under Riley's eye. "You planning to tell me where you were or no?"

"My sister just told you. If you want to ask me any other questions, you'll have to do it with my lawyer present. Not that I have anything to hide. I just know how things can go. I want the protection of someone who understands the system."

He tried staring me into submission, but Riley's condescension and the news of Stewart's murder had pushed me over a line; I glared back at him. Finally, he shook his head. "All right. You don't need to worry about a lawyer just yet. But it might come to that, if we decide that way. You mind writing out a list of all the people you know knew him? You need your lawyer for that? I'm trying to contact next of kin, find out about this man, that's all."

"Sure, I can do that, Riley. I have a notebook where I wrote down everything I could think of, everything I know about Stewart McClaren. I made a list of people who might be able to tell me more about him, when I thought he was the one leaving all those horrible things. But he didn't leave them, did he? Someone else did."

Riley inspected the cuff of his shirt. "That's how it looks. When we found him, your friend had a black bow around his neck."

Already numb, it took all my will to remain standing.

"So it looks like whoever's been coming up here and leaving those things might be responsible for McClaren's death." He scratched the edge of his jaw with a thumbnail. A line of sweat beaded on his upper lip. "That's mostly what I wanted to talk to you about, if you'da given me a chance. Now, I know because I checked, Mizz Cooper, that your husband's supposed to be away until Saturday. I can't tell you what to do, but if you were my wife, alone up here with a little boy, I'd make sure you were far away from this house if I wasn't around."

"Paul's supposed to call at seven tonight," Rosie said without hesitation. "There are no phones, no electricity, nothing at the campsite. He has to walk three miles to the base house. He'd be frantic with worry if we're not here. Maybe we'll do what you're suggesting. But I'm not going anywhere until my husband calls."

Riley wiped the sweat from his face. "I can't have someone out here all the time, just too few people to cover too much territory in the county. If you're not going to leave, at least find someone, a man who don't rattle easily, to stay with you. I'm giving you good advice."

This wasn't the time to argue with Riley's presumptions about testosterone and unflappability. Besides, I didn't want advice—I wanted information. "How was Stewart killed?"

Riley's eyes checked Rosie's face, then mine. "Strangled, it looks like, by someone with fingers way bigger than yours. Marks on his neck, your hands couldn't make bruises like that. That's not public, you understand, not until we have more to go along with it. Between that and the black bow, that's what convinced me it wasn't you." He took my wrist, held my hand up as Don had at the Edgewood, but Riley only inspected my fingers and then let me go.

"So you haven't spoken to your dispatcher in the past hour?" Rosie's voice was sharp. "No one's told you what happened here this afternoon?"

In the wake of the bad news he surely knew was coming, Riley held his ground. "Whyn't you tell me now?"

"I took Andrew to Stissing Lake," I said, "and when we came back, I found some balloons tied with a black bow. There, on the porch. When I was cutting them down, I accidentally punctured one and it exploded." I shuddered at the memory. "It had blood in it, Riley. It got all over me."

"You have them? The balloons, I mean." This time, he didn't sound patronizing; the accusation was gone from his voice, too.

"In the bathroom upstairs. And I'll get the notebook. And the candles. You would have had them a few days ago, if you thought our telephone messages were important enough to follow up on."

I ran upstairs and grabbed the notebook from the nighttable. I retrieved the paper bag from the closet, then went into the bathroom. The balloons were too big for the bag, still damp with blood and water; I fought my nausea as I descended the stairs.

"If you'd come on Monday, you might have spared my sister today's horror." The gray hollows under Rosie's eyes darkened.

Riley took the balloons and the paper bag without examining them. "You let me know what arrangements you make. Best I can do is have a car stop by every hour or so, till we get shorthanded when the eight o'clock shift comes on. I'm gonna go have these checked out." The screen door bumped shut behind him. He stalked to his car, the glasses clinking noisily in the paper bag and the balloons bouncing against his trousers.

"Riley's right about not staying here. We can spend a few days in the city, at my apartment." My three rooms on Tenth Street had the certain appeal of home to me, and the city might even be an acceptable distraction for Rosie and Andrew until Saturday.

"Let me think about it. I'm going to ask Don to come over for a while. Until Paul calls and we decide what to do," Rosie said firmly. "If it were just the two of us . . ."

I knew enough about maternal protectiveness to understand that there would be no arguing with my sister on this point.

"I'd be happy to stay here nights, that's no problem." Don avoided my glance as he laid Paul's rifle on a high kitchen shelf in front of a soup tureen and an ornate coffee service I could never recall anyone using. "But days . . . I just can't miss end of semester, final grades, and graduation. The band has a couple of hard selections this year. Where would you go during the day?"

The thought of Don Ward's long body stretched on the sofa downstairs besieged me with a welter of feelings. His nearness would be tempting. I wasn't ready to test myself, wasn't prepared to keep myself from wandering down the stairs in search of him.

But I held back; it was five minutes after seven, and Paul still hadn't called, and we still didn't have a plan. With her usual practicality, Rosie solved all the dilemmas at once.

"Thanks, Don, you're wonderful to come out now. If I can convince Paul that we'll be all right in the city, going to Lee's for a few days is altogether the least disruptive solution."

Now, Don did turn his glance toward me. He seemed to be waiting for confirmation, of the plan Rosie had laid out and of a future that still held possibilities. I hoped my smile was the reassurance he sought.

"Under normal circumstances, I'd hate to leave," I said softly, "but all in all, I agree with Rosie. Going to New York is the thing to do. Rosie can keep Andrew home from school for a few days. It's only first grade, right?"

"Andrew's going to be unhappy." Rosie glanced at her watch for the fourth time in a minute. "Last week of school. And your place will be pretty crowded."

I understood her concerns, but no better alternative had come up.

"You can turn it into an adventure for Andrew," Don told her. "Bring sleeping bags and roll them out on the living room floor."

I grinned at the thought of all of us lined up wall to wall in the small room. "We can pretend we're camping."

The phone rang, and Rosie sprang up to answer it.

"Paul. It's great to hear your voice, honey. Listen," she said, turning her back on Don and me, "there's something we need to talk about."

We wandered onto the porch, Don leading the way and perching on the rail, watching silently as I arranged my legs and arms to make myself comfortable in the rocker.

"Thanks for not trying to take over, Don. That sleeping bag idea was brilliant." A bat dipped and swooped in the luminous twilight, and Don Ward's eyes glinted with topaz lights.

"Well, I was a little boy once, and I just figured that he needs an enticement to make it seem like an adventure, that's all. Listen, I know how complicated this is. I'm sorry about what happened to that fellow."

Startled, I realized that Stewart's death had been nothing more than a relief and an abstraction to me. Now, it had become a threat to our safety. "Thanks, Don. I'm sure it's all going to hit me later. Right now, I'm mostly numb and worried."

We sat listening to the crickets and a faraway dove as they made music to usher in the night. The silence was comforting; I was pleased that we didn't need a bridge of words to connect us. Neither of us spoke until Rosie emerged from the house.

"Paul was very upset. First he said he was going to hitchhike down. Then he insisted that I drive right up there to pick him up. God, I was so torn. But finally, he didn't like it but he agreed that going to your apartment was, everything considered, the best idea, Lee. He insisted that we leave tonight."

"Fine with me. We can leave any time you say. It shouldn't take long to pack. We're doing the right thing, Rosie. I feel a little better already." Don's presence on the porch had been part of my recovery, and I was grateful.

"Well, I don't. This is that hard part. I'm going upstairs to tell

Andrew. Wish me luck." Rosie trudged up the stairs, calling Andrew's name softly.

Don hopped down from the porch rail. It was almost full dark now, but I could sense his nearness. I stood, too, wanting the reassurance of a last embrace before I started off on the next stage of this strange journey.

"Are you sure you don't want to take map-reading lessons while you're in the city? I'm still not sure how I'm going to find my way without you." His lips brushed my hair and his hands pressed me to him. "You have to promise to call me every day and let me know how things are. Even though I know in my heart that you're all going to be just fine."

In my mind, I saw Don, traveling between schools in the middle of the day. All the black bows had been delivered either around the noon hour or after school. Taconic Hills isn't a nine-to-five kind of place, I reminded myself. A lot of people have flexible schedules, big chunks of free time during the day.

"You cold?" He rubbed my back and peered down at me. "You sure you're going to be okay?"

"Don't worry," I said, scolding myself for my distrust, wondering if it was one more way to keep him at a distance, wishing I'd never thought about his schedule. "We'll be all right."

Not even Andrew would have missed the doubt in my voice.

18

Dinner that night was a hasty and oddly formal affair featuring tuna sandwiches and irrelevant conversation.

Rosie sat across from Don, who was so charming and so talkative that I kept forgetting why he was there. They gossiped about vacation plans and how crowded the county would be when the summer people arrived. A very thoughtful Andrew sat at the table, head propped on a balled fist, dipping his finger into a glass of milk.

"Hey, Andrew, you ready for your adventure?" Don rose and began piling dishes into the sink, surprising me with the unassuming way he attacked this kitchen chore.

Andrew scraped his chair back and carried his glass to the sink. "I guess," he said flatly.

"You know what we're going to do when we get to my house?" I hoped my love of the city would help my nephew over the bumps of his temporary dislocation. "You remember when we found the watercress and I took some pictures for the book I'm working on? We're going to go take more pictures, in a special place in Brooklyn called the Botanical Gardens. It's got all these neat trees and wonderful plants. There's even a special one that eats hamburgers. And we'll camp out in my living room, and we'll buy paper cups of Italian ices, and maybe we'll even go to the Empire State Building and the Statue of Liberty. There's a lot of stuff we can do, maybe even as much fun as building a dam in a stream or picking strawberries. All of which I loved."

By now, Andrew probably knew as well as his mother did that I gave myself away when I was tense by babbling on and on about nothing. From the corner of my vision, I could see that Don had turned around to watch me, and I gave Andrew all my attention. He sucked on his milky finger thoughtfully; his chin dimpled and quivered.

"I don't want to miss the party for the last day of school." His voice was hoarse from holding back tears, and I felt my own eyes fill with helpless frustration. I looked at Rosie, hoping she'd come to my rescue; she nodded and knelt beside her son.

"I already told you, sweetie. We'll have our own party at Auntie Lee's. And Saturday we'll drive to pick up your Dad."

"Of course we will," I assured him, wishing I could rewrite the script so that he could stay for the real party.

Rosie straightened and approached the table, all business as she wiped her hands on a cotton dishtowel. "You better get the compost taken out before we go, champ. The container really is too full."

"And when you're done, we'll get packed. Make sure you take your canteen. Every camper needs a canteen." I reached across the counter and handed him the white plastic scrap bucket. "One quick kiss, all right?"

But he took the container from me and walked away.

Hands dripping soapy water, Don turned from the sink. "I think it will be easier on him if you can get out of here pretty quickly. I'll take the kitten home with me, all right?"

Rosie sighed and nodded. "I almost forgot about Leonardo. Thanks, Don. You've been wonderful."

"Just neighborly," he said, his eyes on me. "Now, you two go ahead and pack and I'll finish up down here."

"You know," I said, watching my sister disappear into the hall-way, "this feels like the longest day of my life. Who would have thought, when Rosie and I were sitting eating our pizza, that all this would happen? Andrew hiding at the lake. The balloons. Finding out about Stewart." I fell silent as I thought about him; for the first time since Riley's announcement, the utterly unchangeable fact of Stewart McClaren's murder hit me.

Don touched my shoulder. "Go pack, Lee. I'll call Riley and tell him about your plans."

I broke away and raced up the stairs, understanding that for me, too, this departure would be easier if I didn't prolong it. I pulled my suitcase out of the closet, gathered my clothes and the picture of Mike, and forced myself not to think about what lay ahead.

"I am too! Auntie Lee thinks Leonardo should come with us."

Andrew's voice carried across the hall as I tossed the collection of cosmetics, hardly used since my arrival, into the front zipper section. My name, invoked in a cause I hadn't espoused—I didn't like being caught in the crossfire of Andrew's battle with Rosie. But I could do nothing about that now. I looked around this lovely room for anything I might have forgotten, then struggled to zip my crammed suitcase.

Don was sitting on the porch when I came downstairs, Leonardo snuggled on his lap. Andrew leaned against the arm of the rocker, stroking the kitten's head; then he pulled the screen door open and padded inside. Sunset had painted magenta streaks across the dark sky. Soon, the moon would rise and slice through the wisps of clouds along the inky horizon. I wouldn't be here to see it.

"Dishes are done," Don said, "the garbage is out, and Rosie is making sure everything's locked up."

His voice was so reassuring, I wanted to keep him talking. "You called Riley?" I asked.

"I was about to tell you. He sounded relieved that the three of you were going away. Oh, and he got a preliminary lab report. I had to practically stand on my head to get him to tell me. The blood in the balloons? Turns out it was animal blood, probably from a cow."

I gripped the porch rail. "What kind of demented mind would even *think* of that?"

But before he could answer, Rosie appeared, keys jangling and Andrew lagging behind her. "Let's get this show on the road," she said briskly.

"Ready, sweetie?" I swept away the lingering horror of what Don had told me and knelt to hug Andrew.

He submitted to my embrace, then shuffled to the car.

"Me, too," Don said, and he held his arms open. For a moment, I felt ready for whatever lay ahead.

It's still one of the great mysteries of life that a drive that seems endless when you're starting out on an adventure is over in a flash when you're headed home. The games Rosie and I played to keep Andrew occupied hurried the time along, but even license plate poker and count-the-signs didn't keep thoughts of Stewart McClaren and his killer at bay.

"He's asleep," Rosie whispered as we made the turn onto the Saw Mill River Parkway. "I'm a little worried about your friend. She wasn't expecting to have to share the apartment with you and your out-of-sorts sister and a grumpy child. You're sure that's not going to be a problem?"

"Maria's wonderful. She's funny and generous and comes from a huge family, so she understands little boys and what it means to have to close ranks sometimes. Don't worry, it will be fine."

I told her about Maria's family, the sprawling network of cousins and grandparents, her five brothers and three sisters, until the George Washington Bridge loomed into sight.

Andrew yawned and stretched, then curled up again and pressed his nose to the window. "I wonder what Leonardo's doing now," he said, his voice quavering. "Is Don going to sleep with my kitten? If he doesn't, Leonardo's going to be too lonely."

I let Rosie soothe him with assurances that we'd soon be returning to home and Leonardo. He was such a dear child; I couldn't help being a little proud that he hadn't forgotten his kitten, a hundred miles away.

"Are we almost there?" Andrew huddled in the back between two sleeping rolls and his duffle bag.

"Soon, sweetie. Not much more now. It's down that way," I said, remembering he wasn't used to calculating distances in blocks. By the time we were headed down Fifth Avenue, he was exclaiming over the towering buildings, staring wide-eyed at a black stretch limo with smoked windows, jiggling with pleasure at the pigeon that fluttered by with the twisted center of a doughy pretzel in its beak.

But as good a welcome as it had been, New York City hadn't managed to provide an empty parking space anywhere near Greenwich Village. "We're going to have to improvise here. How about if we make everyone in New York mad at us and get them to beep their horns while I double park? We'll unload and bring our stuff upstairs and then I'll put the car in a lot overnight."

"If everyone in New York beeped their horns at us, boy, that would make a *lot* of noise."

"And probably get your Auntie Lee a hundred-dollar ticket for blocking the street. Don't do it, Lee. Give us the keys and we'll take the bags up to your apartment while you find parking."

A sensible solution; after all, it wasn't *my* home under siege. It had been Rosie's citadel, up there in the country, and we knew for sure that Stewart McClaren wasn't going to be lurking on the stairway. "Okay," I agreed. "The little round key is for the outside door. The big square one is for the top lock and the medium-size one is for the bottom lock."

"Three keys? You live in a prison?" Her expression thoughtful, Rosie accepted the key ring I handed her.

While a taxi serenaded us with repeated blasts on his horn and Andrew giggled, Rosie and I unloaded the bags. I waited until the heavy outer door closed behind them before I drove away.

Hazy darkness blanketed the city as I maneuvered the car into the last space in the lot. I took a ticket from the sleepy attendant and started walking, exhilarated by the energy of the city, relieved to be back on asphalt and surrounded by commuters, art students, night people in pursuit of amusement. I dashed across the street, dodging between a cab and bakery van; brakes squealed behind me and I pivoted.

In the center of a knot of strollers clogging the intersection, a barrel-chested man, his face splotched purple with anger, pounded with a meaty fist on the fender of a yellow cab. A wizened woman trailed in his wake.

"Get killed, you idiot! You should rot from your goddamn blind eyes to your shriveled brain! *Our* light was green! My mother can't walk so fast, you jerk. You should only get killed!"

A bicycle messenger sped by, nimbly skirting the edge of the gathering crowd. He raised his cap in salute. "Fresh action, Pops! Lay a crease on it for me."

Despite his mother's attempt to drag him away, the enraged man smashed the cab's fender again. The lanky driver stepped into the street, held his hands out in mute apology, then retreated behind the shield of his open door, shaking his head.

the Seduction

The squat and furious man jabbed at the door of the cab with his stubby legs, sending the driver sprawling backward onto the front seat.

Their faces shining with rapture, the crowd hooted encouragement and surged forward. The smell of sweat and perfume jittered against the sharp, metallic tang of excitement. I fought the swell of fear and anger that rose in me as I was shoved forward into the crush of bodies. In front of me, a woman with a silver-streaked chignon and a severe black suit muttered, "Do it!" through gritted teeth.

Pulse racing, I stood on my toes to see over the woman's head. A hand pressed against the middle of my back and I shrugged it away. The muscles in my forearms twitched; I tried to swallow, found that my throat was dry, felt a warm burst of triumph in my gut when the next angry thud landed on the driver's chest.

"Come on, do it!" the woman beside me yelled, the sound of her voice shrill and shocking.

Was I really standing in the center of an excited mob, cheering on a stranger as he attacked a cab driver?

Using my shoulder as a wedge, I maneuvered to the edge of the crowd and turned to look at the gallery of transfixed faces.

Spectator sport—this crowd gave new meaning to the words.

I broke away and headed for Tenth Street.

19

I t was odd to ring my own bell, still stranger to wait for Rosie to call down and buzz me in, but as I breathed the damp, mildewy air of the stairwell, I felt my body relax. The smell of Mr. Klinger's pipe and the gentle odor of incense from the apartment across from me on the second floor weren't exactly flowers and good earth, but they were home.

Rosie greeted me from the open doorway. Andrew stood behind her, peeking down the hall as if he expected some new adventure to materialize. "We've been watching television," she told me. "Is something wrong with the parrot? He's been too quiet."

"Pinky knows when to be considerate." I took in the Indonesian wall hanging, the exuberant Haitian pillows on the sofa, the subtle pastels of the painting beside the bookcase. I even greeted the droning TV set with giddy delight. *Home.* The parrot's raucous squawk welcomed me as I shut the door behind me—could he really have recognized my footsteps?

I shook a handful of sunflower seeds out of the blue ceramic jar and offered him one. He rewarded me with a tilt of his head and a beady stare; feathers ruffling, he finally picked at the seed in my hand and then hopped onto his perch. "You been watching over the house, you green menace? Getting your fair share of sunflower seed hulls on the floor, I see." I knelt and picked the litter from the floor. "Pinky, meet your cousin."

Hesitant at first, Andrew came nearer, inching his way closer and closer, finally reaching out with his plump fingers for the chrome cage.

"Don't do that! This parrot has been known to think of fingers as dinner."

Scowling, Andrew whirled away. He plunked onto the sofa and stared glumly down at the street.

"Come on over here and help me feed him," I coaxed. "You want to see how Pinky eats sunflower seeds?"

But my nephew kicked his sneakers against the sofa, swinging his leg and rocking his upper body. "I want to go home. I want to see Leonardo."

I wanted all of our lives to return to normal—and I was hot and thirsty.

The tiny kitchen, open shelves crammed with pottery mugs and Mexican glass and other reminders of my travels, wasn't any better stocked than when I'd left the week before. Maria had accumulated a melon wedge and three white takeout cartons in the refrigerator; added together, the contents might have made a small snack for a tiny person. Three bottles of Beck's and a can of cola kept the ketchup and garlic olives company on the top shelf.

"Something for the weary travelers." I handed Rosie one of the bottles, then set the soda can on a coaster on the table beside my nephew's chair. Half the beer slid down my throat in three long, icy gulps. "Anything good on?"

Andrew didn't answer; he looked up toward the door a second before I heard a key scrape in the lock. I tensed and then remembered: we weren't in Taconic Hills.

"Hello, honey, we're home," I called. If I'd been thinking more clearly, I would have phoned Maria before we left Rosie's, to warn her that we were coming.

She stood in the doorway, her skin shimmering with cocoa-colored light above her white blouse; she quirked her head and put her hands on her hips. "No notice, you just show up? What's going on, *chiquita?*

You missed the feel of chewing gum under your shoes? Oh, sorry, I didn't know anyone was with you. Hi, everybody."

"I'm Lee's sister, Rosie. You must be Maria. Lee always talks about you."

Smiling to hide her confusion, Maria shook my sister's outstretched hand. "And that has to be Andrew. I've heard that you're the best firefly catcher in Columbia County. What's the secret? Whenever I get one even near a jar, it zooms off and escapes."

Andrew, charmed out of his sulk, gave Maria a thorough lesson in firefly hunting while I got her the last beer. They giggled about using fireflies for nightlights and selling them to the tooth fairy. When the conversation lagged, Maria tossed me a questioning look and drifted back toward the bedroom. I followed.

"What's wrong? You're not here to see the sights, right?" She sat on the edge of the bed, kicked off her shoes, and rubbed her toes.

"Very clever. Listen, I'm sorry about this, but we're only staying a few nights. We have to go upstate on Saturday morning to pick up Paul, you know, my brother-in-law, from the campground. It's a six-hour drive from here so we'll leave really early and you can have the whole weekend alone in the apartment. I'll try to tell you everything. I better start with the rotten flowers."

She listened to the story—the bouquet, the cake, the black bows, the photograph, the candles, Andrew finding Rick's braided bracelet. I told her about Rick running away, and about Riley's announcement that Stewart McClaren's body had been found in a field.

"So, you don't have any idea who's doing this? Gotta be someone more than a little unhinged, right? Why you, why these weird black ribbons? Why kill Stewart?" Legs curled under her, Maria looked at me with uncharacteristic detachment, as if I were one of her clients at the advertising agency.

I shook my head. "I wish I knew. There are possibilities, but one doesn't seem any better than another. The best I can come up with is that whoever he is, he wants to attract attention. This may be just a *very* strange way to get people to notice him."

"But if that's what he wants," she persisted, "what's the point of keeping who he is a secret?"

I couldn't answer.

Maria frowned. "So, what, I ask one question and your theory about his wanting attention is shot down?"

Shot. Down.

"I don't really know what it means. I don't get it. I can't figure out what this person wants from us. Us—we don't even know who he's trying to impress, but the way it's turned out, we're all scared. Andrew, too. Those balloons . . ."

"Balloons?" A dark eyebrow curved as she looked at me questioningly. "What balloons?"

"I didn't tell you that part? Andrew and I came home from the lake today and there were these balloons, seven of them, tied in a black bow on the porch. When I went to cut them down, I popped one accidentally. It had blood in it, Maria. Animal blood. All the other things, the flowers, the cake, the candles. . . . Oh, God, Maria." I swallowed hard. "A birthday party."

Frowning, she stepped out of her skirt and pulled on a pair of shorts.

I sat stunned and motionless while she rummaged through a drawer until she came up with a bright red T-shirt. Two days ago, the notion would have been laughable. But today it had its own sick logic; this explanation was one way to make sense of the weird things that had been left at Rosie's. "How could we have missed it? Cake, candles, balloons, even flowers. A birthday party. I know I'm right."

She tucked the shirt into her shorts and leaned against the dresser, her hands jammed into her pockets. "You know what else sounds right? You guys are in trouble big time. Someone's doing all these whacko things and maybe he just wants you to come to his party. But everything changes when you put your dead photographer in the picture. What are you going to do? What's your plan?" Maria's eyes met mine in the mirror.

Rosie and I had barely been able to manage the present, but at least our future seemed to be settled.

"Like I said, we're going to stay here until we pick up Paul on Saturday. Andrew's pretty upset about missing the party for the last day of school on Friday. I get the feeling he holds me personally responsible, but that can't be helped. That's as far as we've gotten."

Maria pulled her hair off her neck and stuck a tortoiseshell comb through the heavy mass of curls atop her head. "And what's *Paul* going to do if the birthday boy comes by for a celebration? And don't tell me call the cops because we both know too much can happen between a phone call and the time the cavalry actually shows up."

"There's a rifle in the—"

"Oh, come on, Lee, a rifle? A strong man can take him by surprise, grab it and wrestle it away before he has the chance to ever fire it." Her bare foot tapped the hardwood floor.

Maybe. Maybe whoever got to the Springfield first—Paul, Rosie, me—would act more quickly, more decisively, so that our attacker wouldn't have the chance to come close enough to do any harm.

And suppose he was someone we knew, someone we didn't even worry about letting into the house?

"And what if this weirdo tracks you down while you and Rosie and Andrew are here? What if he followed you from Taconic Hills?"

"He didn't. I know it. I drove all the way here with my eyes on the rearview mirror. Nobody followed us." Nobody I'd seen, but that didn't rule out someone who already knew our destination. Maria's questions lay in hard knots at the bottom of my stomach. "So what do *you* think we should do?"

Her dark eyes followed every twitch of muscle on my face. "Go slow, Lee. You're on edge. You have to be careful—"

Now, I'd managed to involve Maria in all this; what was at first only a blot on my vacation had become a stain that sullied too many people I cared about. "I hate this. Whoever he is, whatever his problem is, I can't fix things for him. I won't let him drag me into his nightmare."

"He already has." She tossed me a skeptical smile. "Listen, give your sister and Andrew the big bed, you sleep on the sofa, and I'll go back to my roommates."

"No way. That's not going to help. We need someone to feed Pinky —and we need someone to make us laugh." Before I could tell whether that feeble argument had convinced Maria to stay, Rosie appeared in the doorway.

"Sorry to interrupt, but Andrew's starting to get cranky. I'd like to give him some warm milk to settle him down. If you just tell me where the nearest store is, I'll—"

"Oh, no, you're the guest." Maria sprang into action, checked her lipstick in the mirror and pulled on her sandals. "The three of you need a little pampering and I need some exercise. I'll get the milk. I'll be right back."

Maria had charmed Rosie, too. My sister smiled and shook her head. "You don't have to do this after a hard day's work. I can—"

But my friend waved away Rosie's offer with one red-tipped finger. "Shhh. Now you sound like your sister. Let me do something nice, so that Lee will want me to stay here when she goes on her next trip, all right?"

Rosie's face glowed with pleasure, for the first time all day. "Thanks, Maria. Lee told me you were nice. What she should have said is you're *wonderful*."

20

Rosie looked distant and distracted as I explained my birthday party theory.

"What difference does it make?" She leaned across the dresser and stared into the mirror, dabbing at the dark circles under her eyes as though she could erase them with her finger. "One person is dead, and we've been dislocated, and. . . . Oh, I don't know, Lee. It just doesn't matter. I need to close my eyes for five minutes. Would you see what Andrew's up to?"

I left her in my bedroom, pulled a deck of cards from the table beside the sofa, and tried to interest my nephew in a game of go-fish.

"I'm watching cartoons now," he said as he looked out the window.

I curled into a corner of the sofa. Maria would be back soon; meanwhile, a time out would probably do us all good. But every sound in the hallway, every car that slowed or honked in the street below reminded me of my friend's warning—we were only a little safer here than in Taconic Hills. We simply couldn't let ourselves be lulled into forgetting that.

Twenty minutes later, Maria called out as she opened the door. "The goodies are here. I figured we needed some pastries to go with that milk, so I went to the bakery on Thirteenth Street." She set one paper sack on the counter and cradled another, heavier bag in her arm. "Andrew, will you take charge of heating up these blueberry turnovers? I need to talk to your aunt for a few minutes."

My nephew nodded. "But I'm not allowed to turn on the oven by myself."

"I'll do it," I offered, frowning at Maria's strangely overbearing manner.

"Maybe you can get your Mom to help. Lee, I need to show you something inside, all right?" Maria's face was stern, despite the casual invitation in her voice. Still clutching the second bag, she edged toward the hall, gripping my sleeve. She pushed the bedroom door closed behind me.

"What's going on?" Restless, I moved from the bed to the dresser to the window. This tiny apartment had one drawback—I couldn't pace as effectively here as I could at Rosie's.

"You polishing the floor?" Maria asked. The paper bag lay on the floor between her feet. "Tell me if I'm missing something here. You think your life, and Rosie's and Andrew's, may be in danger, right?"

"If this person, whoever it is, can murder Stewart McClaren, he can kill again. I keep thinking Stewart was just plain unlucky and had to be taken out of the way so that this guy could get to me. Or to Rosie, although that makes less sense. I've managed to make a couple of people angry . . . but enough to kill me?" I shook my head. "I just don't know."

"You willing to take the chance that you or Rosie or Andrew could get hurt? You figure you're safe just because you're here?"

She asked hard questions. "I told you before—no one knows we're here. Well, only Riley and a friend of Rosie and Paul's." I thought again about Don, holding the kitten nestled in his arms, rinsing the dishes, leaning into the curves of his saxophone. Not Don. Surely not Don. "Of course I don't want anything to happen to my sister or my nephew. What kind of thing is that to say?"

"Okay, *chiquita*, now it's my turn to tell you a story and I want you to listen all the way through without interrupting. The old Lee Montara might not be capable of that, and I don't know how well you're going to hear me, state you're in right now, but I want you to try real hard, got it?"

Maria patted the bed and reluctantly I sat down next to her. "What's this about? You think I've gone totally loopy or something?"

"Not everything is about you, Lee. This is about me, and I want you to listen to every word, okay?"

Mystified, and a little embarrassed at my self-absorption, I nodded. "I'm all yours. Tell your story."

"You remember three years ago when I called from Trenton to tell you I was staying with my mother for two weeks? You teased me about running away to the industrial wasteland of the armpit of the mid-Atlantic, I remember exactly how you said it. We used to joke about how New Jersey was a good place to be *from*. You asked why I didn't take my mother and go to the shore or something. You remember that?"

I nodded. I'd carried on over the phone about how she was hiding out in the bosom of her family when she could have at least been getting a good tan at the beach.

"I didn't go to New Jersey because I lacked imagination or because I couldn't afford anything else or even because I wanted to please my mother. I went to recover." Her voice faded and her eyes closed, as though she were powerless against the onslaught of the scene playing in her head.

I tried to think back, but I couldn't remember anything about an illness or any other serious problem during that period of her life. Recover from what?

Finally, she opened her eyes and unfolded her clenched hands. "I was coming home from a class, it must have been about nine, nine fifteen at night. I was at the entrance to my building, that was when I was living on Fifth Street, off Avenue A, remember?"

That neighborhood had always made me uncomfortable; for three years, I'd tried to convince her to move. The East Village had changed; not quite gentrified, it was safer than it had been twenty years earlier. But I never liked the idea that Maria came and went, alone at all hours, despite the comforting presence of Indian restaurants and arty small theaters and the decades-old Italian pastry shops. When I'd visited her, I always went by cab, hating those nights when all the taxis in New York seemed to be avoiding me as if I had the plague, leaving me stranded on the dirty sidewalks. On those nights, I was reminded that my small-town childhood had left its mark: I wasn't at ease with *everything* about my adopted city, at least not east of Astor Place, downtown.

"Well, that night, three guys, I never even saw them in the hall when I opened the door to my apartment, but I heard three voices, they grabbed me from behind. One put his hand over my mouth, the other got me in some kind of hold that nearly squeezed the breath out of me, and the third, man, he must have been a linebacker or something, he tackled me around the knees." The muscles at her jaw worked into a knot.

"Maria, why didn't you—"

"Not yet, Lee. I'd never been so scared or so mad in my life. I kicked. I bit hands, I scratched at faces." The memory of her battle brought a sour smile to her lips. "I know I did some real good damage. And finally, one of them, the one who had his hand over my mouth, he let go and I screamed. I mean, loud, like I never yelled in my life. And you know what? New Yorkers . . . they're not so bad. In only a few seconds there were ten, twelve, I don't know how many people standing around me in that smelly hall. I still don't know where they all came from."

I was breathless, speechless. Why had she never told me this before?

"I couldn't believe it, there I was, half my clothes torn off, my purse I don't know where, and this bunch of street people and hippies and dancers and waiters, even one furious old Italian lady with a string bag full of vegetables, all huddled around me. Took most of them to sit on the three guys until the cops came but that's exactly what they did. And then I went to Trenton, and then I moved to University Place, to a building with a doorman."

And I'd thought, when she had told me she was moving, that it was my good counsel that had finally convinced her to find a tamer neighborhood. I squeezed her cold hand; the attack was over, but Maria still carried its scars.

"That's not the end, *chica*. I didn't talk about it at first mostly because I was in shock, but later I believed that if I didn't have to live through it every time I told the story, I would be able to forget it faster. I'm telling you now for a reason."

"Why, Maria? Does this have anything to do with what's happening to me and Rosie?"

"When I was in Trenton, I couldn't stand it any more, keeping it all in. I got in the car and drove to Fort Lee and told my cousin Jack. I guess I wanted someone to know, and Jack and I, we grew up together and never could keep secrets from each other."

"Jack? Your cousin the cop?" I frowned, not sure where this new information would take her story.

"He gave me something, and you can have it. If you want it. Sounds to me like you got limited options, and I'm going to expand the list. Just a minute." She set the paper bag on the bed, opened it, and pulled out a hard plastic case about the size of a large coffee-table book. A combination lock held it closed.

She spun the numbers on the lock and opened the case like a clamshell. I knew what would be inside, and my breath caught. Not that her story, every bit of it, wasn't plausible. Not that her cousin Jack wouldn't help her cut through bureaucratic tape, if that was required to ensure her safety. What struck me was her calm. She looked as if it were perfectly natural for a gun to be sitting between us on my bed.

It lay in the case, gleaming with a cold, silvery light. Big, lethal, and terrifying—I couldn't take my eyes off it.

"Here, pick it up. It's not loaded. Go on," she urged.

But I couldn't do it.

"All right, I know how you feel. I felt that way too when Jack first gave it to me. I don't carry it with me. I keep it in my apartment, and it lets me sleep at night."

"I can't . . . I don't know, this is . . . *a gun*, Maria."

She got up and stood in front of me, tiny and dark and still angry at what three men had done to her life in a darkened hallway. "You can take it with you or not. But I won't let you have it unless you promise to go with me tomorrow to Ramapo, to the shooting range where I learned how to use it. My cousin Tammy, Tamara but she hates when people call her that, she works there during the week. She'll find someone to give you a private lesson, if I ask her to.

"Maybe I can get Jack to take your sister and the little boy off to the movies or the zoo or something. Tell them I need your help with something, whatever. I'm not going to try to talk you into anything, but if you want the gun, taking that lesson is the only condition I have. Now, let's go see if Andrew is tired enough for his sleeping bag. We can pretend there's a campfire in the living room and tell scary stories."

21

A profound calm settled over me when we walked through the door of the Wyoming Hawk Gunshop. A strong, oily smell filled the shop. Packages containing items whose existence I'd never even imagined hung in neat displays on pegboard racks.

"Maria!"

A woman with short spiked hair and a mischievous, gamine face ran toward us, arms outstretched. "*Ola, chica*, you finally remembered you got family. Oh boy, you're looking good. Some fine guy been treating you right, I bet." She straightened her Hawk T-shirt, brown eyes and dimples flashing as she ran a hand through her hair.

"Hey, Tammy, this is my friend, Lee Montara."

Tammy, her expression at once shrewd and sensitive, put one arm on my shoulder and the other around Maria's. "Scott's here, Jack's friend. You know me, *chica*, I'm not going to ask why the hurry, but I want your friend to sit here a few minutes and make sure she means it. This is no toy you're talking about. Everybody's got a reason, but you better be sure you've thought of all your possibilities before you think about guns."

I'd thought about little else for eighteen hours; I was sure. "Would you tell Scott I'm here and I'm ready?"

They left me alone, clutching the leather attaché case into which I'd slipped Maria's gun case. I stared at the poster on the wall. A cowboy's six-shooter and a pistol that I'd expect a movie gangster to carry stared back at me. I'd seen rifles, the Springfield that Don had pulled out of Paul's closet and stashed in the kitchen, the very old Winchester that was Grandpa Montara's pride. To me, they'd been only tools or antiques, something to display or to use during hunting season so that the freezer could be stocked with venison. Hunting was part of country life, a little different from going into a supermarket and buying pork chops, but not unfamiliar to me.

Handguns, though, had only one purpose, and they looked it.

The range was dimly lit, a row of stalls each with its own small shelf, waist high. Scott Macklin's gray hair was the only thing about him that was paternal; muscular and direct, he laid the pistol on one of the platforms. "For the next forty minutes," he said brusquely as he nodded down the long lane ahead, "you point your gun down range only. No questions, no hesitation."

This would be a new experience in more ways than one. Still, despite my resistance to blind obedience, I understood at once.

"You always check first to see if a gun is loaded. You grip the slide firmly, press down on this slide stop, and pull back to examine the cylinder. Then, press this little release"—he touched a small metallic button scored with hatchmarks—"and the magazine is free."

I nodded, already overwhelmed with information, with words whose meanings had suddenly changed. Cylinders, slides, magazines —I worked for a magazine.

"Okay, set your feet the way I showed you, make sure the gun is resting on the web of your right thumb, and steady it with your left index finger." He handed me Maria's pistol.

I closed my eyes, letting my hands feel the shape of the gun, memorizing the weight against my left index finger and the cold bulk of the grip under my right palm.

"It's the front sight you want to pay attention to, so try to get it lined up with the rear sight. Now, bench your weapon."

Was I supposed to put the safety on now or leave it off? I turned to ask him, but Scott's face got red and he shouted, "Down range! Point that thing down range. Bench that weapon!"

Instantly, I set the gun on the platform.

"You never point a gun at someone unless you're prepared to shoot them. You understand that?"

It would take more than this simple lesson to prepare me to shoot someone. I pushed aside my reservations and nodded. "I won't forget. I wanted to ask you something. . . ."

He pointed out the safety again, showed me how to load the bullets into the magazine. "All right, put on those plastic eyeglasses and replace the magazine. Now, you've got live ammunition in that thing, so pay attention."

His words boomed inside my head: *live ammunition.*

I closed my eyes, took another shaky breath. I could do this: Insert magazine, pull back slide, lift, and sight.

Lift and sight. Twenty-five feet away, a paper target hung from an armature that dangled from a track on the ceiling. A series of concentric circles spread out from the middle of the paper. I looked down the barrel.

"Fire when you're ready." Scott sounded as though he'd just shown me how to use a zoom lens.

I took a deep breath; I squeezed the trigger.

A burst of light, like a camera flash, startled me. My ears rang and my hands were jerked upward from the unexpected force of the explosion but I held on to the gun. A shell flew over my shoulder and landed somewhere behind me on the floor. The burnt-cork smell of gunpowder wafted back to me.

I lowered the gun to the platform and leaned forward to check the target, my stomach knotting. The paper—more than anything, I wanted to have at least hit the paper.

And there, halfway between the bull's-eye and the lower edge of the paper, I saw a round, black hole. I had done it.

"Not bad," Scott said, grinning as though he, too, was surprised that I'd come even close. "Now load up six rounds. And lean your upper body forward instead of back."

Pushing all six bullets into the magazine proved more difficult than I expected. But I'd never let anyone bait my fish hook; I would load every damn one of those bullets into that magazine.

"Okay, this time, when you're ready, fire all six shots. Remember to breathe and remember to lean forward."

I breathed.

I leaned.

My second shot hit the outer circle of the bull's eye. I was so excited I almost whirled around to see if Scott had been looking. Trembling, I stopped myself in time. I was holding a loaded weapon. *Down range.* I steadied myself and fired the rest of the clip.

"You're getting it. Now do it all again."

I loaded another magazine and fired off the entire round.

"We've got two dozen cops coming in for practice in ten minutes. Last round," Scott said as he replaced the target. "Put one shot in the center of each circle."

The new target had five smaller yellow circles, one in the center of the paper and one in each corner. I'd played a fair game of pool a couple of weeks before; I *would* do this. "Center target," I muttered under my breath. I fired into the yellow circle in the middle of the paper. "Upper left," I said, gripping the pistol and adjusting my stance.

Not all of my shots were dead center; two hit the ring just beyond center, but I was thrilled. I thanked Scott, whose eyes betrayed a skepticism he didn't voice, returned Maria's pistol to the case, slipped the whole thing back into my leather attaché, and walked into the bright lights of the shop.

We drove south along the river, in the shadow of the New Jersey skyline. The high-rise apartments and low, waterfront warehouses were etched sharply against the afternoon sky. At the east edge of a park along the highway, blades of grass knifed through the spaces in a chain-link fence that glittered with reflected light. The whole world was bold contrasts and hard edges, the colors so intense I could almost see them vibrate.

"Isn't it incredible? The light, I mean, how it makes everything so perfect and separate. Even the air is sparkling." I flipped the directional signal, tapping my hand on the steering wheel in time to the rhythmic ticking.

"Sparkling? You're kidding. The smog is as thick as my grandmother's bean soup today." Maria groped for the dashboard and held on as I turned off the highway and headed downtown.

"You don't *feel* the light? It's got an electric clarity. Must be me then."

"You're seeing things, *chica*. This ever happen to you before?"

Only a few times, each of them singular moments of mastery; I should have known. "The first time, I was five or six. Wobbling along on my brand new bike, waving away my father and the training wheels. Then I realized that everything had a golden outline around it, even the leaves of a sycamore tree. Same thing when I figured out how to climb out my bedroom window, cross the porch roof, and slide down to the ground, only it was night then and what was magical was how keen the air was, and the stars."

Maria laughed and clung to the dash as I braked for a light. "So shooting a gun made you high? Me, I was just scared the first time I did it. But it scared me more not to, you know what I mean?"

So shooting a gun made you high? I didn't like hearing it, and yet I couldn't deny that proving myself up to the challenge had charged the world with brilliance. I dropped Maria off in front of her building and, miraculously, immediately found a parking spot.

It felt good to be walking, part of the movement of the streets, to be surrounded by people and noise. But instead of an anonymous crowd, this time I saw each person, separate and unique, and I wondered: Do *you* have a weapon secreted somewhere, in a drawer in your bedroom, in your pocket, your purse, your battered canvas backpack? Maria had opened my eyes to a whole new dimension of city living.

Andrew flew to the door and hugged me before I could even put my keys down.

"Jack took us to the zoo. You should have seen the gorilla! He stood on his legs and stuck his tongue out and then—" Andrew's frantic laughter spilled out, stopping the flow of words. He panto-mimed the antics of the gorilla, scratching his belly, leaping to the sofa. Finally, unable to continue, he rolled onto his back and clutched his chest as if to beg for mercy.

Rosie knelt and picked him up gently, cradling him in her arms. "And then we walked down Fifth Avenue," she said, her voice sooth-ing and her cadence steady, almost hypnotic, "and looked in the win-dows and stopped for a milk shake, and then we realized that we were too tired to walk all the way home so we got on a bus and we came home, not five minutes before you did. Jack just left for work."

Andrew had gone limp in her arms; now he turned his weary face to me. "Tomorrow, we're going to see the Statue of Liberty, right, Mom? And you know what, Auntie Lee? Pinky sounded like he knew it was us. He sounded glad we were home."

I grinned. "You're exactly right. He has a different squawk when he's saying hello to a friend. You hungry, kiddo?"

"Not yet. Can I watch cartoons for a while?"

Rosie settled him on the sofa; I waited until she came looking for me, and I motioned her into my bedroom.

"It's going to be all right, Rosie. We don't need to be afraid anymore," I assured her. "I have a gun."

There was no way to make those words sound any different. *I have a gun.* Rosie tipped up her chin and then glanced at the briefcase.

"In that?"

I nodded. "I just took an hour of instruction. How to load it, how to fire it. It does make me feel better to have it. Don't worry, I won't leave it around or anything. Andrew won't ever know about it."

Rosie brushed her hair away from her eyes. Her face was pale. Her mouth tightened and she was silent.

I was suddenly struck with the realization that I had crossed some irrevocable line. It was no longer possible to define myself in old terms. This change was as permanent as a loss of virginity. A few hours ago, I could count on only my knowledge of people and whatever native wit I possessed to protect me.

Now, I had the power to kill someone.

11:30 a.m.

I grip the telephone and stare at the holes in the black mouthpiece, but that doesn't change anything. No dial tone, no static, not a sign of life. I swallow a scream, replace the receiver, start for the door.

No. I can't leave Rosie alone, not even to drive down the hill for help.

I check my watch. I've lost my ordinary moorings and so might have misplaced hours of this day in the emptiness of waiting. Yes, it's still morning. We have time. *I* have time. I wish Rosie were up here with me.

I clutch the door frame to steady myself, and suddenly pale light dances into the room from the window and touches the counter, the gleaming, curved faucet, the books on the shelf above Rosie's desk. The light deepens, turns golden, and I let go of the support.

Amazed, I look around. The whisk hanging beside the stove glints, its graceful curves looping into a perfect, airy teardrop of steel. The teakettle, squat and funny and bright red, catches the spill of sun;

motes of brightness float to the polished surface of the oak table. The silence terrifies me.

The rain, I realize, has stopped. It looks like someone has washed the world for us. But I'm not yet a part of that cleansing. A bird is perched, curious and attentive, on the windowsill outside. He begins a song, and I think I must be standing frozen for him to feel so secure that he lets his song pour out into the new sunshine.

A glass egg with a deep purple flower like a starburst suspended in its center winks at me from the desk in the corner. I am drawn toward it. I reach for the smooth oval; the egg is heavy and it is beautiful and it is Rosie's.

I am surrounded by the things Rosie has chosen for her kitchen, and in their presence I have acquired calm.

Hand in my pocket, I slip noiselessly down the hall as though I weigh nothing. As I approach the door leading to the cellar, the sound of footsteps on the wood stairs rings through the house.

22

Pale gray light leaked between the slats of my venetian blinds onto Andrew's sleeping form. Rosie and I lay side by side in our sleeping bags on the floor, whispering; sirens and garbage trucks rattled the dawn, and we decided that for the sake of my nephew, to keep him occupied and at least offer the illusion that everything was normal, we would leave early, take sandwiches, and spend the day at the Statue of Liberty.

We would be the last ones to board the ferry; we'd check out the crowd, make sure we hadn't been followed. Rosie and I agreed that if anyone was shadowing us, it would be someone we'd recognize.

We were showered, dressed, and out the door before nine. Thick, sooty clouds clung to the spires of tall buildings, and damp city air settled heavily on everything, leaving a fine slick on our skin. But the salty sea breeze was a tonic and the ferry ride perked us all up. Andrew's excitement was infectious as we chugged toward the island. I tucked my purse close to my side; by the time we trailed after the other passengers down the ferry ramp, I'd grown accustomed to the leather strap of my handbag, heavy with the weight of the gun, tugging at my shoulder.

We read every plaque and sign, stood for an hour looking over the brackish water at Brooklyn and Manhattan. As we ate our sandwiches, I thought about that day Andrew and I had built the dam in the sparkling water of the stream. For the "remembering" game, I would keep that memory of my time in Taconic Hills. Other memories would be better left to fade and die away.

By early afternoon, I'd almost forgotten that we'd taken this trip to fill a day of waiting. When Andrew asked if we could go to the South Street Seaport, Rosie and I groaned with mock reluctance, then let him talk us into it. We were exhausted; Andrew was animated, enchanted by everything he saw. We strolled through shops, watched ships pass under the Brooklyn Bridge, ate lobster rolls and french fries, and welcomed in the evening. We had managed the entire day without incident.

One more day to get through.

Then it would be Saturday and we would drive upstate to meet Paul. Arms around each other, we rode the subway to West Fourth Street, rocking sleepily with the motion of the train.

The red light of the answering machine blinked insistently in the shadows of my bedroom, announcing that I had two messages.

"Can I feed Pinky, Auntie Lee? I know how now." Andrew leaned toward the cage, a handful of sunflower seeds at the ready. Rosie stood beside him, smiling indulgently.

"Sure. Just watch out for your fingers," I warned, edging toward the bedroom, toward the blinking light.

I kicked off my shoes, settled myself on the bed, and pressed the rewind button. The first voice I heard when the tape whirred forward was Don Ward.

"I just got to school and I have a few minutes before classes start," he said in his rich baritone. "Leonardo says he's having a good time, and he hopes Andrew is having as much fun there in the big city. I have a rehearsal this evening, but don't worry, even if you get home very late, I still want to talk to you. Call me any time."

Yes, I would, I definitely would. I considered turning the machine off and calling Don immediately, but before I could hit the button, Riley Hamm's monotone filled the room.

"Call me right away," he said tersely. "Work or home."

My hand shook as I punched out the number of the sheriff's office. It was seven o'clock; my thoughts spun wildly while I waited for someone to answer the phone, asked to speak to Riley, was put on hold for what felt like hours.

Finally, that unmistakable nasal voice said, "Riley Hamm here."

"This is Lee Montara, Riley. I just got your message."

For the next five minutes, without giving me a chance to interrupt, Riley told his story. With each detail, my jaw clenched tighter and my anger grew. "I have to go now," he said sharply. "I expect you'll be coming back soon. Just let me know when you get to the house."

I slammed the receiver down. Should I have seen it all along? The signs had been unclear at the time—the incident at the ice cream stand, the apologetic visit to Rosie's, the way he treated his wife—but maybe if I'd been more objective, I would have seen the pattern. I was almost as furious at myself as I was at him.

"Riley's got Hank Steuben in custody," I told Rosie.

Her eyes grew wide; she glanced at Andrew, absorbed in a television program.

I lowered my voice. "He was sitting in his car in your driveway when they arrested him. Four o'clock this morning. Sounds like he was really drunk, ranting about apologies and women who mind other people's business. Peggy Steuben told Riley that her husband's been very upset since the other night at the Tastee-Freez. What a sick, miserable—"

"It's over, Lee. It's all over." Her face was bone white. "Poor Rick. Maybe he'll come back now. I keep thinking about him hiding out, being terrified that he'll be accused of something dreadful because Andrew found his friendship bracelet and you asked him if he'd been around when we weren't home."

Even now, Rosie focused on the Decker boy. Her composure stirred my anger again. I needed her to be outraged along with me; I wanted to shake her until she admitted that she'd been rocked by the events of the past week, that she too had been upset.

"Rosie, listen. Stop all this—"

"And Peggy Steuben, poor thing. They've got three boys, what's she going to tell them? How are they going to afford a lawyer on the wages she makes? Hank probably won't even qualify for unemployment any more."

"Rosie! I can't believe you. This man terrorized us, maybe even murdered Stewart, and you're feeling *sorry* for his family?" But that was her way; without that empathy, she wouldn't be Rosie. I felt petty and instantly regretted my anger. "I'm sorry," I said. "I know you're concerned about Peggy. But you can't take care of everyone, you know that. There's enough to do without you trying to fix things for Peggy Steuben."

"You're right, I know you are, but I just keep thinking about that family. I wish there was someone who knew how to help them."

"Help them? Rosie, Hank is dangerous. Everything he's done is a *threat*, not a request for assistance."

"I wish," she said softly, "that I could just yell, like you do, or cry or something. To get it all out of my system."

It would take a while to absorb the fact that Hank Steuben really was in jail, longer for the vestiges of tension and anger and fear to disappear. All my life, I'd seen my sister take solace from her busyness, making rag rugs or hanging laundry, so that what was once useless or tarnished was transformed into a beautiful, serviceable thing. I preferred my therapy city-style: an hour-long workout at the gym followed by a good, *noir* movie, or a twenty-block walk on crowded streets.

Neither of us could count on old refuges now.

"Well, let's not sit here and stew. Why don't we . . ." I searched for the right activity, but nothing came.

Rosie's face brightened. "You know, Lee, with Hank in custody, there's no reason for Andrew to miss his party at school tomorrow. Why don't we throw our things in the car and drive back to Taconic Hills? What do you say?"

Of course—Andrew, at least, didn't have to give up any more than he already had. "That's exactly what we should do, you're right. You sure you'll be comfortable in the house? It won't bother you to be there without Paul being around?"

Rosie glanced at her son, who was staring mesmerized at my small TV set; when she turned to face me again, she was frowning. "There will be memories for a while. . . . I keep seeing your face up there in the bathroom, your toes curled against the white rug. . . . I can't believe it really happened. I don't want to hold on to it." She shook her head. "If there's a trial, we'll probably have to testify or something."

As she spoke, I felt certain that even if we had to relive the past week again in court, at least the surprises weren't going to keep coming at us like bats at dusk. "Go ahead, Rosie—tell Andrew we're going home."

Hank Steuben—out of work and out of ideas, his manhood already threatened. I hadn't behaved the way he wanted me to and so he had decided to teach me a lesson. Was that it? Stewart McClaren's place in the scenario was murkier. I shoved a bag of garbage down the incinerator chute, wondering if we'd ever know.

"Andrew's so excited," Rosie said when I returned. She followed me into the bedroom and pulled her suitcase from the closet. "When's Maria coming back? I'd love to say good-bye. And you have to give her back that gun, right?"

My sister started for the living room, but I grabbed her arm. "I'm bringing it with me. When I come back here on Sunday, I'll return it to her."

Hank Steuben might be in custody now, but given the vagaries of the legal system, there was no telling when he might be released. He could be free at this moment, for all we knew. No way was I going to leave the gun behind.

She scowled. "It's not necessary any more. And what if Andrew finds it? Accidents happen all the time and I—"

"Nothing's going to happen," I told her firmly. "I'll make sure of it. Hank could get out on bail, no matter what Riley says. I'm bringing the gun, Rosie. If you object, we can stay here."

"But I just told Andrew we were going home. I can't—"

"Those are the only two options." I stepped back and folded my arms across my chest. She could take it or leave it.

"Who the hell do you think you are, telling me what my only two options are?" She spit out the words and glared icily.

I shrugged. "That's the deal. I'm not taking any chances with your safety or Andrew's. Or my own."

"Thank God we're almost home," Rosie said softly, as we spotted the sign for the Pine Plains exit. "You called Don?"

Her question, finally, after two hours in the car without a word passing between us, was a mark that she'd forgiven me at last for the confrontation in my bedroom. Relieved, I said, "No. I forgot in the rush to get out. I'll call him in the morning."

Hearing Don's voice would have been lovely; I'd even make do with sitting and listening to him play scales. I wondered what he would say about the uneasy feeling that had rolled over me again, somewhere between White Plains and Poughkeepsie, of being somehow tainted by the knowledge of how to shoot a gun.

The tires shushed along the road; when I turned to look at Rosie's face, I saw that she was staring out the side window. We whipped past black clumps of trees and boxy houses, some dotted with homey squares of light that blurred into smeary yellow streaks as we drove on.

The moon rose all at once, a full white opal looking down on us as we pulled into the driveway and stepped out into the sultry night. Here too, an uncomfortable edge of humidity had settled over everything, as though the air were too full to be contained. The house, tucked between tall trees and the low, rounded bushes, rose out of the darkness, so much larger than my friendly, compact apartment that it felt looming and ominous.

"I'll carry him upstairs and then come back down for our bags." Rosie bent to pick up her sleeping son; Andrew mumbled something I couldn't make out and snuggled into her arms, one little hand clutching her shoulder.

"I can get it all," I said, reaching into the trunk for our bags and hurrying up the porch steps to open the door for them. "It's locked, I forgot."

I set the bags down and fished through my purse until I found the keys. Rosie went ahead of me into the darkened house. The throat-catching smell of overblown flowers rushed at me as we entered. Finally, I remembered: We'd left in such a hurry that we hadn't thrown away the wildflower bouquet Andrew and I had gathered three mornings ago as he waited for the bus.

I tiptoed behind Rosie, the weight of her sleeping child slowing her down. Staggering a little myself with all three bags—how many pairs of shoes could three people, one of them only six years old, wear, anyway?—I stopped at the landing to catch my breath while Rosie went on ahead.

Her footsteps sounded in the hall, and as I picked up the bags again, I heard the squeak of the hinges as she pushed open the door to Andrew's room.

"Put the hall light on," she whispered to me. "He's always leaving books and stuff on his bed."

I set the bags beside the telephone table and flipped on the hall light, then turned to retrieve the bags.

It was nothing more than a catch of her breath, a ragged intake between clenched teeth, but I knew. Something else waited for us in the darkened bedroom, and I flew down the hall toward her.

She stood in the doorway to Andrew's room, gulping for breath. Then, the little boy still cradled in her arms, she turned and stumbled toward her own bedroom at the end of the hall.

Shadows played along the walls, huge leering things that reached out in all directions. And when I turned on the light in Andrew's bedroom, I understood why she didn't want to put her son in his own bed.

23

The door to Andrew's closet gaped like a hungry mouth. Inside, shirts and pants and jackets, so small, so ordinary when we'd left, hung limply on their hangers. They were nothing more than strips of fabric, rent lengthwise like the pieces in Rosie's scrap basket, a little boy's clothing transformed into yet another unholy testament to someone's madness.

I couldn't bear to touch anything. A pair of blue trousers and a white shirt, probably for school assembly, three pairs of jeans, a lightweight baseball jacket with a Mets patch on the front—all sliced to ribbons. Four cotton shirts, three plaid flannel shirts. . . . Even his winter jacket was cut into strips, shiny red and blue, leaking feathers from the down filling, most of them fallen into a snowy heap atop shoes and ice skates. Nothing was intact.

The macabre wardrobe seemed ready to dance in any whisper of a breeze; a cry could set them all fluttering. A single white sneaker lay in the middle of the floor. I tossed it in with the other shoes; feathers scattered, then drifted lazily back to the bottom of the closet.

the Seduction

Perhaps someone had been in the house when we drove up . . . maybe he was hiding, somewhere near enough to watch our reactions. My chilled fingers closed around the handle of the gun in my purse. A hand touched my shoulder and I spun around.

"Leave everything. I've called Riley. I don't want to disturb any evidence." Rosie's voice was fierce and cold. "This time, he said he'd be here in five minutes. Get it through your head, Lee. It's all over. He's got Hank in custody. Put that thing away. If Riley sees it . . ."

I understood, but I didn't put the gun down. Until Riley came, it was all we had to protect ourselves. There had been too many surprises—I couldn't leave us vulnerable to another one. Maybe our tormentor was in the county jail but until the sheriff's deputy arrived, the gun was our only insurance against the possibility that someone might be here with us in the house, determined to use these five minutes to finish what he'd begun.

"Have you touched anything, any surfaces?" Rosie examined the doorknob as though she could see my fingerprints, or someone else's.

"Nothing, only the light switch. What about the clothes in the dresser? Have you checked?" What would Andrew think in the morning, waking up in his mother's bed, having nothing to wear, knowing, finally, that whatever had hidden in the darkness had chosen him as its target?

"No, Riley will do that. I'm going to sit in my room with Andrew. Go downstairs, Lee. Riley will be here any minute. We'll be all right up here."

I'd go. But first I would walk into each room, open each closet door, make sure they really were alone.

I used the gun to flip every light switch as I went from room to room, touching nothing, looking everywhere. When I heard the now-familiar whine of the approaching Bronco, I slipped the Colt back into my purse and headed downstairs. In the night silence, sounds were magnified, distances impossible to judge. Finally, the Bronco churned up the drive, headlights slicing through the darkness.

Riley rushed up the porch steps, sputtering excuses. "I had a man here at least once an hour between the time you left and when Del Santo picked Hank up. I guess he wasn't too drunk to suss out the schedule. He must have waited until Del Santo drove away. But Hank wasn't quick enough. Del Santo got him in the driveway, pointed back down toward the road. I even came back and checked the doors and windows myself but they were all locked up and I said to myself, ain't no one got into that house. Where's your sister and the boy?"

"Upstairs. In the front bedroom. He's asleep, so please be quiet. We were careful not to touch anything except the light switch in his room. Let me know as soon as you're finished. Rosie wants to make sure the cut-up clothing is out of there so that Andrew doesn't see it. Did Hank say yet why he did this to us?"

I started to follow Riley as he brushed past me and headed for the stairs. "You stay down here and let me do my job," he said over his shoulder.

And that was all he was planning to say? "Wait a minute! Tell me, Riley. What has Hank said?"

One hand clutching the post at the foot of the stairs, Riley sighed and ran his fingers through his sparse hair. "I already told you, Mizz Montara. We picked him up at four in the morning. Parked right up here in the driveway, just sitting there, staring at the house. We've got this all under control, so will you just let me do my job?"

It wasn't enough, what he was telling me, not nearly. "I want to know if he confessed."

Riley snorted. "Hank? He was falling down drunk when we picked him up. Going on and on about trying to say he was sorry and that you wouldn't listen. Said a bunch of stuff I didn't get until I talked to his wife. She said he left the house ranting about why don't some people just keep to their own problems and leave him alone."

"But he's not still too drunk to tell you all the details, is he?"

"Just hung over now. Man was so intoxicated when we picked him up I couldn't believe he drove here without wrapping himself around a tree. When he's that way, that's when he's violent, you understand. Lately, that's been just about every day. Peggy says he's been talking about nothing but this thing that happened between you the other day. At the ice cream place. Now, you wait here while I go check out the boy's room." He turned on his heels and thumped up the stairs two at a time.

I raced up behind him and motioned to Rosie from the doorway of the bedroom. She rose from her seat beside the bed; Andrew was curled into a compact lump under the covers, scrunched against the pillows. His breath rose and fell steadily in the even rhythm of deep sleep as she joined me in the hall.

Before I could tell her what Riley had said, he stepped out of

Andrew's bedroom. He carried the remains of the down jacket and a couple of other articles in a large, clear-plastic bag.

"I'm done in there. No use carting it all with me. I'll be in touch tomorrow. You ladies rest easy now. Get some sleep." He stood at the stairs, waiting for a response, then shook his head. "Better follow me and lock up anyway. These days, you never know."

Riley Hamm tramped out the door; after two noisy tries, the Bronco started up and then peeled down the drive. Riley might be thoughtless, insensitive, incompetent, even, but he was right about us still needing to be cautious. I checked the back door, made sure all the windows were secure. Nobody, not Hank Steuben or anyone else, was getting in tonight.

When I climbed back to the second floor, exhausted and ready for bed, Rosie was waiting at the head of the stairs. "Maybe tomorrow we can celebrate the end of the strangest week in my life, the end of my anonymous telephone calls and all those presents with black bows. Do you really think Hank Steuben killed Stewart McClaren?"

It all came out in one steady stream, the last question following as though it were just another piece of evidence that the nightmare was over. But Rosie had said it aloud, the thing I hadn't been able to ignore, the question that snaked among the strips of my nephew's clothing. Hank Steuben was capable of a lot of things—wearing his wife down, flying into a drunken rage, hitting Peggy Steuben too hard. Was that what happened to Stewart? I wondered where Hank had met him and how they had come to blows, and most especially, why.

"He's certainly capable of it, Rosie. Any one of us is. All someone had to do was say the wrong thing after Hank had a couple of drinks. Maybe they met in a local bar and Hank got mad because Stewart looked at him cross-eyed. Hank could have been driving home from a binge and hit Stewart with his car and then, in a panic when he realized what he'd done, maybe he dumped the body in the field. Sure, Hank Steuben is capable of killing someone."

"Could you do it, Lee?" she asked so softly I wasn't sure I was hearing her correctly. "I think I could. I think I could do it if the life of someone I loved was threatened."

I ignored her declaration. "I'm going to get that mess out of Andrew's room. We can take it to the dump tomorrow. God, Hank Steuben is even more twisted than I realized. What a sick mind, to pick a little child as his victim."

"What am I going to tell him, Lee, when he gets up and wants to get dressed tomorrow? Everything, the bastard ruined every piece of clothing my child owns—"

"Except what we brought with us. What's in the suitcase? Give it to me, let's have a look." I pawed through the duffel bag Rosie pushed over to me, shoving aside underwear and socks, shorts and T-shirts, gray with city grit. Finally, on the bottom, I found a wrinkled pair of jeans and a crumpled plaid shirt. "I'm going to iron these and wash out that ice cream stain. It'll be dry by morning. He'll wear this. It'll be fine."

Her eyes blazed. "It's a good thing Hank Steuben's in jail." Hands clenched and shoulders rigid, Rosie stalked off toward her bedroom.

My dear, sweet Rosie, my even-tempered and generous sister, had become something unrecognizable. I ran down the hall, took her in my arms, stroked her hair. "Ssh, it's over," I said, repeating the words she'd said to me earlier. "It's going to be all right. Everything will be fine, I promise."

In my arms, my sister stood rigid and silent.

24

Every time my eyes flew open to the sullen night, I told myself that Hank Steuben was in jail. But the relief I should have felt, the balm that came from knowing that our ordeal was finally over, never soothed me into sleep. If Riley found fingerprints, a button from Hank's shirt, came up with a witness, I might begin to believe it. If Hank Steuben recovered from his bender and made a full and detailed confession, maybe I'd be able to start letting go.

Several times, unable to lie alone and stare at the shadows on the ceiling, I wandered back to Rosie's bedroom. In the moonlight, I studied my sister's form and Andrew's under the flowered sheets.

Near dawn, I dozed off. I woke with a start; the gun almost fell out of my hand onto the floor. If Andrew had awakened during the night and walked back to my room. . . . I locked the gun in Maria's hard plastic case and hid it under the winter blanket in the closet. Then I took a long, hot shower and went downstairs to wait for Rosie and Andrew.

. . .

"But I want to wear my white shirt," Andrew wailed. "This is just stinky school clothes. Everyone's going to be dressed up."

Despite his distress, Rosie maintained her composure. "I told you, honey. An animal must have gotten into your closet, a raccoon, I bet, you know how sharp their nails are, and everything got ruined and I had to throw it out. I'm sorry. But you look terrific, and I'm sure not everyone will be dressed up. Anyway, you don't have to do what *everyone* does."

"Then I'm not going." He set his jaw stubbornly.

"Suit yourself," Rosie said calmly. "But don't complain to me later that you wish you'd gone to the party after all."

I carried my coffee out to the porch, hoping Andrew would follow and scatter his toast crumbs on the grass and watch the birds swoop down to retrieve them. Some part of me expected the world to look different now that Hank was in jail, but nothing had changed.

Instead of joining the birds and me, Andrew pounded up the stairs. A door slammed.

"Mom! A raccoon couldn't get in here," he shouted, and my heart wrenched for Rosie, having to persist in a lie that her son had seen through from the start. He clomped back down to the kitchen, and I held my breath as I waited for Rosie's response.

I heard nothing. Finally, they appeared on the porch. Rosie carried his lunch box; Andrew fiddled with the buttons on his plaid shirt, brushed at the damp spot where I'd scrubbed away the stain the night before. He blinked his eyes, forcing back tears, unwilling to cry and unable to rage.

At the sight of the school bus climbing up the drive, Andrew's quivering stopped. "It's all right, Mom. I know it's not your fault. I think I better go to the party. I promised Michael I'd be his partner today."

"You have fun at school, okay?" Rosie handed him his lunch box, her fingers closing briefly over his when he reached for it.

"See you later, Auntie Lee." He ran over, touched his lips shyly to my cheek.

"Save me some candy, okay?" I allowed myself to kiss the top of his head.

He hesitated for an instant, swiped at his eyes, and flashed me a thumbs-up sign. Then, hair flying, he raced down the steps and headed for the driveway.

I leaned over the porch rail, ready to wave when he turned around, glad to be cheering him on his way. But as he bounded off the grass onto the gravel of the drive, his feet tangled up and he cried out. His legs shot out from under him and he went down, hard, face first onto the sharp stones. For a sickening moment, he lay motionless and silent. Then, his sob split the morning stillness.

I jumped up, running behind Rosie across the lawn to the driveway. She gathered her son onto her lap and held him, stroking his hair. "Shh, Andrew, it's all right, it's all right," she whispered, over and over until his wails faded and he snuffled against her shirt.

I knelt beside them, frantic to do something to help. The gravel had been pushed into a deep depression where he'd skidded and fallen. A small white sneaker, twin to the one upstairs in his room, lay in the center of the furrow. But it wasn't a twin; the white laces had been replaced. This sneaker had black laces, brand new and neatly threaded through the grommets, tied at the top in a perfect black bow.

Rosie saw it, too. She blanched and stared first at the sneaker and then at her son.

Blood dripped from a jagged cut on his temple, running in a bright, thick stream toward his eye.

Just then, the school bus started its climb up the drive.

"Send him away." Rosie pointed with her head at the yellow behemoth. "Go ahead, Lee. Send him away."

Andrew twisted in her arms and reached up to wipe his eye where the blood ran. My sister grabbed his wrist, dabbing at the blood with her other hand. Still holding him in her arms, she struggled to her feet. "Come on, honey, let me get you cleaned up. It's nothing, just a scratch."

The cut on Andrew's forehead was more than a scratch; he might even need a doctor's attention, stitches perhaps. But Rosie was taking care of him. I brushed off my knees and told the bus driver that Andrew wouldn't need a ride this morning. Panting, I ran to the house, dumped the sneaker in my closet, and ran to see about Andrew.

"There, now you look a little like a pirate with an eye patch that slipped." Rosie wadded up a blood-stained washcloth, tossed it in the sink, and smoothed back Andrew's hair.

"Can I see?" He climbed to the stepstool and frowned into the mirror. Gingerly, he touched the gauze pad Rosie had taped across his wound. "I don't look like a pirate. I look like a dork."

"A dork? Did you ever see a dork with such a cool belt? *I* certainly never did." I ran my finger along the pewter buckle with the Harley-Davidson insignia on it, and Andrew stopped sniffling and smiled.

"Did I miss the bus? I can still go to the party, right? Please, Mom. I'm all right, honest." He blew his nose in the tissue Rosie handed him.

"The bus left a while ago," I heard my sister say. "I'll have to drive you to school."

She was gone for over an hour.

"I just stood in the doorway of his classroom, looking through the glass window. He didn't see me. I had to make sure he was going to be all right," she said as she climbed the porch steps. She sat in the rocker beside me, her hair in disarray and her eyes clouded with worry.

"He's a resilient little boy. I'll bet he was playing with the other kids before ten minutes passed. Kids are amazing." At that moment, I wished for a child's memory, hurts forgotten in the time it takes to choose up teams for the next softball game.

"God, I hate lying. He knows it wasn't a raccoon that got into his room." Rosie glanced over at the pile of boards and sighed.

"You did right, Rosie. He's too young to know how to deal with it. It would have scared him half to death to see those clothes. You did the right thing."

The rocker creaked against the porchboards. Rosie stretched her legs into the patch of sunlight pouring through the railing.

"That sneaker. . . . That's the last thing, Lee. The last damn, ugly, threatening thing tied in a black bow. I'm not going to let *anything* else . . ." She shook her head slowly. "What am I talking about? Jesus, I can't *stand* sitting around and thinking about it any more."

My sister needed to be distracted; I snatched at a solution. "Why don't we finish up the painting? We'll get hot and sweaty, climb ladders, and make ourselves good and tired. What do you say, Rosie?"

"You think that will make it go away? I keep hearing him cry out . . . the blood pouring into his eye . . . the blood splattered on your face . . ."

I reached for her hand. "Try to let go. For a little while. We'll paint the house. Tomorrow, Paul will be back."

Worry lines etched the corners of Rosie's eyes. "Would you mind very much if just Andrew and I went to get him? You won't mind being alone here?"

Despite my fleeting pang at being shut out, I understood. "Well, maybe I won't be alone. How about if I enlist a helper and we make you dinner?" Don Ward wasn't a stranger to the kitchen; we could talk, cook, see if the spark between us still had any life, push away the darkness that had invaded our lives.

"So your menu is going to include bacon and asparagus omelettes?"

I took Rosie's teasing as a sign of her recovery. "It might. Don't you approve?" I asked, and I realized she hadn't heard me.

She leaned forward in the rocker, her spine straight and her hands gripping the armrests. "Andrew didn't say a word about that sneaker, the whole way to school. But he knows, Lee. He knows that something is terribly wrong. I saw him watching me when I walked out of the classroom, with that look, I've seen it before, he's trying to convince everyone how grown up, how unconcerned he is. Inside, he's terrified. But he's being brave. That's the kind of kid he is," she said fiercely.

25

I'd never seen that steely light in my sister's eyes. But it didn't last, and I was relieved when she slapped her hand on her knee and turned to me. "You really mean it about painting the house? Might as well take advantage of an offer like that." She shook her head, the hint of a smile gone. "I have to do *something.*"

Before she could reconsider, I changed into painting clothes and we set to work. The rhythm of each task lulled us: we spread drop-cloths on the bedding plants, hauled out the ladder and the paint cans and brushes, dipped our brushes and watched the thick ribbons of paint slither into the can. We concentrated on each brushstroke and spent what was left of the morning with only the birds and a yapping dog to disturb the peace we craved.

"Break time," Rosie announced an hour later. She wiped her forehead with the back of her hand, leaving a white streak above her left eye. "I nearly knocked over a full can of paint just now. I have to stop, Lee. I keep seeing Andrew's face. Poor baby, he doesn't understand any of this. I shouldn't have left him alone at school. Every time I think I should drive out there and get him, some part of me says that would be foolish, convinces me that he'll be all right."

Andrew wouldn't be home for hours. She still had lots of time to let that internal debate tear at her.

"Okay." I tapped my paint can closed and grabbed both brushes. "You shower, I'll clean up. Then while *I* shower you can make us sandwiches and something cold to drink."

Rosie looked as if she was about to argue, but she rolled up the dropcloths and nodded her assent.

Forty minutes later, we carried plates and glasses to the porch. Molten, silver clouds streamed across the horizon. "Feels good. Hard work, wet hair, warm breeze," I said as I plopped into one of the rockers. "Maybe I'll just sit here for the rest of my visit."

I bit into the lettuce-and-tomato-and-cheese sandwich my sister had set beside me on the table. Rosie fussed with her napkin, then nibbled at a piece of cheese that had fallen onto her plate.

"I'm going all the way," I announced. "I'm going to spend half an hour—no, a *whole* hour—reading in the middle of the day. I need to practice some self-indulgence. Hand me my book, would you?"

Rosie reached into the drawer; a puzzled frown creased her forehead. "What's this?"

A square of folded paper that looked as if it had been clipped from a newspaper stuck up from between the pages of the book.

We were about to uncover another part to our puzzle, I knew. This one hadn't come wrapped in a black bow, but I was certain it would fit somewhere among the other pieces. I wanted to tear the paper into hundreds of tiny pieces and let it fall like summer snow into the wind that was ruffling the maple leaves. By the time I pulled myself out of the chair to stand beside her, she had the paper unfolded.

The article looked as if it had been cut from a tabloid-size paper— no date, no name, no indication of where it came from. My head pounded as I scanned the headline; I had to read the first paragraph twice before the smaller print came into focus.

BOY LONE SURVIVOR OF NOONTIME FAMILY MASSACRE, the black letters screamed. FOUR DIE AT HANDS OF LONG-TIME COUNTY EMPLOYEE.

The paper trembled in Rosie's hands. I read on. A brutal slaying that wiped out a mother and three little daughters . . . multiple knife wounds . . . bodies in the family dining room and kitchen. The details were vivid, and the scene sprang to life in my mind.

Expressions of agony distorted the faces of the children; the mother, found cradling the smallest child in her arms, was frozen in a posture of perplexed entreaty. Upturned chairs, trampled chocolate cake, patterned gift-wrapping and ribbons lay scattered everywhere. Blood stained the walls, soaked into the floral wallpaper, pooled on the floor.

Nausea overcame me. The paper became still in Rosie's hands, "No. Oh, no, no," she repeated, as though she could stop an event that had already happened.

I forced myself to read the last paragraph. The father had been found dead the next morning in the front seat of the family car. Charles Amundsen had been under stress lately, the article reported, because he'd recently lost his job as manager of a county road crew.

"Is this a warning, do you think?" Rosie, white and still, looked as if she'd never seen me before.

"No. No, it's not a warning. It's an explanation." I pointed at the middle of the article, and she read on, tracing the words with her work-roughened finger.

The sole survivor, Jacob Amundsen, was found clinging to his mother's lifeless form. Young Jacob, who turned seven on June 26, saw his birthday party become a nightmare he will never forget. The boy has been unable to speak since authorities found him early Thursday morning.

"A birthday party, don't you see?" she whispered.

"Oh, God, Rosie. Just like I said the other night—flowers, a cake, candles, everything all wrapped in ribbon. That *is* what those horrible things meant. He's re-creating that awful event, and, for some reason, we're part of it." The air seemed thicker, hotter, but still I shivered. She hadn't said it, and I wouldn't, not yet.

Tomorrow was June 26.

"Maybe he's trying to rewrite his own history," I offered, plucking possibilities from air and testing them aloud. "Maybe he wants it to turn out with a different ending."

"Why did he put this in your book? What's the good of telling us now? Does this mean it's over, do you think?" she said quietly.

It is just beginning. It was hardly necessary to say that aloud.

"Maybe he wants something specific from us. I must be on the right track: he's trying to change the ending. But we can't bring back his dead family. Maybe he wants *us* to be his family."

"I already have all the family I want." Rosie raked her thick hair and let her hand drop to her lap. "Why would he send this to *us?*"

I couldn't answer. It was a problem I'd skirted all week. Stewart had made me ask myself the same question. I'd hoped the answer lay not in who I was but in who *he* was, aware that they were bound together in some way I didn't understand. Now, I realized I was unwilling to accept blame—someone had chosen to use Rosie and me as symbols of everything he feared or hated or even longed for but couldn't have. The knowledge made me angry.

"The name of the newspaper is missing," I said sharply. "It's been cut off. You know anyone named Amundsen? No, you don't, of course not. You'd have said right away. That's right, isn't it? You don't know anyone by that name."

"Lee, take it easy." Rosie's vagueness was gone, replaced now by an unfamiliar tightness at the corners of her mouth, a strange narrowing of her eyes. She jumped out of her chair, banging into the table and sending the lemonade glasses crashing. "Look who's talking," she muttered as she bent to pick up the glasses. "No, of course I don't know anyone named Amundsen."

"Well, I'm going to find out about this." I gathered the plates and pushed the screen door open.

Rosie stepped ahead of me, blocking my way. "What do you think you can do about it?"

"Something, I don't know what, but I'm not going to stand around waiting for the next nightmare to descend on us."

"I need to think about this. I don't want you rushing off on some wild chase until I've had the chance to make some sense of it." Her voice was cold; she didn't budge from the doorway.

"And I want you to tell me something: Do you know anything that would confirm that this article is about Hank Steuben?" A challenge— I tossed it at her like a fastball, and waited for her to swing.

But she let it ripple the air, not stepping up to it, not even aware that she was in the game. "No, I don't think it *is* about Hank. We can check, but I remember Peggy saying they were going to see Hank's brother. This spring, around Easter. The article doesn't say anything about a brother. I'm going to call Riley and tell him about this."

"Riley? What the hell do you think Riley's going to do? He's glad he can get back to his damn firebug. He's going to stick Hank with all this and maybe Stewart's murder, too, unless Hank can come up with an alibi, like having dinner with the damn governor or something.

Riley won't drive out here again for a newspaper clipping. He wouldn't come unless . . . someone got hurt." I censored my real thought: *Riley would pay attention if a local got killed,* I had almost said.

"I *am* calling Riley. That's the first step. Then I'll decide what to do next. Andrew will be home in an hour and I won't let him be upset any more than he already has been. Don't talk about this in front of him, Lee."

I glared at her. I could avoid talking about it, but I couldn't pretend that Riley was going to understand the newspaper article or do anything about it.

Her voice, as she clutched the receiver, was calm and assured, and when she told Riley about the article, she might have been explaining to Andrew why the leaves drop from the trees in autumn. Riley's answer didn't take very long.

Tight-jawed, she reported that Riley had told her to save the article. He'd get to it when he could. Meanwhile, he'd said, not to worry. Hank Steuben was still in jail.

26

Rosie sat at her kitchen desk for a long time, silent, her eyes focused on something I would never see. When she finally stirred, she said, "Aunt Christa told me something once."

"Rosie, what are you talking about? What does Aunt Christa have to—"

"Remember the year you went to Girl Scout camp? I guess she decided I'd do as a substitute, and she started to talk to me the way she did to you. Telling me things about how she never liked her hair and how if only she could lose five pounds she'd be a different person and men would find her attractive and what did I think of Harry Crawford and all that stuff."

It would never end, this revision of history, but I didn't care about this particular correction, not now. "What did she tell you?"

She looked past me, out the window. "I never told you she'd confided in me because I wanted you to go on feeling special. I didn't want to take that away from you. Anyway, in that week, I just remembered this, she told me she'd heard this terribly sad story from Mom and Grandma Montara. It was him, Lee, I know it."

Thoroughly confused, I waited.

"It makes a little more sense now," she murmured, "even though I can't remember some of the important details. She said she heard about some poor woman who had to sell all her land so that she could stay home and take care of an orphaned boy. She went on and on about how awful it was to have to give up land that had been in the family for generations, could I imagine if Grandma and Grandpa had to sell this house and the land, how would we feel, what would we do."

Losing this place was unthinkable. Even though I'd moved to the city, I'd always known that a piece of my past remained virtually untouched, within easy access to me. But how was this bringing us closer to the answers we needed?

"Aunt Christa never said who the woman or the little boy were. All her coy teasing—she made me so mad, I remember. But she did say the little boy had been behaving badly in school, refusing to wash his hands before lunch, lining up dead flies in the pencil slot on his desk. *That* I remember. It made my skin crawl when she told me, and I dreamed about dead bugs for weeks. She told me something else.

"I'm sure she said he got sent home every day for a week because he kept cutting up his own shirts in the classroom."

And, years later, crept into my sister's house and slashed all my nephew's clothing? I began to understand why Rosie was telling me this story now.

Rosie stood. She straightened a book on the shelf above her desk, pinched a dead leaf from the philodendron plant she used as a bookend. "I should have remembered this when we came home last night, but I didn't. I'm *sure*, Lee. I'm absolutely certain that the little boy Aunt Christa told me about is the same one in this article. A little boy who survived seeing his mother and sisters murdered by his father surely would develop strange behavior, especially in the first months, even years afterward. He'd have a very hard time adjusting to any new situation, a new school, a new life. Maybe he lives in Taconic Hills or somewhere close by. Maybe he left that newspaper clipping here because he really wants us to catch him. To save him from himself."

Rosie crumpled the dead leaf in her hand. "He'd better not come near me or my child. Because saving him is the last thing on my mind. I *am* going to pick Andrew up from school."

I knew, from her expression and from the terrible coldness in her voice, that her anger was all she had room for. If we were going to find out more about the horrifying events the newspaper recounted, it would be up to me. It just didn't seem possible that Hank Steuben had been responsible for everything that had happened to us in the past week. It had required forethought, preparations too elabora' ` for the simple mind and the visceral hate of Hank Steuben. The more ı turned it over in my mind, the more certain I became: Hank simply didn't have enough imagination to mount an ongoing campaign of terror. But he had been lurking in the driveway at four in the morning, had cursed and sputtered with rage when I cut short his attempt at an apology. I couldn't dismiss him, not yet.

If I could find out his birthday. . . . If someone could prove that his family wasn't named Amundsen. . . . His wife would know, of course, but dropping in on Peggy Steuben would be both cruel and disingenuous. Keen as I was for information, I wouldn't do that. Chances were she wouldn't tell me anyway.

If not Hank, who? If not tomorrow, when?

Several people in every small town were privy to secrets. I didn't want to endure Ruth Hoving's scrutiny; second best but still a good source, Ben Yarnell, the editor of the *Taconic Journal*, would surely have something to report.

The road was deserted. Some other day I would have thought of it as serene, but the lack of traffic only heightened my terrible isolation. Yards, too, were empty of people. The tidy houses, usually so cheery and welcoming, lurked along the roadside like fortresses concealing hidden enemies.

Relieved, I spotted a solitary figure in a distant yard. Stooped over a woody azalea bush, even Dolores Farly was a welcome sight. I raised my hand to offer a wave, and then, impulsively, hit the brakes hard.

Even in retirement, Dolores still kept tabs on the comings and goings in this town and its people. She might be able to tell me something.

I spun the wheel and squealed to a stop in front of a huge white oak, its topmost leaves reaching past the roofline of the modest house.

Four brown hens squawked and scattered. Startled by the noise, Dolores Farley straightened and glanced at the small chicken coop beside the house, a dirt-clotted trowel dangling from her hand. She wiped the other hand on her canvas apron and shielded her eyes, peering at me over the rose bushes that bordered the lawn. It took her a moment to recognize me; when she did, she scurried on her thick legs to the front walk.

"Why, Lee Montara, I didn't expect visitors. Can I get you a cool drink? You look a little peaked. Is something wrong?" A frown creased her forehead.

Through the screen door, I heard the clink of silverware against china. I saw Joseph Farley, dressed in his postal-blue shirt and red bow tie, sitting at the kitchen table, knife poised above a brick of yellow cheese. I nodded in his direction, then turned back to Dolores. I tried to reassure her with a smile; no need to get anyone else upset with details, certainly not Dolores, who would only take it on herself to try to say something comforting when comfort wasn't what I needed.

"No, nothing's wrong. I was just passing by and I thought you might be able to tell me about someone I'm looking for. You always paid such attention to all the kids when you were working at Roe-Jan. I think this person may have been a student at Roe-Jan when you were there."

Her sigh convinced me that Rosie had been right about Dolores missing her old job.

"I'd really like to help you . . ." The trowel still dangling from her hand, she looked down at her soiled shoes and edged closer to the driveway. "I'd invite you in but I'm all muddy and whatnot. Now, what's this about a student?"

I didn't want to alarm her by showing her the article. "I'm trying to track down someone I read about in a newspaper article, a fellow named Amundsen."

Dolores closed her pale eyes and bit her lip, then shook her head. "Maybe you should . . ." She wiped one hand on her apron. "Maybe you should talk to Ben Yarnell, over at the *Journal*. I'm sorry, I can't help you, Lee." She hesitated, then shrugged. "Maybe you should try the school secretary . . ."

But school was out for the day. For the year. I lingered on the concrete step. There had to be some way for me to track down the story that Rosie had dredged up from her memory.

Back to Plan A; Ben Yarnell was still my best shot.

The offices of the *Taconic Hills Journal* were half a mile outside of town in a squat brick building that shared a parking lot with the Columbia County Historical Society. I hadn't seen Ben Yarnell since a Fourth of July party two years ago at Ike Kronenburg's farm, but I'd gotten the feeling that Ben admired me for taking myself so completely out of my old country life and creating another that suited me so much better. Ben had done the reverse: a privileged childhood in Boston had been traded for the editorship of a twice weekly newspaper in Taconic Hills, and both the town and the *Journal* had become the passions of his chosen life.

I knocked on his door and took his distracted grunt to be an invitation to come in. Pleasant and almost scholarly in his glasses and white shirt and tie, Ben's smile broadened when he looked up.

"Lee. Have a seat, I'll be with you in a minute." He waved me to the one chair in the room not piled with papers and books. I picked up a scuffed blue Frisbee and turned it in my hands while he made a quick notation on a paper in front of him. He propped his feet on his desk; red socks winked out beneath the cuff of his trousers. "You play? Hurt my shoulder last month, so I have to lay off for a while. Give that to Andrew, why don't you. One less thing lying around here. Listen, you must be a mind reader. I was just about to call Rosie. Is this a social visit?"

Smiling, I shook my head and ran my finger along the grooves on the plastic surface of the Frisbee. "Not that I don't like your company, Ben, but I need some information. I know the paper won't be out until Monday, but you're already working on the Hank Steuben story, right?"

His face became grave. He clasped his hands behind his head and said, "Well, it's the body in the field that's big time for this burg. For now, I'm concentrating on the details of the murder, where the body was found, what the law enforcement officials did in what order, that kind of thing. Riley's being weird about saying any more than the bare facts. I did try to get hold of you and your sister not five minutes ago to ask about this Steuben business but the line was busy. You've all been through a bad time, from what Riley tells me."

Close-mouthed about his corpse, Riley *was* willing to talk about us. The last thing Rosie needed now was a reporter, even one as sympathetic as Ben, asking her questions. I hoped she wasn't being hounded by reporters from other local papers while I was off hunting down the Amundsen family.

"Listen, Ben, I don't have much to say right now, on or off the record. And Rosie *is* worn out from all this, so if you can, I'd really appreciate your waiting a day or two to ask her anything."

His feet dropped to the floor and he leaned across his desk, his eyes steady and serious. "Can't promise. But if I can avoid it and still put out a decent newspaper, I will. So why are you here, Lee?"

"Two things. Have you ever heard of a Jacob Amundsen? And second, I want to know Hank's birthday and where he grew up." It didn't take someone as astute as Ben to know these weren't idle questions.

"You're not going to tell me what this is about?"

Maybe, after I'd found out what I needed to know, I'd have a story for him, but I wasn't ready yet. "How about if I tell you Sunday, at the latest? I'm going back to the city then, and I promise to spill everything before I do."

Ben laughed. "The old exclusive interview trick? Sometimes I really do feel like life is one long movie script and by now, the words are starting to sound familiar. Okay. Two pieces of information, in return for an exclusive on Sunday. You got yourself a deal. First of all, I never heard the name Jacob Amundsen before. As for Hank—" He opened a manila folder and tossed papers, one at a time, in a heap on his desk. "Here. Hank Steuben blah blah blah. From Plattsburgh, New York, parents still run the same appliance repair business there. Born December fifteenth nineteen hundred and—"

But the year didn't matter. Whatever Ben Yarnell said after that was lost to me, because my mind was reeling. Still holding the Frisbee, I left his office and sat in my car, desperate for inspiration.

The pizza place in Millerton was bustling; Debbie Decker looked overwhelmed, racing from kitchen to patio with a full tray of drinks, returning with dirty dishes and glasses, stopping before she picked up the next order to hastily total a check. I waited until she pulled the green slip from her pad. Then I approached her.

"Hi, Debbie. I'm Lee Montara, Rosie Cooper's—"

"I know. There's a seat at the counter if you want. Excuse me, I have to get this order out." She swept her hair back and grabbed the pizza with a hot pad, then disappeared outside.

A line had begun to form behind me. I wanted to get this over with, so I stood in the doorway. When Debbie came in, she looked startled to see me blocking her way. "When is Rick's birthday?" I asked before she had the chance to get around me.

"Why don't you just ask *him?*" Her smooth skin wrinkled with her frown.

"Ask him? Is he back?"

"Yesterday. He came home in the morning. You can tell your sister, she'll want to know. Now, if you'll excuse me, there are customers waiting. I have to—"

I stood in front of her. "His birthday, Debbie, when is it?"

"April eighth. Now please get out of my way. I have to get these people seated." Frowning, she hurried past me to the next group on line.

Her response was too automatic to have been a lie, unless it was one that she had been told all her life and believed. Still, one thing was clear: Rick Decker, whatever his birthday, had returned to Taconic Hills in time to be around on June 26.

I'd used up my best sources and now I had to reach for straws. Mom would require endless explanation, why did I want to know, what was wrong, how did I come up with the name Amundsen, but if nothing else seemed fruitful, I would have to phone her in Florida. Maybe she would remember what Aunt Christa claimed never to know. Besides, all of this frantic running about had kept me away from Rosie long enough.

"It's started," she said before I even set my purse down. "The newspapers have been calling, asking questions about Hank and what happened here. I'm not sure they know there's a connection to Stewart McClaren's murder yet."

"I should have warned you that would happen." I sighed. "Not that a warning would make it any easier to deal with. It's just that you'd have been prepared. You have to listen to me, Rosie. I don't care what Riley thinks. I don't believe it was Hank who did all those things. Ben Yarnell had some background information. He told me Hank's birthday is in December, and that his parents still live in

Plattsburgh. It doesn't work. And unless his sister is a very good liar, it's not Rick either."

"Rick . . . You know, it made me feel good to have him look at me that way. I held on to it too long, that's all. I go through these times, they don't last long, when my life seems so uneventful. I start a new project or take a class at the community college and that's usually enough. It took me too long to see the truth, that's all." She touched her hair, then let her hands fall to her lap.

She was telling me something important about her choices, and about what hadn't changed in her. I had never been my sister's keeper, and I didn't need to be now.

She shivered and her back straightened. "I remember when Rick was born. His parents are both still alive; nothing like that ever happened to him. Anyway," she said, her voice crisp with authority, "I figured out what to do."

27

If you examine your life very carefully, you realize that some of the truly important milestones, perhaps even the most significant changes, often hinge on a moment. You have a choice, maybe many options, and you pick one and everything after that springs out of the single moment in which you said, "Go this way," instead of taking any of the other roads in front of you. Robert Frost knew; now I did, too. Faced with whatever Rosie had decided and what I thought we could expect, I needed to be sure we were headed in the right direction.

The first step was to cut back the speed and stop this forward hurtling.

"Where's Andrew? I want to give him this Frisbee."

My sister stared dreamily into space. "After I picked Andrew up at school, I drove over to Don's. I asked Don about his birthday. He gave me the oddest answer at first. He said John Alden should speak for herself. What did that mean?"

My patience snapped. "Just a joke about why didn't I ask if I
wanted to know. You said 'at first.' Did he *ever* tell you?"

"He's a Pisces. March sixteenth."

March sixteenth. I wanted to believe that. I wanted Don's line
about John Alden not to have been a stall for time in which to think
up a lie. It had to be a joke intended for me, a way to say that even if
he didn't celebrate occasions, I should ask him myself if I wanted to
know his birthday.

Most of all, I wanted to trust him, as Rosie did. But I couldn't reach
that deep now.

"Andrew's with Don," Rosie said, and she picked at the seam of
her jeans. "I brought the kitten back with me. I told Don I was worn
out and didn't know if I could handle the drive upstate. They're on
their way. Don says they'll drive for four hours, stop somewhere for
dinner, maybe find a motel with a pool near Paul's campsite. Andrew
loved that idea. Then they'll only have a short drive in the morning.
Paul can't leave until eleven tomorrow morning. They won't be back
until early afternoon. I promised Don and Andrew we'd have a special dinner tomorrow night."

What had she done? "Why, Rosie?"

"Before I went to Don's, I called Riley again. He's still insisting
he's got his man. He told me he was leaving for Vermont, that they
think they got the arsonist, up in Manchester. He said there was no
need for me to get all worked up over the article. It didn't mean
anything, he said. I should be relieved that Hank is in jail. So I had to
ask Don. Andrew will be safe with him. It's almost over, Lee."

I forced myself to sit very quietly and look into my sister's face; her
composure, I knew, had nothing to do with Riley's assurances. What I
saw behind her eyes was the cold, brilliant light of conviction and the
heat of contained fury.

"Why Don, Rosie? What makes you so sure Andrew's going to be
safe with Don?"

"I know," she said firmly. "Paul and I have known Don almost a
year now, and I can tell about a person. I even met his mother, she
came for Christmas. Nice woman. You'd like her. Besides, he really
was born on March sixteenth. I made him show me his driver's license."

Rosie and I lived in worlds so incomprehensibly different that I
couldn't tell if either of them corresponded to the truth.

My sister didn't understand why I was looking at her with such horror.

And I couldn't believe that Rosie had let her son go off with a man she hardly knew, simply because he had a driver's license that claimed his birthday was not tomorrow.

"Don showed you his license?"

Rosie frowned, as though she didn't understand my question. "Yes. His birthday. It was right there. March sixteenth. Now, listen, we need to talk about this."

I couldn't have agreed more. "Rosie, people can get phony birth certificates and driver's licenses. It's ridiculously easy to falsify documents."

With her hand, she brushed away my objections. "We have to talk about tomorrow, Lee. What we're going to do. How we're going to stop him. You know, it doesn't even matter who he is, not really. The thing that counts now is what we do. We need to make preparations. Personally, I think it's pretty clear."

Only someone who knew her could tell that her flat voice and those eyes were evidence that something in my sister had slipped over an edge.

"Rosie, wait, it's not at all clear. We can't do what you're proposing. We're not talking about some reasonable person you can say the right things to and then he'll stop. Whoever this man is, he's already killed someone. And he's very clever."

"And is his cleverness a match for my determination, do you think?"

There was no good answer, and I knew it. Either way, Rosie wouldn't hear my answer.

I didn't respond, and that brought me a little closer to the path she intended to take.

"So here's what we'll do, Lee. We'll wait. We'll stay home tomorrow. We'll wait for the party to begin. And when it does, you have the gun, we'll subdue him and call the sheriff's department. Someone will come get him and he won't ever bother us again."

It sounded so simple. And so wrong.

"And if he has a gun, too? What then, Rosie?"

I wanted her to see the flaws in her logic, to realize on her own that she wasn't thinking clearly. As the seconds ticked on and she didn't answer, I wondered if she was capable of hearing anything at all.

Finally, she spoke. "If we have to, we'll shoot him."

I'll shoot him. That's what she was really saying. "I can't do this, Rosie. I can't talk about shooting someone. There has to be another way. You stay here. I need to be by myself for a few minutes. I'll be back."

Afraid to leave Rosie alone for too long, unable to sit with her and give my approval to her bizarre plan, I sought temporary refuge in the kitchen. Was it really as simple as she suggested? Subdue him and call the police. Use the argument of the gun to convince him that we would never again let him turn us into victims.

Him. Who was he?

I dialed the number of the Florida apartment to which Mom and Dad had moved the year after I went to the city. The phone rang interminably but no one answered. I hung up just as Rosie entered the room.

She sat down across from me at the table, her hands folded, and began to talk as though I hadn't interrupted our dialogue to search for a little quiet and some answers. "Two more days. You're going back in two days."

Caught up in the concerns of the present, I'd forgotten that I'd be sleeping in the little bedroom with the eyebrow windows only two more nights, would have two more breakfasts on the porch with my sister and her family.

"But I'll come up and visit every once in a while. Weekends, whatever." This wasn't the time to say that I'd been meaning to keep more in touch; I was certain of my intentions, but I might forget them, gradually, in the press of my daily life. . . .

"I'm glad you're here with me *now,*" she said adamantly. "You're family; I can count on you. Remember when you called and asked if you could come for a week. I never told you, but I had this feeling, just a little flash but it was there, of resentment. That you would think my life was so, I don't know, interruptable. I had no idea just what kind of interruption I'd have."

Confused and offended, I wanted to avoid an argument. Still, I couldn't help defending myself. "But you said anytime. When we spoke a couple of weeks ago. That's exactly what you—"

"I know." Rosie smiled and reached out; I let her fingers cover mine. "I meant it, too. The resentment didn't last, but it made me see something about us, about the way we lose touch with each other."

I took a deep breath to release the tightness in my chest. "I love you, Rosie," I whispered.

the Seduction

"All our resolutions won't last, you know. Even if we're careful, Lee, there are going to be times when we'll fall back into those old ways. But it can never be exactly as it was before. *Nothing* will ever be the same. I want you to understand, so I'll say it again. This is my home, Lee." She let go of my hand and curled her fingers into a fist. "He invaded it and made my child afraid and turned everything about this place into something ugly and terrifying. I won't accept that. I have to do something to take it back. I've been thinking—it's a way to make things clean again."

My sister had careened back to the problem of Jacob Amundsen; I struggled to shift gears and keep up with her. "That's not your job, Rosie, it's too—"

"I have had to wipe away too much blood!" Her face was pale with fury; the muscles along her jaw tightened. "Those balloons. And my baby . . . *he* did that, he left that sneaker and Andrew fell and . . . all that blood streaming down his sweet face, Lee. He did that to my baby. I have to make it clean."

"No, Rosie. You don't. Riley will—"

"Riley *won't*. You said it yourself. Go ahead, try. Call him. See if you can do any better than I did. There's the phone, go on."

It was a dare, and Rosie knew I could never resist a dare.

I took another step down her path when I reached again for the phone.

The dispatcher answered; I asked for Riley.

"I'm sorry, he's away until Sunday, maybe Monday. Can someone else help you?"

I almost laughed aloud. I doubted it; I'd have to help myself through this one. "This is Lee Montara, Rosie Cooper's sister. Listen, I want to talk to someone about this newspaper article my sister found in—"

"Ma'am? Officer Hamm already told your sister that Hank Steuben is in custody. She's called several times, and I told her and Officer Hamm told her not to worry. Maybe you should get a doctor, see if he can give her something to help her relax. Honestly, Miss Montara, I know it's been hard on you both but you have to accept that there's nothing to worry about."

I couldn't bring myself to say good-bye. When I hung up, I turned to look for Rosie, to tell her I understood her frustration.

"He's coming at noon, Lee. That's what the article said—the party was at noon. And I need you to stay with me."

At that moment, I made my choice.

I would walk beside my sister down the road she had chosen. God help us, we were going together.

11:45 a.m.

The whirl in my brain has slowed and now I can grab onto my thoughts. All this time, worrying about keeping the house locked, we have forgotten about the cellar door. He has been using the cellar door to come and go as he pleased. What else have we missed? I don't know, but I cannot begin down that spiral of wondering and worrying.

What I do know, clearly and without question, is that it's up to me. Me and Rosie. Getting out of this whole and unharmed is something we must do on our own. Remembering this only serves to make me more certain, to screw my resolve more firmly in place.

Without a telephone, I'll have to make an adjustment to our original plan. I have to get Rosie away from him. And it should be simple, knowing what he's done and what he's capable of, to figure out the next step and make sure he understands that we're finished with letting him have his way.

The weight of the gun is soothing. The shaft glitters coldly in the overhead light. I remember the instructions: Two hands, legs planted;

both sights lined up. And I feel in my outstretched arms the recoil, and hear the blast of sound, and remember the small black tear in the target, and the unholy feeling of transformation.

Before I can get my thoughts clear of the gun, Rosie appears in the doorway. He is behind her, and his face looks exactly as it always has, without enough expression to gauge what he might be thinking or feeling. *Feeling.* I can't allow myself to suppose he has feelings, it takes too much from me that I need.

"Well, now, look at this. We're both well equipped," he says in a voice that is deeper than I remember, and when they step into the hall, I can see that he is pressing a deer-skinning knife against Rosie's ribs, where a lung opens and empties, opens and empties, just beneath.

"You don't want to hurt her, Joseph." The calm words are coming from a place that is not me, from a place I have never been.

"You're right. I don't want to hurt her. But that doesn't mean I won't. I like my new knife. Do you know—when I was a child, I never had new things. I always got stuff that had someone else's smell on it, but this knife, it's mine. Nobody else has ever used it. Now, let's go into the kitchen. It's easier to clean up in a kitchen, don't you think?"

Thoughtful. I picture Don Ward, hands plunged in soapy water, and I am glad it was someone else in the cellar. Joseph pushes Rosie forward and steps closer to me. He whirls around when he hears my nervous laugh. His nostrils flare with anger.

"You think I'm joking?"

Rosie is pale, like almonds, like pearls, and she hasn't spoken since she's come up the stairs. Can we understand each other without words? *Don't worry, I'll take care of him,* I signal her with my eyes, and I think I see her shoulders relax, it's only a small difference but it is change.

"No, Joseph, I don't think you're joking. This isn't something to joke about, not at all. Okay, let's go into the kitchen."

I move ahead, and they are right behind me. I can smell him, excited, sharp, like lemons about to rot.

The light in the kitchen is too bright, and I can see every spidery capillary on his nose, every pore on his chin. He looks around, then waves me to the chair at the head of the table.

"You sit there. We're going to stand here for now."

For now. *How long will this take?* I move to the table, my hand protecting the gun in my pocket so that it won't thump against my hip as I pull out the chair. I leave it far from the table so that I can move quickly if I must.

I have to get him talking. This is our plan, and Rosie and I have choreographed it so that we can entice him to join our dance, he will be unable to keep his story from waltzing out, and that will give us time and the opportunity to surprise him.

"Joseph, we know you're upset. This isn't going to help anything. Now, let's see if we can figure out what to do."

His face twists into a painful smile and he keeps his grip tight on Rosie's collar. "We? What do you mean *we?* You and her, you're family. I'm out of it, right?"

I watch his hand, white and smooth and almost feminine, clutching the fabric of my sister's shirt as though he has reached into a bin of corn to grasp a handful of feed for the chickens his aunt Dolores keeps. He opens his fingers and the collar stays in the same crumpled place.

Rosie shrugs away from him, but he waves the knife again, close to her pretty, freckled cheek, and she stops moving.

Did one of his sisters have freckles?

"Why don't you leave her alone and we'll figure out how to help you?" I offer. I register how he blinks his eyes, how his breathing moves his shirt slightly where it's sticking to his skin. I imagine his chest, white, bald like an infant's, and the thought makes my stomach knot.

"I know the kind of help I need. I need your fire to make me clean. I laid the kindling, and your sister here is the spark. And you're going to burst into flame until there are only ashes left." His face is blank. He tilts his head and asks, "Do you like ashes?"

Before I can answer, he continues. "I do, soft, powdery ashes, silky like a child's hair. Like my hair when I was little. He used to touch my hair and my face while he read the newspaper. He called me his boy."

He is focused on the past: He is not paying attention to us. I slide closer to the edge of the chair. Rosie ducks and her right arm flies out toward his throat, the fist of her hand tight and small.

Startled, Joseph jumps away and her wrist comes down hard on the edge of the sink.

"Don't."

That's all he says. He backs up his resolve by holding the knife at her ribs again and pushing her toward a chair. Rosie sits down, and I do, too.

It takes all my strength not to rush up and grapple with him for the knife. But I am unwilling to risk Rosie getting hurt, at least not this early. We haven't used up all our chances yet.

"You know," I say, watching his hands and his face, "Dolores has been very worried about you. Sometimes, when people are under stress, they don't sleep and they don't eat. They behave in ways that aren't, well, in their own best interests. You do need help, Joseph, a hospital where they'll work with you and get your body and your mind healthy again." I do not say *your tortured* mind; it seems unnecessary.

His snort is contemptuous. "She's not my mother, she doesn't know what I need. I have my own interests in mind, don't you worry. I'm thirsty," he says. "Don't move."

He reaches into the cabinet and takes down Andrew's Mets cup, fumbles for the faucet. Rosie, I can see, is tense and waiting, seeking the right moment to make another move. He twists the faucet shut, drinks the whole cupful down in three gulps.

"We've been thinking about today, Joseph," Rosie says evenly. "We knew you'd come today. We read about your birthday."

His expression hasn't changed, he isn't showing us anything that's going on inside. "You *what?*" he rasps as he grabs a fistful of Rosie's shirt again. "How?"

I think what he really means is how did we know and not let him or anyone else know about it. I don't want to explain to him that he was, at least in some measure, successful at preparing us for this moment because he forced us to fall back on our own resources. I like to think of it that way; it's so much less vulnerable than saying we were afraid.

This is risky, what I am about to do, but Rosie and I have decided it will tip him into a quagmire filled with his own demons. We must do this: This is the only way we will have a sure advantage.

I fumble in my pocket and lay the newspaper clipping on the table. "*She* gave this to you." He reaches for the paper, releasing Rosie as he snatches up the faded, brittle page.

Rosie slams both her hands down, fingers clasped together as though in prayer, on his wrist. The knife clatters to the floor. Rosie and I jump up. Amid the confusion of arms and legs scuffling for the steel, I try to push him aside. Rosie is closest, can reach the knife more easily, if only I can keep him out of her way.

Chairs crash against the table. The sickening thud of a head hitting the floor doesn't stop the flailing, and I don't know anymore where the knife is, I know nothing except that I've got Joseph's arms pinned for a moment and when I look up, Rosie is standing by the sink, panting. The knife is in her hand.

"Get up, Joseph, and stand right here." With the knife, she points to the bare center of the room. Her face is transformed. It is as though she sees nothing but that spot in the middle of the floor.

I let him go and he pushes up onto his hands and knees, like a wary cat. He struggles to his feet and stands there, mouth open and arms hanging at his sides, palms toward us. "You have the knife now," he says.

"You've had your turn," Rosie says quietly, "and now it's mine." She doesn't say *ours;* I am not included in this moment.

Rosie takes one step toward him, then another. She is standing so close to me that I can see the fine beads of sweat on her face.

She touches the tip of the knife to the soft skin under his jaw. His head jerks up, his eyes wild.

"You have given my son nightmares," Rosie says, and her hand moves, ever so slightly. "You have made my son bleed."

When she drops her arm to her side, a spot of scarlet, bright and glistening, springs up from his neck.

"Get your camera, Lee."

Her voice seems to come from somewhere else. I am confused, and I cannot move. She waves her free hand in the direction of her neat little desk and says it again. "The camera. Get it, Lee."

Joseph moans and he clutches his neck, eyes widening at the sight of his own bloodied hand. He brushes his disheveled hair back into place. A smear of blood darkens his temple above his right eye. He moves toward the sink, but Rosie pushes at his shoulder.

"Sit in the chair and put your hands on the table."

He obeys.

I am still frozen, wondering what she is thinking, unable to look at her face, which has become fixed into sharp planes of dark and light. Her softness is gone. The blade of the knife is now pointed at the place where his cheek is round and fleshy.

"Take his picture. I want everyone to know. Do it, Lee."

I am breaking with sorrow. Rosie has already broken, and has been put back together into something I don't recognize. I have no bearings, no guide for what to do next, and I stand and move slowly toward the desk. I want to delay her action, so that she can come to her senses. Can I struggle with her and still keep watch over him? I accede to her demand.

The camera is cold to my touch and feels almost as heavy as the gun I haven't yet taken from my pocket.

12:00

"You didn't have to do this. Just because you were suffering, you didn't have to take us along with you. Go ahead, Lee, full face, left profile, right profile. The way they do in the jail." Standing behind him, she places one hand on his chin, plants the other on his crown where the part of his hair ends. She twists his head roughly. A cry snags in his throat. My sister is waiting for me to take his picture, and I lift the camera.

I point the lens somewhere near his shoulder; I cannot focus on his tortured face; I will not include Rosie in this picture. When the flash goes off I am startled, expecting an explosion and a kick, like firing the Colt on the shooting range. Still in my pocket, the gun no longer seems like a protection but this isn't over and I'm unwilling to discount it.

Joseph looks so small with Rosie behind him, his long, fat, smooth fingers twined together on the table, frightened and harmless.

I imagine those fingers clasped around Stewart McClaren's throat. "Did you kill him?" I ask, knowing there's no need to say who he is, wondering why I am bothering to engage him in talk. This is not the way I thought things would go, but it seems necessary to postpone something happening that will shatter us all.

Joseph Farley's snort is contemptuous. "He never even heard me until I tripped over his feet. He saw me with the flowers. I knew those telephone calls wouldn't be enough; I needed her fear, you see?"

Rosie's mouth twists into a grotesque smile. "You thought I would just disintegrate in fear? You forgot about *anger*, Joseph."

But Joseph is too intent on his story to notice the interruption. "I made another plan, and he was about to ruin everything. What was he doing in your yard, watching you with binoculars? Thought he could scare me off with dirty words. Words. They're sounds, that's all. It's what you do that counts. I can do things that matter, you know. You looked at me when I came by with the mail and you never once saw me. Like I was a tree or a barn, just part of the scenery. But I can do things. He was in my way. Afterward, I tested the knife on his hair. Just to see how sharp it was. I had a plan," he says, squirming in the chair, "and he wasn't going to stop me. You understand?"

Rosie yanks his hair back. "So that's how you proved you could *do something*? By killing a human being? By bringing us things tied up in black bows? By breaking into my house to cut up my son's clothes? Why didn't you just kill yourself and finish the job your father started?"

"Rosie!"

I can't help the cry that escapes me, but she is braced for it and doesn't move, doesn't blink. Whatever she is thinking, I can't see it and I wonder whether she is thinking at all or merely saying things aloud to prove to herself that she can bypass her own rules. My sister seems to be exploding out from some center of her that is beyond my understanding.

Joseph Farley's chest is heaving and his pink skin has no shine; it is waxy now, as though he has been dipped in a preservative to keep him from losing more color. But his eyes look out with a victory light; he is basking in the sick pride of what he has done. "You're the one going to finish what my father started. You, you're the one."

"You did this to me," Rosie says, her voice bright with bitterness. "You shouldn't have."

A grimace cracks the triumph on Joseph's face. "I had to. Those other times, the milk truck, the ladder, they were all wrong. It has to be the same way for me as it was for them, for my sisters and my . . . You're so smart. I'm sure you already know that."

I feel as though I am watching a play performed by people who speak a language I've never heard before.

Rosie jabs at him with the knife, and the fabric of Joseph's shirt rips with a screech. "You tried to lure *me* into finishing what Charles Amundsen began, didn't you?"

The words come with their own blinding light, and it shows every moment since my arrival in Taconic Hills for the dark, manipulated performance it has been.

The child who blamed himself for what happened to his family, who managed to survive a bloody, horrible rampage, who desperately needed to share the fate of his mother and sisters.

The adult who tried and failed, who walked in front of a speeding truck and threw himself from a ladder and recovered both times.

The man who, ultimately, required an executioner.

"You don't know everything. You or her, I didn't care which. After she got here, I thought she'd be the one, not you." He nods in my direction. His smile mocks me, taunting me with his belief that I would say yes to his seduction.

He saw a need in me, that night at the ice cream stand, to make things right. Because it suited him, he decided I loved justice in the abstract, that I was capable of killing someone who invaded the lives of my family. He saw in me only the seed of anger, thought he could coax it into violence, the violence he'd decided was his salvation. He doesn't understand the tempering effect of time. For him, the years have only gnawed at the edges of his wound until emptiness is all that's left in him. Instead of blind anger, he has awakened my pity.

"We can get you help, Joseph. You should have been treated when you were a child. Someone should have made sure that you saw a therapist. . . ." My words trail off and the quiet that fills the room feels dangerous.

Outside, quicksilver drops fall from the leaves of the maple tree and plink onto hard surfaces. I had no intention of speaking of this but it may be the wedge I need. We all share this knowledge but I go on, trying to forestall any action from the other two. "She must have known for a long time, two years at least, that you were cracking apart. Since that day you stepped in front of the milk truck, your birthday, wasn't it? And then last year, falling off the ladder. But that wasn't good enough. It had to be a knife, I see that now. She shouldn't have let you suffer without making sure you got help."

Joseph, oblivious now to the knife Rosie holds near his throat, begins to speak. "Who would that have been to get me help? My father's sister? Tried to get me to call her Mommy, she's so stupid. Dolores Farley didn't know what to do with me, not from the minute I arrived at her house thirty years ago until today."

A quiver of his lower lip is cut short. "Anyway, that's not the way it's done around here. She wouldn't even know to think like that. She asked me about the black bows, did I hear about them, what did I think they meant. After a while, I knew she knew. She told me she was going to bring that box of fabric here, and I knew she was going to warn you."

Not then, but eventually Dolores did find a way to tell us. I don't remind him of the article. I am suddenly afraid for her. "Dolores is all right, isn't she, Joseph?"

His smile is sly. "Dolores can live off her fat for weeks. But she won't have to. You tell them that she's locked in a closet in her own bedroom. Tell them that when they come for my body."

"Why did you lock her up? You shouldn't have—"

"A lot of things *shouldn't have.* They don't matter any more. This is what is. Are you going to protect your sister or not?" And he jumps out of the chair and grabs Rosie's hand. Her face turns red, and she struggles to hold onto the knife.

I take the Colt out of my pocket. My hands are slick with sweat and I squint at Rosie and Joseph. They are locked in an angry embrace, a grappling beast, two-headed and thrashing about. Whatever I learned on the gun range, it had nothing to do with this confusion.

I will not take the chance that I will hit Rosie instead of him. I replace the safety. I put the gun back in my pocket, lift the wood cutting board from the counter behind me, and bring it down, hard and swift, on Joseph's right hand.

I am both startled and pleased to hear his scream. He crumples, howling in pain and fury, clutching the injured hand with his good one. Rosie picks up the knife, and I pull an extension cord from the utility drawer.

"Sit down, Joseph, and put your hands behind you."

I watch him consider my order, but he is too taken with his own pain to complete the action.

Rosie, her mouth open and her breathing harsh, flings the knife onto the counter. She tosses it from her hand like an object that has already burned her once, or bitten her. Joseph sits on the floor, an awful, bloodless smile stretching his thin lips as he cradles his injured arm.

Rosie takes a step toward the counter. If my sister moves any closer, the knife will be within her reach again. "Rosie, I want you to get in the car. Go down to the Smiths' and call Riley. I have the gun. I won't let him go anywhere. He's sick. He's hurt. He needs to be in a hospital."

She doesn't move. I want her to come out of this trance on her own, without my forcing her, so that she can live with her choice, but she doesn't appear to hear me. Then she steps forward. She picks up the knife and holds it out in front of her. Her expression doesn't change.

"Maybe you're right," she says, in a stranger's voice. "I think that would be a better thing to do to him."

Joseph struggles to his feet and stumbles toward the table.

I am ready. I can do this. I can lift the gun, push the slide back, my hands remember.

Joseph is rocking, swaying, a whimper coming from high in his throat.

But Rosie steps in front of me, lays her hand on my outstretched arm, pushes my arm down. The gun points at the floor now.

"I think we'll make him live with it. What do you think, Jacob? It *is* Jacob, isn't that right? That's how I'll punish you for what you did to my family. You wanted to upset me so that I'd kill you the way your father killed the others? Well, maybe you've upset me so much I'll let you live."

A roar of anguish fills the kitchen. Joseph falls to the floor and grabs Rosie's knees, pressing his face against the fabric of her jeans. He reaches up and clutches her arm. His hand leaves a bloody print on her shirt.

Rosie bends her neck gracefully until it is curved like a swan's, and she looks down at her sleeve, at the crimson stain with which he has marked her.

Her eyes fill. She shudders and reaches down to touch his hair with her empty hand.